The Caine Prize for African Writing 2015

Lusaka Punk
and other stories

The Caine Prize for African Writing 2015

Lusaka Punk
and other stories

New Internationalist

Lusaka Punk and other stories
The Caine Prize for African Writing 2015

First published in 2015 in Europe, North America and Australasia by
New Internationalist Publications Ltd
The Old Music Hall
106-108 Cowley Road
Oxford
OX4 1JE, UK
newint.org

First published in 2015 in South Africa by
Jacana Media (Pty) Ltd
10 Orange Street
Sunnyside
Auckland Park 2092
South Africa
+2711 628 3200
jacana.co.za

Cover illustration: Memory Locker of Things Remembered
© Victor Ehikhamenor (victorehi.com)

Design by New Internationalist.

Printed by T J International Limited, Cornwall, UK
who hold environmental accreditation ISO 14001.

British Library Cataloguing-in-Publication Data.
A catalogue record for this book is available from the British Library.

Library of Congress Cataloging-in-Publication Data.
A catalog record for this book is available from the Library of Congress.

New Internationalist ISBN 978-1-78026-228-4
(ebook ISBN 978-1-78026-229-1)

Jacana ISBN 978-1-4314-2262-3

Contents

Introduction

Selected from a record number of eligible entries, 153 stories from 17 African countries, this anthology contains the five stories from the 16th annual Caine Prize shortlist, which was announced in May 2015. In a sign of the established calibre to be found in African writing and as the Caine Prize matures in its 16th year, the shortlist includes one past winner, Segun Afolabi, who won in 2005, and two previously shortlisted writers, Elnathan John (2013) and Namwali Serpell (2010). A £500 prize will be awarded to each shortlisted writer in addition to the travel and accommodation grant to travel to London in June/July for a series of public events and the award dinner in Oxford.

The Chair of Judges, award-winning South African author Zoë Wicomb, described the shortlist as: 'an exciting crop of well-crafted stories'.

'For all the variety of themes and approaches, the shortlist has in common a rootedness in socio-economic worlds that are pervaded with affect, as well as keen awareness of the ways in which the ethical is bound up with aesthetics. Unforgettable characters, drawn with insight and humour, inhabit works ranging from classical story structures to a haunting, enigmatic narrative that challenges the conventions of the genre.' She added: 'Understatement and the unspoken prevail: hints of an orphan's identity bring poignant understanding of his world; the reader is slowly and expertly guided to awareness of a narrator's blindness; there is delicate allusion to homosexual love; a disfigured human body is encountered in relation to adolescent escapades; a nameless wife's insecurities barely mask her understanding of injustice; and, we are given a flash of insight into dark passions that rise out of a surreal resistance culture.'

'Above all, these stories speak of the pleasure of reading fiction. It will be no easy task to settle on a winner.'

The 2015 shortlist comprises:

- Segun Afolabi (Nigeria) 'The Folded Leaf' from *Wasafiri* (Routledge, London, 2014)
- Elnathan John (Nigeria) 'Flying' from *Per Contra* (Per Contra, International, 2014)
- FT Kola (South Africa) 'A Party for the Colonel' from *One Story* (One Story inc, Brooklyn, New York City, 2014)
- Masande Ntshanga (South Africa) 'Space' in *Twenty in 20* (Times Media, South Africa, 2014)
- Namwali Serpell (Zambia) 'The Sack' in *Africa39* (Bloomsbury, London, 2014)

Joining Zoë Wicomb on the panel of judges are the distinguished television and radio journalist, and Chairperson of the Royal African Society, Zeinab Badawi, Indian author and Man Booker Prize shortlistee Neel Mukherjee, Assistant Professor of English at the University of Georgetown Cóilín Parsons and Brian Chikwava, the winner of the Caine Prize in 2004. Once again, the winner of the £10,000 Caine Prize will be given the opportunity to take up a month's residence at Georgetown University, as a Writer-in-Residence at the Lannan Center for Poetics and Social Practice. The award will cover all travel and living expenses. The winner will also be invited to take part in the Open Book Festival in Cape Town, South Africa, the StoryMoja Festival in Nairobi, Kenya, and the Ake Festival in Abeokuta, Nigeria in 2015.

This book also contains the stories that emerged from this year's Caine Prize workshop, which was held in Ghana. At the Coconut Grove Beach Resort Hotel in Elmina, thanks to the generosity of the owner, Kwesi Nduom, we assembled 12 talented writers to compose short stories by the beautifully clear Atlantic Ocean beneath graceful queen palms that swayed to warn of pending storms and provided slim shelter from the equatorial sun. We are immensely grateful to Akoss Ofori-Mensah, Nii Parkes and Martin Egblewogbe for their useful advice and assistance and to Prudential plc and

Groupe Nduom for providing the majority of the funding for the workshop. Three of the writers who took part were shortlisted in 2014 and 2013 and four were local Ghanaian writers; the others hailed from Kenya, Nigeria and Malawi. During 12 days of peace and quiet the workshop participants were guided by the accomplished novelists Zukiswa Wanner (South Africa) and Leila Aboulela (Sudan), who won the inaugural Caine Prize in 2000. Halfway through the workshop the writers visited four schools near Elmina in groups of three or four to speak to and read to the students about writing, reading and storytelling. The writers were also visited by the esteemed Ghanaian writer Kojo Laing, who spoke of his first love, poetry, his experiences in Scotland and imparted some personal advice: 'I'm very stubborn. You should listen to your publishers, fellow writers... but I don't.'

After the workshop the group returned to Accra for an event (on Saturday 18 April) at the Goethe Institut in partnership with Writers Project Ghana and Sub Saharan Publishers. Workshop participants Jemila Abdulai and Kiprop Kimutai read from their stories published in this anthology: '#Yennenga', and 'Princess Sailendra of Malindi'; and workshop leaders Zukiswa Wanner and Leila Aboulela read from their latest novels *London Cape Town Joburg* and *The Kindness of Enemies* respectively. Pede Hollist hosted a conversation about African writing with Jonathan Mbuna from Malawi, Nana Nyarko Boateng and Jonathan Dotse from Ghana and Nkiacha Atemnkeng from Cameroon. Questions from the audience included whether it was acceptable to use local languages in English writing, to which there was a resounding 'yes' from all panellists, as well as curiosity around African sci-fi, women writers from Malawi and reaching young readers. A very stimulating evening was enjoyed by everyone.

The success of the co-publishing arrangement with Sub-Saharan Publishers in Ghana, which has sold over 25,000 copies of Caine Prize anthologies in the last 18 months, suggests there is a great appetite for literature in Ghana, and yet there have been no Ghanaian Caine Prize winners to date. We hope that holding the first workshop in Ghana since 2009, providing the opportunity to meet Caine Prize authors and to talk about books and writing will have encouraged locals to keep up to date with all the Caine Prize does each year. Most importantly, we wish to encourage entries from Ghanaian writers, strengthening and supporting local and pan-African literary networks. The anthology is also available in Zimbabwe, Uganda, South Africa, Zambia, Nigeria and Kenya through our co-publishers, who receive a print ready PDF free of charge. It can be read as an ebook supported by Kindle, iBooks and Kobo and, via a partnership with the literacy NGO Worldreader, some award-winning stories are available free to African readers via an app on their mobile phones.

The principal sponsors of the 2015 Prize were the Oppenheimer Memorial Trust, the Booker Prize Foundation, the Miles Morland Foundation, Sigrid Rausing and Eric Abraham, and CSL Stockbrokers. Prudential and Groupe Nduom primarily supported the workshop, and travel grants for workshop participants were also provided by The Beit Trust, Commonwealth Writers, an initiative of The Commonwealth Foundation, and The Morel Trust. There were other generous private donations, and vital help in kind was given by: the Royal Over-Seas League; Bodley's Librarian; the London Short Story Festival; the Royal African Society; Marion Wallace of the British Library; Tricia Wombell, Co-ordinator of the Black Reading Group and Black Book News; the Southbank Centre; Rich Mix, Numbi, Jinaka Ugochukwu, and Brixton Library. We are immensely grateful for all this help, most of which has been given regularly over the past years and without which the Caine Prize would not be Africa's leading literary award.

Lizzy Attree
Director of the Caine Prize for African Writing

The Caine Prize 2015
Shortlisted Stories

The Folded Leaf

Segun Afolabi

'Bunmi! Bola!' the cry rings out, Toyin calling from the other side of the road. At first they don't hear it, but I do. We're sitting in a circle around Reverend Abbe: Mrs Kekere, Tunde and Mr and Mrs Folorunsho's eight-year-old, Sam. Mama's here too, as are Bola and Mrs Folorunsho, the six of us contained within a tight knot around the reverend, her thin white hair wrapped around her scalp like a halo, everyone says so.

Reverend Abbe is 80 years old. She came late to the church and she's only a deaconess, but we rarely refer to her as such. By we, I mean Papa, Mama, Bola and I, and most of the parishioners along Leke Street. We have an actual reverend, in fact – Reverend Okulaja – but he doesn't seem to resent Reverend Abbe.

'Bless Samuel, Father Jehovah,' she says. 'Today, today – please send him new legs.'

I am trying not to giggle. Bola is shuddering beside me. At 14 he should know better than to be disrespectful towards the reverend. I'm two years younger, so I use age as an excuse.

'Allow your messenger to heal your son Tunde this very today. Touch each of your children, Lord – Bunmi, Samuel, Tunde. And Mrs Kekere. Make them to be reborn in your presence. Make your spirit to descend down on top of them, to make them well and whole.'

'Yes, oh!' Mama says, standing, raising her arms.

The *messenger* the reverend referred to is Pastor Adejola

Fayemi, or Daddy Cool as he is better known on account of his helicopter and Gulfstream jet and his homes in Florida and Switzerland and somewhere in the Caribbean. He has a penchant for wearing dark glasses and Tunde swears he's never seen the pastor's eyes before – not on TV, not in magazines or in the newspapers.

'They are calling you!' Toyin shouts, this time from the entrance to the church, which is just a room off the street in a series of rooms in a low-lying building: Musa's suya bar, a soft-drinks shop, Daniel's sewing parlour, Mama Yinka's Emporium of Weave. Toyin falls silent when she realizes we're in the middle of prayer.

'Holy Father, allow no harm to meet your children on the road, no wickedness to touch them in Lagos,' Reverend Abbe says. 'Return them safely – today, today – with your holy blessings.' She stops speaking, then after a full minute of silence she exhales and claps her hands and says, 'My, my – what a wonderful day!'

The sun streams through the window, warming the back of my neck. The morning cool has lifted. Sweat stains are certain to bloom across my Sunday dress and disgrace me in front of Papa.

'I beg, Ma,' Toyin says. 'The driver is here. They are waiting for you.' By *you* she means Tunde, Sam, Bola, Mrs Kekere and me. By *they* she means Mr and Mrs Ejiofoh. And Papa.

'Wonderful!' The reverend claps again. '*Oya* children – time to go. Mrs Kekere, let us *commot* from here.'

Three or four wooden planks connect the church to the road. Beneath the planks, a ditch filled with whatever anyone has chosen to discard. Tunde pushes Sam's wheelchair behind me. Mama's to my right, whispering 'Sweet Jesus!' on account of the stench. Bola's gone ahead, sulking because he'll miss football practice as he has to accompany me on this trip. Mrs Kekere trails behind us, clickety-clack with her canes.

Tunde is 16. He has a hole in his heart. One day he might get out of bed and not have enough energy to take another step and flop down and die. It's very dramatic, the way he describes it, as if he were talking about someone else. As if he hasn't played football every other day alongside Bola or beaten Femi Adeleke to a pulp (Femi is a year older than Tunde) or played the Akpala sisters like a pair of slide guitars, strumming them both, Bonnie and Elizabeth, insensible, sending them scurrying to Ma Benga who performs her own brand of abortion. People think I don't know.

'What is taking so long?' Mr Ejiofoh shouts from the minibus. 'What and what are these people doing?'

'Cannot you see we have been waiting?' his wife chimes in.

'"Cannot you see we are waiting?"' Tunde mimics behind me.

Sam giggles.

'In the Lord's good time,' Reverend Abbe says, which silences everyone, although I hear Mrs Ejiofoh release a little *pfff* of displeasure.

'Yes, Mama.'

'Wait, oh!' Reverend Abbe says. 'Bunmi, come here.'

I shuffle back to the sliding door and the reverend brushes her fingers against my cheeks, my lips, my eyelids. Onion and garlic, a hint of sage. Has she no-one to cook for her? Her fingers are trembling. 'Blessings be with you, Bunmi, my dear. Blessings to all of you.' And she steps back. It's a mystery why she and Mama can't join us, why the Ejiofohs are here instead. Papa says Bola is here to support me and help with the wheelchairs, but surely Mama could do that?

'Come and sit down, Bunmi,' Papa says from the back row. He guides me to the space between him and Bola. I brush past Sam, who's next to the sliding door, but what I notice is Mrs Ejiofoh beside him; her perfume overpowers even the reek of the ditch. I lower myself in increments before I can settle in the seat, which has been gently baking in the sun.

'Humph,' Mrs Ejiofoh says. 'Where is this woman? What and

what are we waiting for, heh?' A waft of floral notes tumbles over me as she flourishes her paper fan with abandon.

This woman – Mrs Kekere – is beside Bola, making her way outside the bus. Her canes drag along the road and then the passenger door squeaks open. 'Help me with these things, *joh*,' she says to Tunde, who will also occupy the passenger seat. She grunts as he helps her up and the minibus sinks a little to the right.

'Okay!' the driver calls.

'Make we *dey* go now!' Papa says.

Mrs Ejiofoh slaps her hands twice, heavily, against each other, and says, *'Hey-e-yeh!'* as if she's never experienced anything as absurd as a bus load of invalids.

We weave through town, along the unpaved roads. First there's a whiff of thrown-up dust, then dry-fish pepper soup and the aroma of *moyin-moyin,* so we must be near Mama Boyega's *buka*. Every so often a pedestrian taps against a window.

'Blessings!' Mr Olawale shouts.

'Pray for me, oh!' Auntie Ugome calls. Everyone knows where we're going.

'Sammy, you will be dancing tonight, oh!'

I don't recognize the last voice, but Sam replies, *'Eshay,* Ma.' I'm none the wiser, but I'm concerned about offering such encouragement to an eight-year-old boy.

In no time we're on the highway and the wind billows in and Mrs Ejiofoh screeches, 'Close up that window!' Her head tie has partly unravelled and whips against my cheek. She's wearing embroidered lace so soft it must have cost a fortune. Last year Mr Ejiofoh took his family to Rome and they stayed at the Intercontinental. Bimbo, his daughter, drives a Volkswagen Passat. That's why they're on the bus, Mr and Mrs Ejiofoh, because you can never have too much. You give and then receive in abundance. They're famous for their church donations.

Sam obliges with the window.

'Bunmi, you want to sit here?' Papa asks. 'You are not hot?'

'I'm fine, Papa. A-Okay.' Our code to indicate all is well. It's pleasant with the wind sailing through the bus, my body no longer drenched and Mrs Ejiofoh's perfume mitigated by the breeze.

'We have left town now,' Papa explains. 'We are on the road! We will be revived!'

'Amen!' Mr Ejiofoh says in front of him.

'Amen!' Mrs Kekere calls from the passenger seat, although she probably can't hear Papa above the din of the engine. I can hear her talking to Tunde, though, and to the driver. The odd word: city, celestial, Okene, *ewedu* soup.

'What do you see?' I ask Bola, who is noticeably silent and likely fuming since he was forced to give up his place beside Tunde.

Bola doesn't speak for a moment. He likes to take his time. 'We just passed a woman carrying a metal bucket on her head and a girl washing her legs under a tap. There was a building, a blue building with a large Pepsi logo painted on one side, but now we've left that village and there's nothing.'

'Nothing?'

'Well, just trees all around, but not close to the road. There are two or three metres of path on either side of the tarmac, then long grass, then the trees. Oh, and a lorry ahead of us – I think our driver is going to try to overtake it. It's covered in green tarpaulin, strapped down with ropes. And there's a sign at the back. It says *DO NOT...* One minute – it's a bit far away.' He waits. '*BE AFRAID.* All the letters are written in white. In capital letters. What else do you want to know?'

'Hmm, I wonder what's underneath the tarpaulin. Do you think it's cows?'

'Bunmi, how would I know?'

'But you'll tell me if you see something, won't you?'

'Of course I will, you know that.'

He doesn't speak after this and I fear he may descend into one of his moods.

'*Daddy,*' I begin to sing, '*Daddy Cool,*' and in the end Bola joins me. I can tell from his tone that he's smiling. '*Daddy, Daddy Cool.*' Our private joke concerning Pastor Fayemi. '*I'm crazy like a fool.*'

Papa leans towards us. 'There are one thousand things to see and do in the city. Just you wait. This is just bush, there's nothing to see here.'

'Things like what, Papa?' I ask.

'Never have you seen so many cars before, Bunmi. Mercedes, BMW, Rolls Royce, you name it. More cars than people. And bridges – one bridge can stretch for miles. When we get there I will let you know.'

Mrs Ejiofoh lets out a low chuckle.

'You think we will see a Rolls Royce, Papa?' Bola asks.

'Why not? More than one. And offices that rise up to the sky. And swimming pools.'

'Really, Papa?' I am sure he's making it up.

'Bunmi, I am telling you. And the arena – just wait. Bola, open your eyes today, we will see wonders.'

'The wonders of Lagos,' Mr Ejiofoh says, without enthusiasm.

'Just make sure you keep close,' his wife says. 'Don't wander.'

But I can sense the excitement in Papa's voice, and in Bola's too, and for the first time today I feel light enough to levitate above my seat, above the bus, above the landscape around us.

'Me, I want ice cream, oh!' Sam says.

'Me too!' Tunde says from the front.

'Ice cream, Papa?' Bola asks.

'Of course,' Papa says. 'When we see the vendor, I will buy you one. Each of you.'

'Don't worry,' Mr Ejiofoh says. 'Today the ice cream will be on me.'

'We are here to serve the Lord!' Mrs Kekere pipes up from the front. Her hearing is sharper than I give her credit for. 'Let us forget about ice cream and swimming pool and place our mind on prayer, isn't it?'

'It is, *shah*,' Mrs Ejiofoh replies.

This has the immediate effect of silencing everyone, even though we know Mrs Kekere would be the first to demolish an ice cream and then appeal for another.

For a stretch we listen to the churn of the engine and the roaring road and the thud of percussion instruments from the front of the bus. The driver must have switched on the radio. I pick out the pluck of a steel guitar coupled with a man's reedy voice and then backing singers as they belt out a chorus. That's when I notice the wind dying down, the engine become a mere grumble. 'Papa, are we stopping?'

'Road block!' the driver says as he pulls to the side of the road. The radio is switched off.

'*Pfff!*' goes Mrs Ejiofoh.

Mrs Kekere begins to hum.

'What do you have inside?' a voice demands from outside the bus.

'Police,' Bola whispers.

'Just people,' the driver says. 'We go Lagos.'

'How many of you?'

'Well – '

The driver probably didn't think to tally up his passengers.

'Excuse,' Mr Ejiofoh says. 'We are nine in total.'

Someone else is pacing around the bus. Footsteps halt somewhere between Papa and Mr Ejiofoh.

'So, you are not carrying something?' continues the policeman beside the driver. 'If we make our check, we will not find something, *na so*?'

Mrs Kekere appears to be humming the tune to 'Great Is Thy Faithfulness'.

Footsteps continue behind the bus. A shadow lingers on the back of my head. A set of footsteps stops beside Sam, followed by a sharp rap against the door. 'Open, *joh*!' a policeman says and Sam begins to fumble with the latch. When the door slides opens, the policeman must see Sam's withered legs. He *must* see them. His wheelchair is doubtless folded in the space in front of him. Or perhaps the policeman is not focused on Sam at all, he's drawn to Mrs Ejiofoh and her soft lace and perfume.

Mrs Kekere is humming at a gallop now, though she appears to have lost the capacity to hold a tune.

'That bag?' the policeman asks. 'What is inside?'

'Ah, ah! What is this?' Mrs Ejiofoh says. 'What is your business?'

The policeman pauses, then speaks almost inaudibly. 'What did you say?' He sounds as if he is about to climb aboard the bus and illustrate why Mrs Ejiofoh should never answer back to a policeman.

Papa pats my leg. I cannot hear Bola breathe.

'Mr Man!' Mrs Kekere says so that everyone can hear. 'What do you want with us, heh? We are going to praise the Lord. In Lagos. We are not richy-rich people. Leave these sick children, *joh,* and let us not to be late. God is watching you.'

What follows is a period of silence or contemplation, a quick shuffling of clothes, the unfurling of an *agbada.* 'Please,' Mr Ejiofoh says. 'Please take this for your trouble, you and your colleagues.' There's a pleading quality to his voice I have never heard before, a slight tremor, an absence of dignity.

'*Eshay, sah,*' comes the reply. 'Thank you, *sah.*' The sliding door is slammed shut. The bus shudders. '*Oya,* let these people go!' The policeman bangs the side of the bus and we draw away from the sound of guffaws.

Mrs Kekere resumes her humming; another tune this time – 'Sweet Is The Light'. Minutes later the driver switches on the radio, or perhaps Tunde has had enough of Mrs Kekere's warbling.

'Did they have guns?' I ask.

'Let us think no more about it,' Papa says and he begins, perhaps unconsciously, to hum along with Mrs Kekere.

People ask me sometimes what I think Papa looks like and Mama and Bola, how I imagine myself. I have always been blind. How they appear to me, and my own understanding of myself, might not compare with other people's perceptions. But do any of us identify the same thing in exactly the same way? The shape of an egg, the colour blue, the smell of a leaf? That's what Bola says sometimes. So don't worry, he says. And Bola's right about most things.

Mama is taller than me – for now – and I'm shorter than Papa and Bola. She has a heart-shaped face and sometimes she places my fingers on her dimples when she smiles. She smiles constantly, unlike Bola, who hardly ever cracks a grin.

Papa broke his leg in a motorcycle accident before he met Mama, so he walks with a slight limp, but he's the strongest person I know. Stronger than Tunde. He visits Elias the barber every two or three weeks because he has so much hair, which never seems to stop growing. I love the feel of it against my face when he reaches down to say goodnight.

A car toots. Another responds in kind. We are no longer driving at speed.

'Where are we now?' I ask.

Silence.

'Bola?'

'Hmm?'

'Were you sleeping?'

'No. Maybe. What did you say?'

'Are we nearly there?'

'I don't know. There are more houses. Not many trees. And cars. Lots of cars.'

'Can you see the offices in the sky?'

'No, not yet.'

'We have some time until we reach the city,' Papa says. 'This is just the suburbs. That's how big it is.'

'This *is* Lagos,' Mrs Ejiofoh says. 'Only there is so much traffic you cannot get from A to B without hypertension.'

'Are we going to be late?'

'Bunmi, stop worrying,' Papa says. 'There will be worshipping long into the night.'

Thirty minutes later the boom of a car's speakers buffets the minibus like a gust of wind.

'*Hey-e-yeh!*' the driver says. 'Lagos people *dey* craze!'

'What kind of car is making that noise?' I ask Bola.

'It's not a car. It's coming from a shop.'

We drive on and the volume subsides behind us. It's confusing not to be able to recognize sounds, the sources of sounds. I'm having difficulty building a picture of this world in my mind.

The honking and snarling around us swells into a new kind of language, like a million crows crying out at the same time. We move forward a few metres, then idle, again and again.

'What do you see?'

'A traffic jam.'

'Please, Bola.'

He exhales. 'Okay, let's see. There's a market to your left. Just clothes and vegetables and one or two electrical shops and a place selling generators. Lots of cars in front of us and behind too – most of them yellow taxis.' He hardly pauses this time. 'There's a pot hole in the middle of the road, so all the cars are steering around it and there's a boy there. Maybe seven or eight years old. He's moving from one car to another. I don't think he has any legs.'

'Oh,' I say. Now everything is upside down. I was trying to gauge the size of the pot hole, hoping the driver would do his best to swerve away from it, bracing myself for a potential bump. Now there's a child in my head, with no legs. I am trying to understand what that looks like, how he is able to move between cars without thighs and knees, ankles and toes. I shift closer to Bola. 'What does he look like, that boy?'

'Like a boy,' Bola says. 'What do you mean?'

'How can he... Is he in a wheelchair?'

'No – he is using his hands. And his arms. He's actually moving very fast.'

'The road, isn't it dirty? Is he not low low down? What if the drivers can't see him?'

Bola doesn't reply straight away. He says, 'Well, I think they can see him. The cars can't move very fast in this traffic.'

'But what does he look like?'

'Bunmi, I told you already.'

'I mean his face. His expression. Please, Bola.' I can't explain it exactly, even to Bola.

'Bunmi... Well, he seems – his tongue is sticking out a little. He's pushing hard with his hands and his singlet is dragging on the ground. He is trying to get money, from the drivers and from the people sitting in the back seats, but they're not winding down their windows.'

'His face, Bola.'

'Okay, he looks... not tired, but maybe like he needs to rest. You know? Remember when you walk home after school, then run a little, then walk again to catch your breath?'

'Yes.'

'Like that. He looks like he needs to catch his breath for a minute. But he's smiling too when he holds out his hand.'

'Yes, I think I see it.' I'm building a picture of velocity and metal and chaos and heat. And in amongst that, a tiny, scuttling bundle of flesh. A smile. 'It doesn't sound as if he's paying attention to where he is. Isn't it dangerous in between those cars?'

'I think you're right,' Bola says. I feel him turn, look behind. 'I can't see him any more.'

We are quiet now, listening only to the honking and shouting, a ripple of laughter to my right. There may be an intersection nearby, a crowd attempting to cross the street. Right now I don't want to know.

'What do you think will happen to that boy when he is older, when he is as old as Papa or Mr Ejiofoh?' And then I remember Sam, sitting in front of us and I am ashamed of my relentless curiosity.

'I don't know,' Bola says after a while.

'God does not like the poor!' The pastor's voice booms

through loudspeakers all around us. We've been instructed to take notes and I can hear the frenzied rustle of paper. 'We have all the riches of the world right here, right now! He gave us wealth, more than we can imagine. There is no excuse not to partake. Listen to this: "A fool wallows with the pigs in the pen." You write that down!'

We're at the back of the arena listening to Pastor Fayemi, who has a voice like the man on the six o'clock news, only he sounds angry, as if we have done something to displease him. When we arrived, Mrs Kekere was crestfallen not to be invited to the front row, but she has begun to sing, calling out her *amens* whenever the spirit takes her. Tunde hasn't yet spotted an aeroplane or a helicopter, and of the pastor, he says, 'The stage is miles away.'

Mr and Mrs Ejiofoh were whisked away to the VIP area. One glance at Sam and Mrs Kekere and me and the staff ushered the rest of us to the back of the arena. Talk of ice cream and bridges and buildings that puncture the clouds has long since faded.

'Jesus, this place is wheelchair city!' Tunde says with such awe it might go some way to alleviating his disappointment about the lack of aircraft.

'Do not use the Lord's name in vain,' Mrs Kekere says.

I wonder what he's wearing, the pastor, what he looks like up close, whether there's a holy aura around him like Reverend Abbe.

'How will we reach the stage?' Bola asks.

'When they call us, we start running,' Papa says. 'You hold your sister. I will push Sam. Tunde – you hold Mrs Kekere, you hear?'

'Yes, *sah.*'

'Wonderful. We are ready.' I can hear the wide grin in Papa's voice.

'I feel hot,' Sam says.

It's true – it's stifling in here. My dress is already limp with the humidity. The flutter of a thousand paper fans fills the air like flamingos taking flight.

The choir begins to sing and all around me people join in.

'How do you know the words?' I ask Bola. 'I don't know these new songs they're singing.'

'They're up on a screen.'

'Sing along if you can,' Papa says. 'But don't worry, Bunmi. We are going up soon, Jehovah!' He gives my arm a quick squeeze – his hand hot and clammy – and continues to sing, his voice ringing clear above others around us.

Something is happening to Papa, to the congregation. Thousands upon thousands of voices bellowing in unison, the choir electrifying the stage, the presence of the pastor like a fire in our midst. And this heat, like fear or happiness, coursing through my body.

'How now, Bunmi?'

'A-Okay, Papa.'

The choir launches into a medley of hymns, and then the pastor cries, 'Hallelujah! Hallelujah!' and everyone roars, 'Hallelujah!' in return.

'And is it not good to be in the presence of the Lord?' the pastor shouts.

The congregation responds with a resounding, 'Yes, oh!'

'I am telling you,' the pastor says. 'There will be healing tonight. Stand up from that wheelchair!' And a hush descends upon the crowd.

'Not you, Sam,' Papa whispers. 'He's talking to someone on the stage.'

'To give is to please the Lord,' the pastor continues. 'So give generously my children!'

'Did you see someone get up from their wheelchair?' I ask.

'They didn't show it on the screen,' Bola says. 'And I can't see anything from here.'

'Not long now,' Papa says. 'Mrs Kekere – prepare yourself.'

'I am already prepared,' she says, 'even before today.'

Silence. Noise. Silence again. The sounds slipping away, returning – a seashell back and forth against my ear. I am both giddy and fearful. I have always been afraid, I know, of the night, of silence, of losing Mama or Papa, of Bola running away, never hearing from him again. More than anything, I am afraid the pastor will see right through me to my sin, my doubt, my disbelief. I am frightened because, in spite of myself, I want so much for something to happen.

'Tunde, Mrs Kekere – take this,' Papa says. 'Sam, Bola – one one for each of you.' He must be distributing the funds we've raised in church, months of donations sealed in envelopes, used partly to pay for the driver and the minibus and today's collection.

'Stop trying to stand,' Tunde says. 'He wasn't talking to you.'

'But I can feel something,' Sam says.

'Give all you can!' a voice booms, though not Pastor Fayemi's. 'He sees into your hearts. Don't cheat Him, oh!'

'Who is that?' I ask.

'There are many pastors up there,' Bola says. 'They're taking turns to speak. They're wearing suits, mostly black suits. Daddy Cool is wearing white.'

Sweat trickles down the sides of my face and each intake of breath in this humidity is increasingly hard-earned. Halfway through a hymn the music fades and a voice from the stage shouts, 'Did you see that? Cancer has just left that girl! Did you see it fly away? Hallelujah!'

Gasps escape throughout the arena and people begin to call out names – of loved ones, their own names, Jehovah, Jesu, Lord. I want to see the girl who was healed. I want to see the cancer leave her body, the fetid lump of it flung into the air, her face now she has been healed. I want to see. Now. I am ready.

'Time to go up,' Papa says. 'Bola, hold Bunmi tight. Don't let her get lost, you hear?'

'Yes, Papa.'

'Tunde, Mrs Kekere – you go first. Sam and I will follow.'

And we're off, Bola with an arm around me, half-running to keep up with Tunde and Mrs Kekere. Is Tunde carrying her? Perhaps someone from the congregation is helping. I miss my step and stumble. I cannot find my balance at this speed. Bola props me up, holds me tighter. 'Sorry, Bunmi.'

Bola is so lean against me, perhaps I should be offering the support. I hadn't realized how thin he has become. It makes me wonder if he is eating properly, whether the hours of football are taking their toll.

'Follow those people!' a woman says behind me and I'm aware we are part of a mass headed for the same place. It gives me hope, this communion, this flock of kindred souls. I no longer care that I'm sweating, that I'm stumbling like a drunk. I am only in love with love, with the thought that love is on the stage and, when I reach it, when I touch it, I will be made whole.

'An old woman is dancing on stage!' Bola cries. 'She just threw her cane down! Bunmi, she's really dancing!'

'Bola, hurry.' I have never heard him so engaged. 'Let Sam and Mrs Kekere dance too. And Tunde, let his heart be healed. And that boy with no legs, we will pray for him.'

'We will all see healing tonight,' Bola says, half-dragging, half-carrying me now.

'Are we there, Papa?'

'Not far, Bunmi. You will see each of us tonight, He has ordained it. He is watching over us today today. You will see the green leaves and the white clouds and your Mama's face.' His voice begins to break, from the strain of the day, from pushing Sam, from pushing all of us to flourish.

'Mr Man!' That can only be Mrs Kekere. 'Mr Man, move away! Cannot you see you are standing in the road?'

'Wait, Bunmi,' Bola says. 'Slow down.'

'Let us pass!' This is Papa.

'*Commot* for road!' Tunde says.

'Who and who is going where with this wheelchair?' It's a man's voice. Calm, but firm.

'What are you talking?' Mrs Kekere says. 'I beg, let us pass, *joh.*'

'Have you received healing?' another man says.

'Who are those people?' I ask.

'They're wearing suits,' Bola says.

Have we received healing? Are we not all waiting to be healed? Have we not driven all this way to be renewed, touched, reborn?

'Brother, what do you mean?' Papa has a smile in his voice, as if he understands that the men have made an error which they will no doubt soon correct. 'We are going up there, for the healing, don't you know?'

'Better sit down,' one of the men says. 'No obstruction or wheelchair. Pastor Fayemi can reach you wherever you are. Please, move back so these people can pass.'

'Move, *joh,*' someone says behind me.

'No, no – you don't understand,' Papa says. 'We have been travelling all day, you see. Here is my daughter, Bunmi. She must meet Pastor Fayemi. My son Bola, Mrs Kekere, Sam – '

'What is this?' A new voice. Movement, a brisk kerfuffle, someone drawing close to Papa.

'Reinforcements,' Bola says.

'Move from the road, my friend,' the new voice says. 'Who asked you to move from your seat?'

'But – ' Papa says.

'You sit down now. All of you.' The man speaks so quietly, his words can only be meant for Papa, but I hear them too. It does not sound like a request. His voice has the timbre of someone who could knock Tunde to the other side of the arena.

'Oh, okay.' Papa gives a half-hearted chuckle, but I hear anxiety and capitulation in his voice, as if an invisible hand has reached down and folded him in half, and half again, like a leaf or a scrap of paper.

'Bola, you go,' Papa says. 'You run and don't look back.'

'But Bunmi – '

'Just go, I said. You pray for your sister. You pray for all of us. Go now.'

Bola leaves without a word and I am left with the hubbub of the crowd, dread in my stomach, people jostling me from all sides and the floor tilting now against my volition. Mrs Ejiofoh's words come rushing back to me. 'Keep close, Papa.'

He catches me just as I am about to slide to the floor. His arms are damp, almost wet, and I can smell his perspiration. Papa never complains. He perseveres. 'I am sorry, Bunmi. Sorry. Hold onto my arm.'

He guides me with one hand and manoeuvres Sam's wheelchair with the other and we return to our seats. It does not seem so difficult for him to manage and it occurs to me that Bola needn't have come. Could his space in the bus not have been given to Lola or Osawe or Jibola, who has been diabetic for most of his life? As we trundle back it dawns on me why Mama and Papa insisted Bola join us today. He isn't here to help me or Sam or Mrs Kekere; he too has come to be healed. How could I have failed to understand?

'*Atcha!*' Mrs Kekere slumps to her seat. 'What kind of people are these people? That we can come all this distance, for what? For water? Heh? Tunde, don't mind me, *sef.* Go up there and join Bola. I can stay here by myself.'

'Don't worry, Ma,' Tunde says. 'It's okay.'

'What and what is okay? Go up and receive healing.'

'Don't worry, Ma,' he repeats. 'Sam, stop trying to stand up. You are going to exhaust yourself.'

'But I'm not tired,' Sam says. 'See?'

I hear his wheelchair creaking from side to side, his little groans of exertion. But more than anything, I hear Papa's silence. 'Sam, stop,' I say. I try to be as gentle as I can.

'Keep praying, Sammy dear,' Mrs Kekere says. 'We will each of us see healing in our lifetime, don't you worry.'

Papa has not spoken in so long, I don't know what to do or say. I don't need anyone to describe the expression on his face.

'Another arthritis has been healed!' a man shouts from the stage. 'Hallelujah!'

'Hallelujah!' the congregation choruses.

'Praise Jesus!' Mrs Kekere calls and I am amazed at the strength of her conviction.

'Not yet,' Papa says at last, rubbing his hands together, letting out a little clap at the end.

'What's *not yet,* Papa?'

'The pastor has not yet blessed your brother. I am watching on the screen. So many people are waiting in line. When he goes up, I will let you know.'

Papa must return home to face Mama and Reverend Abbe and Reverend Okulaja and all the members of our congregation. He will have to explain how we came so close and how we were turned away, how we gave away all the donations in a single collection.

'You are disappointed, Papa.'

He remains silent and I wonder if he has not heard me. Cries go up throughout the hall and I assume another person has been healed.

'No, Bunmi. I am not disappointed. Remember what the steward said? We can receive blessings from here. He sees all of us, all of the time. Don't forget that. Don't allow your faith to grow dim.'

'Yes, Papa,' I say. But how can it be dimmed if it is barely lit to begin with?

'Bola is on TV!' Sam says.

'Really?' I imagine a lanky boy with hair about an inch long, like Papa's, cut and combed by Elias especially for today. Thin cotton trousers. A smart, button-down shirt. I forgot to ask him about the colour.

'Really, Bunmi. I am not joking you,' Sam says. 'He is up there with Daddy Cool.'

'Yes, he is,' Papa says, his voice filled with pride.

I cannot guess the colour of Bola's shirt. I can't envisage him on the stage. And how I wish I were back home, back in the familiar. Mama would know what to say to Sam, how to console Papa, how to calm this wildness in my chest. Is Bola

overwhelmed by the adoration of the crowd? Is he frightened
as he's thrust in front of the pastor?

'He is coming down from that stage,' Sam says.

'That was quick. Papa?'

Papa doesn't speak.

'Sam, what does he look like? Can you describe him for
me?'

'Who, Bola?'

'No, Daddy Cool.'

'Pastor Fayemi,' Papa says.

'He is wearing suit. A white suit and white shoes. Very fine.
And cap. A white cap.'

'What kind of cap?'

'I don't know.'

'A cowboy cap,' Papa says. 'Like in the movies.'

'Can you describe his face, Sam?'

'Ah, ah – *I* don't know.' He sounds unnerved by my request.
I forget sometimes how much I rely on Bola.

'He is wearing sunglasses,' Sam says. 'I don't see his face
well. Maybe he has *craw-craw* skin.'

'Stop talking nonsense, Sam,' Mrs Kekere says.

'Sorry, Ma.'

'Sunglasses,' I say. 'I forgot about that.'

We're in the bus, driving home in the evening. I am thinking
about the pastor. His sunglasses, his aeroplane and stage
show, his homes across the world. I'm thinking of Papa
beside me, folded and put away like a letter. What a fool I
have been to be drawn into all this when I have known, from
the beginning, that I will never fully comprehend what Papa
looks like or see Mama or witness the twinge of pain on
Bola's face when Elizabeth Akpala and Tunde walk by hand
in hand and he only sees Tunde, but Tunde does not see him.
I understand this. Bola can play football alongside him till
kingdom come, but this will change nothing. Sam will not
dance tonight, Tunde will still have a hole in his heart and

Mrs Kekere will have to live with her arthritis after all.

'Are you sure you can still see it?' Mrs Ejiofoh is playing *I Spy* with Sam, but she is not doing so well.

'I can, Ma.'

'What can begin with *S* in this darkness?'

Sam giggles. 'You must guess, don't you know?'

Papa is breathing heavily beside me. He must be exhausted. From the radio comes the lull of a Hawaiian guitar and a woman's voice, uneven as sandpaper.

'What can you see?' I ask Bola. 'Can you describe it for me?'

Silence.

I know he isn't asleep.

'Trees,' he says eventually. 'At the sides of the road and in front of us. I can see them in the headlights. And up there are many stars.'

'Stars!' cries Mrs Ejiofoh.

'That's not fair!' Sam says. 'Bola helped you.'

'My turn now,' Mrs Ejiofoh says, regardless. 'I can spy something starting with a *T*.'

'Mrs Kekere is sleeping,' Bola continues. 'Her head is against the window. Mr Ejiofoh and Papa are sleeping too. I can't see anything else.'

'What about Tunde?'

'Tunde!' Sam says.

'Oh, you're good at this,' says Mrs Ejiofoh.

'What about him?' Bola asks.

'Is he sleeping too?'

'Bunmi, we're not even halfway home. Aren't you tired?'

I sigh and lean my head against his shoulder. There isn't much to it, just bone and sparse muscle behind a thin cotton shirt.

'What colour is your shirt?' I whisper. 'I forgot to ask.'

'It's blue, Bunmi. Bright blue. Azure. Like the sky and sometimes the sea, remember?'

'I do, I remember. Bola, are you healed?' The roar of the

road against the tyres is like the crash of ocean waves. I imagine the forest ambushing the minibus from all sides, being held back by the glare of its headlights, folding in again, pursuing us from behind. I feel Bola exhale and lean against the window and when at last I think he will speak, he says nothing.

I wanted life, my life, to mean something beyond this sightlessness. I wanted it to be a gift, a sign from God, from somewhere, that there was purpose behind it, a larger plan. But I'm beginning to understand that I will not be led to grace. There will be days when I rail against my inability to appreciate the pattern of a leaf or the colour of a cotton shirt or witness a boy with no legs eking out a kind of existence. I am beginning to understand that this is my life, that it is good enough. I have Mama and Papa and Bola to thank, Reverend Abbe, our congregation, all the people on our street.

As I am considering this, Papa yawns, shifts in his seat. 'Bunmi, there is nothing – ' he says and stops. 'Bola does not need to be healed, you hear? He is with the Lord and he is in our hearts. Why don't you get some rest and stop chattering? Other people are trying to sleep.'

'Yes, Papa.' And I feel Bola tense up against me, his heartbeat thump wildly. After a long minute he begins to relax. I was convinced Papa was sleeping.

'*I* know,' Mrs Ejiofoh says. 'I see something starting with *A* – *A* for apple. You are never going to guess, young man.'

'I *spy*,' Sam says. 'Not, I *see*. You are not playing well.'

When I am grown, will I remember Reverend Abbe's onion-scented fingers, her kindness, Do Not Be Afraid splashed across the back of a lorry, the sweat and fervour of the arena, Bola's desire to be reborn? A boy dragging himself along the road in the middle of traffic? How could I forget him? I pray he has shelter at this hour and people he can rely on. Good people. His smile. I pray he never loses sight of that.

Segun Afolabi was born in Kaduna, Nigeria, and grew up in Canada, the Congo, Indonesia, Germany and Hong Kong. His first novel, *Goodbye Lucille*, was published in 2007 and won the Authors' Club Best First Novel Award in the UK. His first book, *A Life Elsewhere*, a short-story collection, was published in 2006 and was shortlisted for the Commonwealth Writers' Prize. Afolabi was awarded the Caine Prize for African Writing in 2005. He lives in London. 'The Folded Leaf' was first published in *Wasafiri* (Routledge, London, 2014).

Flying

Elnathan John

I fly when I sleep. Not the *tatata* wing flapping of pigeons and doves. More like the stationary gliding of a plane. My hands are my wings – I run, leap forward chest out, and will myself to fly. The engine that propels me is my mind, so if, when my eyes are closed, anything bothers or distracts me, I glide for a while, then start to descend sharply and crash. This happens at least one out of every five times. When it does, I wake up sad and with a headache. But when I am happy, I soar so high I start to feel breathless.

Aunty Keturah asks me questions before she states her theories. Do my wings have feathers or are they *wings-wings*? Do I usually fly alone? How high do I fly? If my wings have feathers, then I was a bird in my last life. If I fly alone, then I was an eagle, and if I was in company, a vulture – but only if I was bad in the life before that. If I have *wings-wings*, however, like a butterfly or a bat or the stiff wings of a plane, then maybe I was a bat or pilot. But God forbid bats, she says, God forbid bad creatures caught between lives, neither bird nor mammal. Bad people get trapped between worlds, between bodies, so that they are half this, half that; neither this nor that. You have to be really evil to become a bat. She is afraid of getting a child like that. A bad person from an old life.

I am normal so I must have been good in my last life. Except if this getting wings at night means I am part one thing and part another. Aunty Keturah knows so much of this stuff that I wonder what she was in her old life. To know so much, she had to have been something great in her past life, maybe a seer, something that would have shown her these secrets of how and why we return as one thing or another. Sometimes, I fear for her because of her temper and swearing. I fear she may become something dreadful in her next life. 'Your mother's cursed womb,' she says when any of the boys on window duty forget to clean some of the louvers or leave them open at night or when someone wets the bed. Good thing though, she doesn't stay angry for long. She protects us like a dog protects its puppies.

Once a man tried to lure Adnan, the albino boy, out of the house. Adnan had wet the bed and tried to hide it by turning the mattress upside down. The smell was so strong she turned the entire dormitory upside down until she found the guilty mattress. She slapped Adnan and said that his penis would wither for making the whole place smell and told him to kneel down outside between the two cactus plants by the short broken part of the fence. The dark man wore a beard like Che's face on the t-shirt I got from the clothes donated by the Cherubim and Seraphim church on our street.

The man was telling Adnan to climb over the fence and take something when she spotted him. She alerted the guard, Bimbol, with whom she went through the back gate. They caught the man. Another man on a motorcycle, who was waiting to whisk Adnan away, sped off. Aunty Keturah bit the man on the neck and hit him with the guard's stick until she had to be dragged away by the Policeman who had come from the junction.

Aunty Keturah is not really my Aunty. She is not anyone's Aunty. She started Kachiro Refuge Home when they told her in the hospital she couldn't have children and her husband went off with a woman who had six toes. I have heard Aunty Keturah tell that to some visitors she was giving a tour round the Home. She refuses to call it an orphanage because she says the word orphan has too much stigma around it. Moreover, she says, most of the children are really not orphans. Many of their mothers, whose wombs she always curses, dumped them by the roadside, in garbage dumps, in wells, in churches or just left them in the hospital.

Our home is also a school. The school is mostly for the children who are in the Home but we have some children who come from outside and leave every day after school. The rest of us live in the dorms. The babies are in a house called the nursery. I have just started JSS3, the most senior class in the school, and I am both class prefect and dorm leader for the boys' dorm. There is a separate dorm for girls and no boy is allowed to go in there. Aunty Keturah says that the greatest sin you can commit is to insult God. The second greatest sin is to be caught in the girls' dorm.

Far in the distance, beyond the football field, are the staff quarters. Aunty Keturah lives there, as do the Principal and his family, some teachers, the school nurse and the cooks. No-one is allowed across the football field. The Principal, a bald-headed man whose suits have hands that are longer than his, has a quiet voice that people can hardly hear during morning assembly.

As dorm leader, Aunty Keturah expects only that I clean her office, early in the morning. I can take a junior boy from JSS1 or JSS2 to do the work, but I like being alone in her large beautiful office. She has many books and paintings and a fridge that she doesn't lock. The big black table, the TV, the two cushioned chairs, three plastic chairs and the floors, I clean every morning before school. The high cupboard, the books, the louvers, I clean once every week, and twice during the dusty harmattan. I clean the table last because then I sit and flip through the books on her table or check her drawers. There is always something to find in the drawers. Sweets, dates, left-over biscuits.

Last week I found a big old brown book called 'Kachiro Memorial Refuge Home Records'. It has details about everybody. Names are arranged alphabetically beginning with Aaron and ending with Zichatt. There is no name under X. I can't think of any name beginning with X. I started reading from the first page and after a few pages decided to read only a little, three pages, every day. Reading the book gave me then, as it gives me now, a breathless feeling, like I feel when I fly too high. I feel my stomach almost empty and my heart suddenly fill my entire chest. Knowing everything about a person's life, where they came from, where their mother dumped them, what sickness they came with, makes me feel I have some kind of power over them. It was in that book that I saw that Adnan was dumped by his mother in General Hospital. In the column called 'Remarks', she wrote that Adnan was abandoned because he was an albino and that the whereabouts of his mother are unknown. I thought for a long time when I read it what he must have been in his former life. Maybe a white man. A bad white man. Perhaps that is why, big as he is, he still wets the bed. The sun hurts his eyes and skin and his eyeballs cannot focus on one thing. They keep darting back and forth like someone searching for something.

I have deliberately refused to jump to my own page. I don't know the feeling I will get if I read my own history: who dumped me and why.

The large field behind the dorm, where there are groundnuts, tomatoes and sweet potatoes planted, has three mango trees, which are forbidden to climb. During mango season, we have slices of mango served at breakfast and dinner. There is never enough for anyone, especially for those who really like mangoes. When we were in JSS2, Bakut, who has the biggest head I have ever seen, started telling the boys that the reason why we couldn't get whole mangoes was that Aunty Keturah was selling the mangoes. Abednego, who stammers and always gets knocked by teachers for his dirty collars, swore that he saw women leave with sacks full of mangoes. Aunty Keturah heard and made all the boys in our class spend the entire break kneeling in the sun and made Bakut and Abednego cut grass for two days. Abednego's bow legs make me laugh. He walks like a duck. I wonder what he was in his last life.

Another mango season is here. The boys in my class are planning to steal mangoes instead of getting one slice at breakfast. It is break time and the boys, all ten of us, usually head to the last desk in the classroom to play biro soccer. Today there are no biros on the table. Bakut, Gideon and Bosan – the fat boy we call Biggie – are talking about how to sneak out in the evening to steal mangoes. Biggie says that, when the guard goes to say his evening prayers, they will sneak off and climb the trees. Gideon has found a way of removing the louvers in case they need to come in through the windows. Me, I don't like their plan and I tell them I won't go with them.

Bakut stares at me. He says that I am a sell-out and that he thinks it was me that told on them last year.

'How come you didn't serve punishment with us that day?' he says.

'Because I am dorm leader. And she sent me to count the new exercise books that they brought to her office.'

'Why are you always in Aunty Keturah's office then?' Biggie asks.

'Yes, why is she always asking you to come?' Mindat, the fair boy with the curly hair, joins in.

'But she is not even there in the mornings when I clean her office,' I protest.

'OK, but in the afternoon when she asks you to come she is in the office,' Bakut insists.

'I tell her about...'

I stop. They will laugh at me if I tell them what happens to me when I sleep. They will not believe if I tell them that the reason I am always talking to Aunty Keturah is that she is the only one who understands my dreams and she doesn't look at me like I am crazy when I tell her. I tried to tell Samson, the tall boy whose hair never stays combed for more than five minutes. Samson is more my friend than any of the other boys and even he laughed at me. Samson is quiet when they question me.

'I help her arrange her books!' I scream and walk out, pretending to be angry.

'Lie-lie,' Bakut shouts out.

I don't care that they think I lie. The things I know about them – Bakut's mother was 16 when she was raped and she refused to touch him or breastfeed him and Biggie was found in a toilet, wrapped in plastic bags – make me feel bigger than them.

I walk to the dorm to eat the biscuits I took from Aunty Keturah's drawer yesterday. I think of the day she told me she had a baby once who looked just like me. Same nose. Same face. The ground under my feet started moving and I had a sudden urge to pee. I didn't want to hear her talk with a shaky voice about a dead baby who looked like me.

'Can I go and pee, ma?' I asked her when I couldn't bear it any longer.

'Yes, use my toilet. Just don't mess it up.'

Nobody ever used her toilet. Even though I had seen the toilet every morning when cleaning, I was excited about the prospect of actually peeing in her toilet, so excited that I couldn't actually pee. The reflection of the fluorescent bulb on the floor and wall tiles made me dizzy. I sat on the toilet seat and thought. That was when I decided that if I had to listen to her story, I would tell her mine.

'Wash your hands in the sink,' she shouted when she heard me flush.

When I came back in and sat down, she continued.

'Sometimes I think you are my baby that came back,' she said and stopped. Her eyes looked at me like she wished she hadn't said it. She went quiet for a while. Afraid, I began.

'I fly.'

She didn't say anything. Perhaps she didn't hear, I thought. But it was already out, already in the air between us and I knew I had to continue.

'I fly. When I sleep, I fly.'

She looked at my hands that were rapping on the table. I stopped. She leaned forward.

'Who else have you told about this?'

'Nobody. Emm, just Samson.'

'And what did Samson say?'

'He said I am mad and he laughed at me.'

'OK, first thing. You will not tell anyone else about this. Do you hear me? Nobody!'

'Yes, ma.'

'Second. You are not mad, Tachio.'

For the first time I wasn't afraid to talk about my flying, not ashamed. Flying wasn't such a bad thing. She made it all so real, people being born before and coming back. My dreams took on new meaning and I looked forward to the night. Flying became more exciting and I gradually started being able to choose where I would go, where I would fly to. I stopped crashing. It was in that month, that first month of secondary school, the month she created the post of dorm leader and put me in charge, that I started enjoying flying.

The bells ring and I run back to class. I am in the E section in the records but tomorrow I will jump to G just to check Gideon's story. His big scattered teeth make me think he was a donkey in his last life; he acts like a donkey.

The boys in the class are looking at me funny and passing little notes behind me, and everyone, it seems, knows something I don't. Their murmuring has become loud and Mr Ezra the Mathematics teacher with dark lips, who holds the chalk like a cigarette, asks what the matter is. They go quiet and he continues teaching. The notes still fly around and I am getting really annoyed. I want to punch somebody in the face and tell them their life history.

I think of Bakut's accusation and of the day, last year, when I had a cold drink in Aunty Keturah's office. She asked me if the boys were unhappy about anything. I told her about the mangoes and the stories Bakut and Abednego were spreading about her selling mangoes. I thought of mentioning Samson, but Samson borrows me his extra clean socks when mine are dirty. Did I do a bad thing by telling Aunty Keturah about the lies they were spreading? Did they not cause it by saying things that were not true?

I walk to the dorm alone after the last class. Some JSS2 girls walk past me, turning and laughing. The Principal has forbidden senior boys from punishing junior girls, otherwise I would have stopped them and asked them to kneel down for an hour. When I take off my shirt in the dorm, I see why they were laughing. Someone has glued a sheet of paper reading 'I am a big fool' behind my shirt. I wonder how long the paper has been there. It could have been any of the boys in my class.

Bakut sits whispering with Biggie on his bunk below mine. I know they are talking about stealing mangoes. They make me feel like I have a disease. No-one is talking to me. Even Samson just waves at me as he goes to sit with Bakut and Biggie.

I know they want to go this evening. My head struggles between telling Aunty Keturah or Bimbol the guard, between getting the boys punished, being hated, and joining the boys and sealing my lips if she asks me who went out to steal mangoes.

Gideon sneaks out first and taps the window from behind the dorm to say that it is safe to come out. Then Bakut and Biggie follow, taking pillowcases to fill with mangoes.

I get down from my bed and walk around the dorm. At the other end of the dorm, where the JSS1 boys are, some louvers have been left open. I walk toward the louvers and ask them who it was that left them open. Before the boys around the window begin scrambling to shut it, I see the Principal and Aunty Keturah walking toward the farm from a distance. My heart races and I run to our end of the dorm.

'Aunty and Princi are going to the farm,' I shout to

Abednego, who is standing by the window waiting for the rest to return. He slides out through the louvers they have removed to alert the others.

They come in one after the other, panting, barefoot and sweaty. They have plucked only four mangoes. Under my bunk they laugh loudly. Gideon puts back the louvers gently.

'Men, dey for catch us o! Who told you Princi was coming?' Bakut asks Abednego.

Abednego points at me. They are all surprised and look away. Bakut takes the four mangoes out from the pillowcase. There are seven boys that will share them. Two of the boys, Ishaya and Monday, don't like mangoes. As suggestions fly between the boys on how to share the mangoes, Bakut throws me a mango. I understand it. It is his way of telling me they have forgiven me.

I wake up in fright, earlier than I used to. I felt like I was disappearing. My night had no dream. No flying. No running and gliding. No choosing where to fly to. Nothing. Not even crashing. For the first time since I remember dreaming, I did not fly. I am afraid.

The minutes are passing slowly and my hands are trembling. I am sure Aunty Keturah will know what this empty night means. The earliest I can see her is during break and I don't know if I can hold on for that long.

After cleaning the office, I sit in her soft black chair, with the record book in my lap. On Gideon's page, I read, 'found crying and abandoned in the market.' Maybe someone even stepped on him as they went by, I think, feeling sorry for him. Then it comes back to me – my night without flying – and I am afraid again. I turn to my name in the book even though I told myself I wouldn't look at it yet. I can hear my heart beating and it is hard to breathe.

Tears are gathering in my eyes. I am scared of seeing my story. Not left in a toilet like Biggie, I pray. I trace the words with my forefinger. *Place of birth: Ridgeway Hospital, Kaduna.*

Mother's name: Ruth Kachiro (deceased). Father's name: Bobby (whereabouts, unknown). Just Bobby, without a surname. I take out a sheet of paper from the top drawer of the table and start copying quickly, thinking how I will ask Aunty Keturah about this without her discovering I have been reading her records. I have questions: what killed my mother, why my father has no surname, how she found me.

At the morning assembly two girls from JSS2 are standing in front, between the Principal and Aunty Keturah. After the Muslim and Christian prayers, we hear that two girls were caught with lipstick and will be given six lashes each. One of the girls, a thin, dark girl with big eyes, cries as she stretches out her hand. Aunty Keturah's lashes don't look so painful. The second girl looks very stubborn and has her eyebrows raised and her mouth squeezed like she doesn't care about the lashing. Everybody is stretching to watch this girl. Her mouth makes me think of the rats we sometimes chase out of the dorm. Aunty Keturah is breathing hard as she lashes. The cane drops before the sixth lash and Aunty Keturah staggers a bit and falls to the ground. Girls scream and I rush to where she has fallen.

'Go and get the nurse!' the Principal screams.

He and the other teachers try to lift her up. They fan her face and call out her name. Then they pour water on her face. Their voices sound like voices from a dream – far away yet near. I am getting dizzy. The nurse comes with a car and the teachers help carry Aunty Keturah into the car.

It is the third period and I haven't heard a word of what the two previous teachers have taught. I try to pay attention as the Social Studies teacher talks about civic duties. He is writing on the board when a teacher from the Primary section comes in and whispers something to him. She is short so she has to stretch to reach his ears even though he has lowered his head to hear her. He drops the chalk and runs out.

My heart is beating and I stare out the window. I see a big brown chicken with a limp in one leg. The chicken is staring at me in a way that chickens shouldn't stare at people. I have not seen this limping chicken before. Everyone in the class is talking about Aunty Keturah. Some girls are saying that the girl being caned was possessed. Flogging a girl with an evil spirit could make one collapse, they say. I would ask them how they know but I don't like talking to girls.

The whole day passes like a breeze and the school is more quiet than usual. Those who are talking about what is happening are doing so in whispers. Everyone is behaving right. No-one is walking on the lawns, no-one has left a window open and at lights-out everyone is still. Aunty Keturah is everywhere, in the breeze, in the whispers, in the dorm.

I wake up in the morning, relieved that I flew. I flew higher than I had ever gone, above white clouds that looked like balls of cotton wool in the sick bay. I saw big brown chickens like the one that stared at me in class. This is a good sign, something to show me that all is well with Aunty Keturah.

Everyone is on time for the morning assembly, properly dressed; I can't even see anyone chewing gum. Aunty Keturah will be happy if she comes. For once everyone is obedient without waiting for her to chase them around.

The Principal climbs the concrete podium and takes off his glasses. He is wearing a dark blue caftan and a light blue cap. I can't remember the last time I saw him in a caftan.

'Today,' he starts, but is barely audible. He clears his throat.

'Today,' he says again, this time shouting too loud. Everyone is still and silent and I can hear the wind sweeping the dry leaves across the ground.

'Today is a sad day. The Bible says there is a time to be born and there is a time to die…'

I can no longer breathe and my nose hurts. Hot tears form in my eyes and I can't see clearly.

'Let us have two minutes' silence for the soul of our dearly departed mother, proprietress and founder.'

The Principal takes off his cap. He does not need to tell us to have two minutes of silence. We came silent. The tears are rolling down my cheeks and my stomach rumbles like when I am hungry and drink water. The teacher by my side, the fair French teacher whose rings seem to be too tight for her fat fingers, holds my hand when she sees I am crying. Her hands are trembling and she holds me tight. I wonder how someone who was not sick or very old, can just fall, and die. Aunty Keturah should not just die like that, I think.

By the time he is finished talking, the Principal also has tears in his eyes. He dismisses us. No-one walks fast or runs or chatters.

I can feel her in the strong wind that blows. More hot tears roll down my cheeks. Some girls ahead of me are crying. Bakut is also a little ahead of me, wiping his eyes with the back of his hands.

After the first period, which the English teacher spent mostly wiping her face and telling us how Aunty Keturah is now happy in heaven, I clean the chalk board and go to the tap behind the class to wash my hands. I see the chicken of yesterday limping toward me. It comes a bit closer, stops and stares at me. It looks around. I look closer and suddenly, I recognize the stare in the chicken's eyes. I am not so sad any more. I smile and watch Aunty Keturah turn and limp away.

Elnathan John is a full-time writer who lives and works in Nigeria. His writing has been published in *Per Contra*, *ZAM Magazine*, *Hazlitt*, *Evergreen Review*, and Chimurenga's *The Chronic*. He writes political satire for a Nigerian newspaper and his blog for which he hopes some day to get arrested and famous. He has tried hard, but has never won anything. His first novel is due from Cassava Republic Press in 2015 and Grove Atlantic's Black Cat in 2016. He is a 2015 Civitella Ranieri fellow. 'Flying' was first published in *Per Contra* (Per Contra, 2014).

A Party for the Colonel

FT Kola

All evening, groups of white people came up to shake the Colonel's hand and to say sweet things to his wife. The Colonel was the nickname his son had given him, though he had never been in the military. It was due instead to his bearing, which was splendid. The Colonel exhibited no anxiety at being admired. Not even in the grand, rose-coloured ballroom of the Johannesburg La Fontaine, a hotel that a man of his race – Indian, as he and his wife's identity documents declared – could not normally enter as a guest. But the Colonel's wife was uncomfortable. Whenever, from within the room of round tables with their peach tablecloths and bouquets of flowers, a new and unknown lady approached her and told her she must be so proud, she could barely form the words to respond. The Colonel's wife was a stout woman, as sweet and cautious as a milking cow, with a face permanently crumpled into pre-emptive embarrassment. She had never been around so many white people in her own country before. She had, as a girl, patched together the facts of the Apartheid laws she lived under and her own meagre education to form the idea that every single one of them hated her, and so the evening for her proceeded as a series of mounting terrors. Each sparkling smile and jewel-laden hand on her shoulder filled her with panic. She sat, traumatized and still, holding her toddler grandson in her lap like a shield, offering mute smiles to anyone who spoke to her.

Now and then she threw a helpless glance in the Colonel's direction, but he never so much as met her eyes. He had made a show of avoiding the sight of their grandson, whose presence so annoyed him. But it was also clear to her that the Colonel was entirely unaware of her agony for the simple reason that he was enjoying himself, for this was a party held in his honour.

The Colonel had become the first agent of the Gold Lion Insurance Company in South Africa to earn more than 25 million rand in insurance sales. He sat erect, surveying the scene before him with conscious nobility, as if he were a king looking at his subjects for the pleasure of knowing that they were looking at him. He wore thick-rimmed glasses in the fashion of 20 years earlier and a moustache, neatly clipped and carefully waxed. His hair was pomaded into tight, mildly greying waves. When he stood tall – and he always stood tall, because he had excellent posture – he conveyed a sense of natural authority. His skin was as brown and smooth as a hazelnut, and he always smelled of clean linen, thanks to Eunice, their African maid, who, under his strict orders, spent an hour painstakingly hand-washing his clothes every evening.

On the drive toward the hotel, the worries that the Colonel's wife had managed to ignore all day began to blossom, uncomfortably, inside her. At first she had only concerned herself with her grandson, but now she imagined what would happen once they actually turned up at the party. Although the Colonel could well have afforded it, they had never so much as stepped inside one of the fancy downtown hotels before. She worried that they would be denied entry outright, and that her husband would make one of his scenes. Sure enough, when they arrived the Afrikaner security guard outside the hotel had taken one look inside the Colonel's forest-green Mercedes and held out a palm to halt them, before leaning his body through the window to ask exactly what they thought their business was. The Colonel's wife sat stiff against her seat, holding her grandson's face against her neck, a panicked sweat instantly bathing her lower back, anticipating the ensuing conversation with dread, and as it happened – as the Colonel angrily ordered his driver to move on and park the car, because they were going in, no matter what this bloody *boer*, this *rooinek* said – she heard herself desperately trying to placate everyone, saying that they had an invitation but of course the guard was only doing his job, that there was no need to argue. They would wait politely until someone could check that they were supposed to be there. But everyone had ignored her. The Colonel sat stubbornly; barking at his driver to drive on while the security guard grew increasingly red-faced and furious and threatened to call the police. The police might really have been called, and the security guard would have been in his rights to do so, except that the wife of the Gold Lion Company's President had turned up to rescue them.

The woman had appeared breathless, coming down the lighted pathway from the lobby in a light jog, holding the silk skirt of her salmon-coloured gown above her ankles, her face all flushed. With a sort of natural elegance that the Colonel's wife found herself immediately envying, the woman sweetly explained to the guard that the Colonel was her guest and hadn't this been prearranged and discussed with the management? She would have to complain. And so the Colonel's driver had driven them right up to the marble pillars that flanked the hotel's entrance, and a slightly confused African bellboy had opened the car door, and the Colonel had stepped out of the car, upright with pride. The white guests milling around the entrance were too polite to do anything but stare, curiously. The Colonel had floated through the lobby and into the ballroom like a debutante, and the Colonel's wife had followed behind, her little grandson a burning weight in her arms, all too conscious of the eyes upon her.

As a girl, the Colonel's wife had frequently wondered what the grand ballroom of the La Fontaine would look like. It was a place that often appeared in the wedding announcements at the back of *The Sunday Times*, a section that she and her sisters would liberate from their father as soon as the newspaper came, and go into a corner to examine carefully. They delighted in the sophisticated-sounding English names in particular, ones that sounded like characters from films or Enid Blyton books; the curious details of parental jobs (judge, chief of police, government minister); and, most of all, the always sparse details of the wedding reception, which only lent a heightened glamour to their imaginings.

Once the Colonel's wife was actually standing in the ballroom that she had pictured as a girl, she was disappointed to see that it was not at all how she had imagined. There were no chandeliers. Instead there were strangely shaped light shades that hung unevenly, perhaps artistically, from the ceiling. The room was not marble. Everything, including the walls, was carpeted in dusty shades of pink and pale browns. She had expected classical music, assuming it to be omnipresent on all such occasions, but there was a band playing jaunty jazz-like numbers instead. With a hot, embarrassed feeling in her stomach, she noticed that the other women gathered around tables or drinking champagne wore long gowns or fitted jumpsuits, mostly silk and satin, in pastel colours, with little jewellery. Somehow, they had all known what to wear. She herself wore a wool suit, olive-coloured, with lace trim on the sleeves and collar, that she had thought appropriately glamorous. She had taken out her best jewellery – her wedding jewellery, heavy and gold. There were no other children at the party. Her grandson, three years old, stood shyly behind her legs.

The President of the Gold Lion Company and his wife walked rapidly towards them, the President clapping his hands with delight. A girl, blonde head lowered, in a flowing dress the colour of rust, had followed.

'Mr Ibrahim!' the President had said. 'Well, hello! What an honour it is! What do you think of all this?' He gestured to the party behind him. 'I told my girls, what a brilliant achievement this is for Gold Lion South Africa! That is, a great achievement for you, yes, but also for all of us. Even in London they're talking of our – your – great success. Let's have a big bash, for once. Leave our restraint at home.'

'Bravo,' the Colonel said. 'You have done a wonderful job, Mr Greyling.'

The President had reddened with pleasure, examining the Colonel with admiring eyes. When his wife leaned over to tap him on the hand, he started. 'Oh,' he said. 'This is my wife, Justine.' The President's wife was smiling tightly at him, and he seemed to remember something. 'Oh yes, you've already met. And my daughter, Elizabeth. Come on, Elizabeth.' He waved his hand impatiently at the girl.

Their daughter was perhaps in her early twenties, the youngest person there after the Colonel's grandson. The girl had a broad, freckled face, the freckles disappearing at her jawline and then reappearing, floridly, all over her tanned upper arms. Her blonde hair hung loosely around her face. She said nothing, but stared at the Colonel's wife with a look of apology on her face that the Colonel's wife did not understand.

'Mrs Ibrahim,' the President's wife Justine said, extending a gracious hand. 'It is so lovely to meet you, properly. And who is this? Your son?'

The Colonel's wife had not even been able to open her mouth to speak. No words would rise in her throat.

'It is our grandson,' the Colonel said, and his wife knew it must bother him even to explain. 'He is called Riyaz. He is three.'

'Your grandson!' Justine exclaimed. She bent down to the little boy, who clutched his grandmother's leg with renewed fervour. 'Oh, he is all suited up. What a sweet boy. Well, hello, Riyaz.'

'But you should have told us,' the President said. 'Of course it's wonderful to bring him, just wonderful, but if we had known, we would have brought Elsie, our maid. She loves children. Of course, the rest of your family would have been welcome too, Mr Ibrahim.'

'Dad,' Elizabeth said, a tone of embarrassment in her voice.

'Well, come on, let's introduce you to everyone,' the President said, gesturing toward the room. 'We have space for the little man, of course. And you must consider Elizabeth here your nanny for the evening. She is at your disposal. Mrs Ibrahim, feel free to hand the little fellow off to her right now if you like. This is your night, you must enjoy it.'

As soon as the President had turned away, his hand on Justine's lower back, the Colonel had turned to his wife and, in a voice that stung, whispered, 'You see? Mohammed is destroying my celebration and he is not even here. Now we must treat the President's daughter like a maid. An old woman like you dragging a child around. She was mocking you when she asked if it was yours. They think you look ridiculous.'

Mohammed was their only child, the father of the little boy. He had been arrested six months ago. It was the fourth time in two years. Selima, his wife, had come by yesterday with tears in her eyes, pressing the grandson on the Colonel's wife, full of explanations about her own sick mother and the impending drive of over a thousand kilometres to Cape Town before her. 'What does she think?' the Colonel had asked, when he had come up from the office that night to find Riyaz sitting at the dining-room table and sticking his fingers in a bowl of chocolate Maltabella porridge. 'She can take the child on protest rallies and get him sprayed with tear gas, teach him all that ANC nonsense, but she can't drive in a car with him? Lazy. Irresponsible. Doesn't even want to look after her own child. These feminists are like that. I knew she was no good.' The Colonel's wife had said nothing in response to this. When they went to bed, she had nestled the little boy between them, ignoring the Colonel's disgruntled muttering, holding the child close to her, away from the Colonel's broad, irritated back.

She had forced herself to disregard her husband's complaints, and had used the money he allocated each morning for fresh fruit and groceries to buy a tiny suit for Riyaz, even though she knew he would not want the boy at the event. She and their maid Eunice had gone shopping for the suit together. The streets had been half-empty in the pale morning light, closed off because of a protest happening at the university a few blocks away. Now and then the Colonel's wife could hear the sounds of the distant crowd: the static-filled cries of *Amandla!* shouted by some young man through a microphone, followed by the responding roar of the crowd's *Awethu! Power – to us!* The two women had quickened their pace; spoken less than they usually might. As the Colonel's wife silently filled Eunice's arms with paper bags of food and the child's suit wrapped in a sheath of plastic, she thought that Eunice must be thinking about Mohammed, too.

When her husband found Riyaz sitting beside her on the plump leather seat of the Mercedes, the child's chestnut curls carefully brushed and his new suit ironed by Eunice, the Colonel had erupted with anger. But his wife had simply watched him from the inside of the car, detached, pretending that she couldn't even hear him, though the little boy himself had burst into tears.

What she could not tell the Colonel was this: she had come to believe that the moment she let go of her grandson she would be letting go of her son. That the instant her skin ceased to have contact with the child's warm body, somewhere in some dark and unknown place her son would cease to exist. All she could do was to keep the little boy close to her, to imagine that, by some transitive property, her own son would be safe. And so in the grand ballroom of the La Fontaine, she did not hand the little boy to the President's daughter, who was waiting by expectantly, but instead lifted the little boy back up into her own arms. Avoiding the Colonel's glare, she stepped forward to follow the President to their table.

For the rest of the night the Colonel and his wife sat like a bride and groom whose futures had been arranged, newly revealed to each other and instantly dissatisfied. At intervals, people came to offer their congratulations, and left again. Waiters moved around them almost clinically, filling water glasses and replacing cutlery, offering bread and folding abandoned napkins. The Colonel's wife watched the impassive faces of these Black men, some so young they must have been barely out of school, others older than she was, entranced by the deliberateness with which they completed their tasks. If Mohammed were there, no doubt he would have spoken to the waiters, declaring that he was not interested in engaging with whites, only those that he called his brothers. But the Colonel's wife found herself as unable to speak to them as she had to the ladies who visited her table, unable to ask them for juice or a soft drink, instead of the untouched wine that sat before her. For however out of place she felt, they seemed not to notice her.

The Colonel and his wife had been seated with the President and his family, who were almost never at the table, but spent their time moving about the room, dispensing small talk and sharing laughter. Every so often the Colonel's wife would catch glimpses of them, in between the movement of waiters and elegant ladies in their gowns and men in tuxedos. Everybody had natural groups to fall into, she noticed, the women in particular greeting one another enthusiastically. She realized, with a faint surprise, that of course these people all knew each other before this evening – they had been to each other's children's weddings and summer houses and dinner parties. It was only she and the Colonel who were new.

At turns, the little boy crawled under their legs, held his grandmother's hands and hopped to the jazz music, ate spoonfuls of broiled sole and lemony rice, banged the cutlery against the table and crawled into his grandmother's lap to kiss her. At one point, when the Colonel had been beckoned away by the President, and she was wiping Riyaz's mouth with a heavy pink cloth napkin, a group of women came to sit down at the table, taking up all four abandoned seats across from her, and cheerfully declared that they must speak with her.

'Mrs Ibrahim!' the first one, a woman with a brown bob said. 'We've been admiring your lovely suit from across the room. Congratulations, by the way, we all know that your husband's success must really be down to you.'

'Yes,' said another, wearing bright blue eye shadow. 'But it's just so dreadful, going on all those long trips in a car to drink tea in a stranger's living room and talk insurance. How can you even bear it?'

'I know I can't,' said brown bob. 'My husband talks so long too. The other day we drove all the way to a farm in Nelspruit. *Ag*, I thought we'd be there for days.'

'Nelspruit!' a chubby one with green eyes said. 'That's *baie ver*.'

'Is this your grandson?' asked blue eye shadow. 'I heard Justine Greyling mention that you brought him here. Isn't he handsome?'

The women all cooed over the little boy. The Colonel's wife was gratified to see that he never left her, never ran around the room, but stayed beside her as if tethered. Now, with the attentions of four strangers focused on him, he hid under her chair, one tiny hand around her ankle.

'Riyaz,' she said gently, and felt the little boy head-butt her calf, like a cat.

'Oh shame, he's so shy,' the fourth woman said. She was very tall with androgynous features, so slim she looked as if she could be folded in half like a piece of paper.

'You know, Mrs Ibrahim,' said brown bob. 'We were just discussing the seasoning on the fish and I said, it doesn't taste very fresh. I'm sure it's all from a box, you know how places like this can be. Cutting costs every which way. The Oriental Plaza – now my girlfriends say that is a curious place to shop. They must have wonderful spices and such things there. Is it true?'

'But is it good quality?' demanded blue eyeshadow. 'I don't like to spend any money if it's just going to go *vrot* or break.'

The Colonel's wife did not know how to reply. The fear, still tight inside her, was mitigated only by a realization that her silence was not an impediment to the conversation continuing. Still, she was relieved when the President tapped a microphone and hushed everyone into silence, and the four women retreated, with many whispered apologies and vows to speak with her again later, back to their seats.

Some minor awards were handed out; one to blue eye shadow's bashfully stooping husband, and then the President began to speak of the Colonel. His was a remarkable achievement, the President of the Company said from the podium. What an auspicious start to 1977. And the Colonel had been so inventive, seeking out new markets. What a privilege it was to award a man who was not only an accomplished insurance agent but also an upstanding member of the community, who was a motivation to them all. And a native of Johannesburg, the President added, a city which the company had always thought had a great potential for business. What was not said by the President – and what the Colonel's wife realized could never be said – was the reason that the Colonel had sold so many insurance plans where other agents had not. It was due to the same fear that she felt now, the fear that beat in the heart of everyone who was not permitted to enter a hotel like this. No white agent, turning up to a family home on a Sunday afternoon, in an area unfamiliar to him, selling things to people who believed he wished only to do them harm, could dispel it. But the Colonel was different. He was the same as the people that he sold to, and this, his wife had realized, was his gift.

The Colonel and his wife lived in a near-deserted part of inner-city Johannesburg. When they had first moved there,

Mohammed was just a few months old: an infant boy whom the Colonel's wife clothed lovingly in white knitted dresses and embroidered bonnets. At that time the area had been lively and crowded – a chaotic mix of African fruit stalls and Malay cafés and Indian bazaars and Chinese grocery stores. It was the kind of place the Colonel's wife had grown up in, the kind she was familiar with – there had always been someone for her to talk to, someone to help her when Mohammed got colicky, to chat over the garden fence with while their children played in the street. She had been happy, but had quickly realized that the Colonel was not.

When they first married, her husband worked as a high-school mathematics teacher, a terrifying presence who was more than willing to belt a student for a misdemeanour, yet wise enough that his students began to rely on him for advice in matters of marriage, career and family. In their small community he had become a figure of respect, and she was proud when he began to court her. It wasn't until after they were married that she discovered the Colonel had been born in a remote area of the Transvaal, that his family was poor and that on top of that he was the illegitimate son of an unmarried Malay woman, his father's mistress, a fact for which his stepmother never forgave him, for which she had made him sleep outside, and denied him even the tiniest kindnesses. For the Colonel, becoming a teacher had only been the first step in proving himself.

They had wanted more children after Mohammed, but two years into their marriage the local doctor, a heavily bearded and religious man, had told them that she would never give birth again, that something inside her was twisted up. Fortunate, he had added, that you have already given your husband a son.

Something had cooled between them after that. The Colonel worked harder, taking on more classes, until one day he came home and announced that he had quit. It was money, he declared to his wife, that was a man's ticket out of whatever limits others may place on him. Money was the great equalizer; it would take them places, it would open doors for their son, and lubricate even the most stubborn parts of the Apartheid system. And so, the Colonel had signed up with the one company that would have him. He became an insurance man.

It was natural that his former students, continuing to seek his advice, should also buy insurance from him, and the Colonel found that the government-created ghetto had left him with a niche market. White people preferred white insurance agents, and so he confined his business to fellow Indians, Muslims, and Malays, Coloureds, and Blacks, and they, reassured by the fact of him, had given him their business. The Muslims were the easiest. He could extract from his glove box a seldom used *topi* to place upon his head, assume the language of the pious and enter any living room on a wintry Johannesburg evening to settle comfortably into a chair and ease himself into a conversation by virtue of sheer goodwill, smoke endless cigarettes and accept numerous cups of tea. No white agent could have done that. No white agent would even have been in these areas at evening time, when shops were closed and groups gathered to gossip and eat. The people felt comfortable with him. They trusted that he was genuinely concerned, that he knew best – after all, he was an educated man, and he was one of them. The Colonel was good at his work. He visited grieving widows, gave advice to fatherless sons, helped mediate in difficult marriages, sent boxes of fruit and flour and a joint of meat to the people he knew were struggling. When clients turned up at the door, often unexpected, seeking some urgent advice or hoping to assuage a worry, the Colonel's wife would assume her own face of confident cheerfulness, and would set the table with her finest china. Platter after platter would come sailing out of the kitchen, as if a prince had come to dine.

The tendrils of trust he had cultivated spread ever outward. There was no-one he would not sell insurance to. The Coloured man that the Colonel's wife bought fish from in the market, the ministers of the Homelands and fresh-faced Black teachers who were eager to participate in the professional classes, the Hindu family next door to every Muslim one. He would even try, now and then, to convince a maid or gardener on his way out of a home that they too might benefit from life insurance, though they had not a penny to spare. After another day of successful sales, he would come home and assume his place at the head of the table, eat the same sparing dinner he ate every night (he did not believe in overconsumption), and remind his wife and his increasingly uninterested son again of the secret of his success: that he treated everyone as if they were *important* enough to buy insurance. The lives of these people had value, the gift was in telling them that, and if you could put a price on their life – it only proved the point.

The more money the Colonel made, the more he was convinced that all along he had been right. But the Colonel's wife, in private moments, thought differently. The Colonel's money did not bring them favour, or let them into the forbidden places from which they would always be excluded; it merely let them pretend, sometimes, that Apartheid didn't exist at all. Where the fact of inequality crept into their daily lives, the Colonel simply replaced the inevitable with the illusion of choice; going only to the Indian cinemas because there were no 'for use by white persons' signs since no white people ever went there at all; sending Mohammed to a private school in Botswana; telling his wife to take a more scenic route from the market rather than the direct path through the cemetery where white children would hide behind the gravestones to throw rocks at her; never going to the annual Rand Easter show where a man of his colour would be denied entry on certain days or to the nicest pavilions no matter how much he might pay for a ticket, but where the poorest white would be allowed to enter.

In the summer, the family went on trips to places where one could be treated as an equal: to Spain, to England, to

Botswana, to Portugal. The Colonel managed eventually to buy the largest building in their area, one that took up the whole corner of the block, and had given himself a spacious set of offices downstairs and leased the rest out to a café. He had tasked his wife with transforming the upper floor (which the Colonel preferred to call the penthouse) into a charming warren of imported marble tiles, costly fabrics and modern conveniences. They had hired Eunice, and the Colonel had built a sparse, four-by-four room on the roof for her, a room in which she would live for the next 30 years. For the Colonel's wife, Eunice soon became like a friend and daughter, as well as an older sister to her son, so much so that she often forgot Eunice had a family of her own, in far-off Transkei, a husband and child whom she saw just once a year.

It had stung the Colonel's wife a little when Mohammed, at 16, had come home on school holidays to admonish his parents for hiring Eunice, claiming that they imprisoned her, and asking why she was not permitted to eat dinner with the family. He followed Eunice around while she made beds and chopped vegetables and washed the floors, lecturing her on Communism. The Colonel's wife had to shoo her son away – *Can't you see she's busy?* – and the Colonel and Mohammed had fought in the evenings once Eunice was safely away in her own room. The Colonel claimed that hiring Eunice was practically charity, and besides, this life was something he had earned, while Mohammed accused him of trying to live like a white man, blind to the fact that he would never be one. Though she would never say it to her husband, the Colonel's wife agreed. They did not live in Houghton, or Hillbrow. The view from their windows was bleak, and the stink of frying from the café below made its way into every gold-embroidered sofa cushion and filigree cedar-wood shutter. They would never be able to go any further than they had come.

The President's speech ended, the strings of the orchestra stirred, and couples moved to dance. The Colonel's wife watched as her husband sat back with an expression of immense satisfaction and surveyed the scene. The little boy was now asleep, his head in his grandmother's lap, the rest of his body on one of the cushioned pink seats next to them. The Colonel turned to his wife for the first time in the evening and smiled, a genuine smile. It was so unexpected that she wanted to say something kind to him, when she saw a man approaching.

'Hallo, Mr Ibrahim!' the man bellowed, pushing four fat fingers into the Colonel's shoulder. 'Mind if I sit?' He was large, and stunk strongly of alcohol.

'Please do,' the Colonel said.

'Congratulations to you,' the man said. 'I tell you, five months ago I tried working those same streets as you – Lenasia – and I couldn't get a penny from anybody. I'd say, what the hell's the matter with you? Don't you want life insurance? What will happen to you and your little bambinos if you pass away? And the bloody fools would just look at me like I was an alien.'

The Colonel leaned forward. All night, the Colonel's wife noticed he had relished the ability to tell people about his various sales techniques, his little mechanisms to earn trust and to ingratiate himself with his clients, but now, the large man would not give him the opportunity. He slapped the table.

'I tell you what,' and here the man leaned forward, 'if more people were like you, keeping their heads down and making their living, we would be a different country. There's a lot of complaining here but no-one works hard and gets himself a forward momentum. No matter who or what you are, I believe you have to prove yourself, you understand?'

'That's what I tell my son,' the Colonel said.

'Good man,' the man replied, slapping the table again. 'I hope he's like you.'

'This is my wife,' the Colonel said. The Colonel's wife half expected the man to make some terrible joke, but his bleary eyes barely settled on her. Instead, he bent his face low to the table.

'I've got a wife too,' he mumbled, and reared up and shouted so loud that several people turned to look. 'Anna!'

A smiling woman, with bangs that fell over her forehead like little sharp teeth, was bustling towards them, a concerned expression on her face. 'These are the Ibrahims,' the man said, winking. 'He's the bastard who's been stealing all our business.'

'You're awful, Rodney,' Anna said. 'Oh, Mr Ibrahim, Mrs Ibrahim, I hope my husband hasn't offended you. He says whatever comes into his head when he drinks.' She sat down at the table. 'Is that your little boy?'

'No, he belongs to our son,' the Colonel said.

'So you're a grandfather! How nice. And what does your son do?'

'He is a doctor,' the Colonel said, hesitating for only a moment. 'Almost. He's only halfway through medical school.'

'Oh, wonderful,' Anna said. 'It's simply a marvel that your people always seem to be doctors, isn't it? Just the most intelligent of the bunch, you must be. Our children don't have any discipline. Lorraine is a dancer and Henry a lawyer, well, we'll see if he makes it.'

'Bloody fool won't make it,' Rodney said, thumbing the sleeve of a passing waiter and pointing at his glass.

'And you, Mrs Ibrahim? How do you spend your time? Do you work?' Anna said, leaning forward over the table as if she intended to reach out and touch the Colonel's wife. 'I'm mad about book clubs. Host them for the mothers in the neighbourhood. We raise money for charity. Recently we've been quite political. We spent at least four meetings discussing all the rampages. My word. Even Rodney was shocked. Our maid Onika's daughter was there. I told her as soon as I saw the news, go home, find your daughter, don't worry about the ironing, we were so shocked. They were just children, you know? To shoot at them like that! Lorraine was in London, she told me all about the BBC footage. But then what choice did they have? And we all said, where were the mothers? Would I let Henry go out that way, and act like that? Burning down your own school, not learning Afrikaans, how can you be trusted if you can't act civilized? How can you get a job? That's how you get respect. It's absolutely essential. Look at you, Mr Ibrahim, you are so successful.'

The Colonel's wife felt herself nodding away, though she had barely taken in any words Anna had said. She wanted to ask how old Onika's daughter was, and if Onika had found her. It was in those same riots in Soweto that Mohammed had been arrested. The last time she had seen her son, the last time she had hugged him – the warmth of his body beneath his woollen jumper, the scratchiness of his beard on her ear – had been that morning. He had turned up at their door asking for money – the Colonel had cut him off after he was expelled from medical school for his political activity. The Colonel's wife had stood by the kitchen window hearing their argument echo up from downstairs, before her son ran up, furious, brushing aside her offers to make him breakfast, which is all she had to give him, though she would have given him anything.

After the riots she had telephoned every hospital in the city, but no-one matching his description had been found. Selima had finally found out from someone that Mohammed had been arrested, and detained, either at John Vorster Square Prison or some farm somewhere, some remote place where they took terrorists. The Colonel had made inquiries through a lawyer that had come to nothing, and then he had given up, saying that Mohammed had made his bed and should lie in it.

John Vorster Square was only a few blocks away from the La Fontaine Hotel. The Colonel's wife wondered what would happen if she got up right now, left the ballroom, walked out into the street, knocked on the door of the prison, and asked the security police for her son. Demanded him back. That was what a mother should do. But she could not even bring herself to move. The sleeping boy was a weight in her lap, his little hand curled around one of her fingers. She wondered what Onika's daughter looked like.

'Bunch of bloody idiots chattering, those women,' Rodney was saying. 'Don't know their arses from their elbows. Think they're fashionable to be radical. I tell you when I see those bloody crowds all lifting their fists up like that and jabbering in the air, *Amanda* or whatever it is they say, my blood turns cold.'

Anna ignored him, smiling apologetically at the Colonel. 'The President said you live in Johannesburg. Is it true? I thought all your people lived in Lenasia or Bosmont. Or is it Newclare? I think that is terrible, by the way, forcing people to move. Just unacceptable.'

'We live in Pageview,' the Colonel said, clearing his throat. 'We have always lived there.'

It wasn't entirely true. If it had been her, the Colonel's wife would never have said it, because Pageview was only the most recent place from which the family had not been forcibly removed. Just a few years into the Colonel's insurance business, when they still lived in a small cottage and Mohammed had been just eight, the community had been upended. Paranoid that all the non-whites were plotting revolution, the government had vowed to create separate ghettos for each race. Early one morning the Colonel's wife had been hanging out the washing when the telltale white car with its government number plate had cruised into the narrow street, delivering a pair of official-looking white men with sheafs of papers in their arms. Removal orders. The Colonel and his wife had been evicted maybe four or five times in their lives, and they knew what happened next.

For the next four weeks, as his wife silently served the Colonel his breakfast, they heard the unmistakable rumble of bulldozers and voices shouting in Afrikaans that all must vacate their houses on threat of arrest. The Colonel's wife had repeatedly asked the Colonel where they were to go, watching anxiously as her neighbours packed up and left, as street signs were removed, yet the Colonel remained distressingly silent, until one day he arrived home and in a confident voice told her they were not going to move at all. While stooping down to pull up the metal cover from the front of the insurance office that morning, he had stepped into the velvet green coolness of desks and filing cabinets and simply decided that they would not leave. Let the government knock everyone's house down. Let the new white residents occupy every house, every apartment. The Colonel's family would remain.

Every morning the bulldozers and German shepherds arrived to hector and terrorize. The Colonel sat stoically at his desk surrounded by papers while his wife hid, terrified, in the bathroom of their home upstairs, Mohammed pressed to her skirts. She prayed out loud for them to remain safe, envisioning the claw of a bulldozer breaking through one of the concrete walls of their living room. That is where the Colonel had found her every evening, the dinner uncooked, their son distressed and confused. It seemed only to make him more insistent that they defy the order, though she often tried to persuade him just to move. What did it matter? Wouldn't it be less trouble? But the Colonel ignored her. He employed the talents of a young Jewish lawyer who sent increasingly lengthy and dense letters to the Department of Community Development with a regularity bordering on harassment. The Department had eventually stopped responding, which the young lawyer counted as a victory, and since no police had turned up to forcibly evict the family, they assumed they had been consciously forgotten.

It turned out that the white people the government had cleared the area for did not want to live there, and so the rubble of bungalows and bazaars and cafés lay where it had fallen. Now, over a decade later, the area was still near empty.

A few families here and there, and businesses that relied on trade passing through: a cemetery, an auto salvage yard run by a deaf man of indeterminate ethnicity with a drooling mastiff, and a big open square that the Colonel's apartment looked over, in which nothing but a couple of sad trees, bent drowsily, had survived. To his wife's surprise, even after the area was deserted, the Colonel's business continued to thrive. The clients still came in from the Indian ghetto, a lonely concrete development in the open veldt with half-built and neglected structures everywhere, and from Eldorado Park, where the houses crowded against one another and tumbles of barbed wire sat atop every roof.

'Oh, yes, Pageview,' Anna said. 'Rodney, are you too drunk to dance? What about you, Mr Ibrahim?'

'Well?' the Colonel said, turning to his wife. Her grandson remained sleeping in her lap. The boy looked like a tiny, drunken elf, his suit crumpled, his cheeks flushed, one little hand entangled in his curls. The Colonel's wife was surprised at the suggestion. Her husband had never before wanted to dance. Their wedding had been traditional and religious, only her parents and an imam, no dancing, and he was not a romantic man. Even when they went on their trips to Spain, when they sometimes went to restaurants in which people danced after dinner, and she had sometimes wished that he would take her hand, he would not do so. Today, though, he apparently wanted to dance in front of all these white people.

'Rodney!' the President said. 'What are you telling Mr Ibrahim? Nothing troublesome, I hope.'

It seemed like the Colonel's wife was perpetually being rescued by the President and his wife, who were heading towards their table, their daughter again in tow.

'We were just seeing who wanted to dance,' Anna explained.

'Ah ha! We noticed that you were not dancing. No-one wants to dance, until they do. As I said, Elizabeth is here, and she is a competent babysitter.'

The Colonel stood up. 'Thank you,' he said. 'My wife would appreciate that.'

'Excellent,' the President said. 'And you too, Rodney. Your wife is waiting. Don't fall over just yet. Come on, Mr Ibrahim.'

They all got up, except the Colonel's wife. Elizabeth sat next to her, and spoke breathlessly. 'Don't be nervous,' she said, 'I'll take good care of him. You go and dance. By the way, I really admire your husband so much, I've been supporting the Progressive Reform Party, you know. Though don't mention it to my dad. I try to go on the protests when I can, though it's difficult... we're the laughing stock of the world in South Africa. I was in Amsterdam for three months earlier this year and I found it so refreshing, to be able to mingle.'

'I don't usually dance,' said the Colonel's wife.

'Oh, go on,' Elizabeth said, reaching out to pluck the child from her arms.

For a moment, the Colonel's wife tightened her hold on Riyaz. But Elizabeth's hands were already on the boy's waist, and the Colonel's wife briefly envisioned each of them pulling the child away from the other until he snapped in two. Elizabeth was smiling at her, beseechingly, and staring into the girl's eyes the Colonel's wife had a moment of sudden, terrible realization. Whatever bad thing she had tried to avert by gripping onto this boy, it had already happened. That Selima had handed him over, that the little boy was with her, was the sign she had been dreading all along, the proof she had been waiting for so anxiously. Nothing she did, and nothing she could do, mattered. She relaxed her grip on the little boy, felt him suddenly lighten as Elizabeth took the bulk of his weight, and the Colonel's wife let one of her hands run down his chubby little leg to his foot, so that when Elizabeth finally pulled him away she was left with nothing but a single tiny leather shoe in her hand. The Colonel's wife looked at it, turned it around, as if she had never seen it before.

The boy opened his sleepy eyes, and reached up to grab a

fistful of Elizabeth's hair. Elizabeth laughed and reached out to take the shoe, and nudged the Colonel's wife gently. 'Go on,' she said. 'Don't worry about him.'

The Colonel was waiting by the dance floor and, with halting steps, in a pair of brown suede pumps that made her feet ache, the Colonel's wife moved toward him. Couples nodded appreciatively as they joined. 'Well done!' a man said, raising a glass full of champagne. The Colonel's wife realized how desperately thirsty she was. A waiter was nearby with a silver water jug and a napkin folded over one arm, but he passed by before she could say anything. She felt even more nervous now. Everyone was looking at them. The truth was that neither of them really knew how to dance. But the Colonel gripped her hands, and made a show of doing what the others around them appeared to be doing.

'Maybe now,' she ventured, feeling bold, 'we can move to London. All of us.'

The Colonel did not reply, but instead turned her awkwardly in his arms. She looked for her grandson. Elizabeth had taken him away from the table. He was dancing around in circles near the band, with Elizabeth looking on, saying something to him.

The Colonel was smiling broadly, looking at everyone but his wife. A couple nearby were dancing in an elaborate way, tracing their fingers along each other's arms and spinning around, and the other couples had moved back to give them space. The Colonel's hands felt heavy and stiff on his wife's shoulders, manipulating her clumsily like an unyielding toy.

'We are doing just fine here,' he said. 'What would we want in London? You want me to live like my brother in Manchester? And run a fruit shop? He can't even afford heating in the winter.'

'No,' the Colonel's wife said, her voice small, 'but there is Gold Lion there also. You have more money than your brother. He will sponsor us for the visa. And Riyaz, he could go to school...'

'There is nothing wrong with where we live now.'

'But Mohammed,' she said, and the Colonel tightened his grip on her shoulders.

'I don't want to hear his name,' he said, 'not tonight. He has destroyed things enough as it is.'

She looked into her husband's face as he gritted his teeth. It was an expression she knew well, one that her son had not inherited. His face was always open, even in anger, wide-eyed, astounded. But in his resoluteness, he was like her husband. She wondered sometimes if this was why it stung the Colonel so – that not only had their son been arrested, not only had he been in prison, not only had he failed at medical school and been rusticated for political activity, but, in doing all of that, he had rejected the Colonel himself. The Colonel had always had big plans for their son, ones that he had tried to sell Mohammed on with little success (that Mohammed could become a property developer, that he could open up a chain of clinics and pharmacies from here to Zimbabwe, that he could become the President of Gold Lion himself) and while Mohammed received these with irritation and eventually outright contempt, when the Colonel spoke of them his wife sensed an enthusiasm born of love, of belief. Mohammed – he liked to tell her, in the sleepy moments when they lay in bed – was destined to do something great. He was a boy who would never be merely content to live in the safe shadows of those bigger than himself.

The music was coming to a slow stop. A sigh went up from the dancing couples. The President was back up on the stage, clapping his hands together.

'Forgive me, forgive me,' he said. 'I will resume the music shortly. But we do have one more special presentation before the evening comes to an end. A very special presentation.'

A red-haired girl wearing a very short white dress was shimmying through the crowd, holding out a large object before her and smiling mischievously at everyone she passed, all bright lipstick and gums. As the girl ascended to the stage, hobbling a little awkwardly on an absurdly high pair of shoes, the Colonel's wife could see that the object was a large square, wrapped in string and brown paper. 'Look at that dress,' the Colonel's wife heard someone whisper disapprovingly behind her.

'Wonderful,' the President said, and then, loudly, 'Mr Ibrahim? Would you do us the honour of joining us on the stage?'

The Colonel stepped away from his wife, and, conscious of everyone waiting for him, slowly ran a hand over his hair, and then both hands down the front of his tailored blue suit. He stepped carefully and slowly to the stage, as if bathing in the murmurs of appreciation that flowed around him. He did it with the kind of self-composure that suggested he had known all evening that this moment was coming, as if he never doubted that at some point, everyone would be officially asked to gaze upon him.

The Colonel's wife stood below the stage. A few people nodded at her encouragingly. She looked around for her grandson, but in the dim lights could not quite make him out. At a corner in the back, she saw Rodney's face illuminated by the lamplight at their table, drunk and half asleep.

'As our honoured guest makes his way to the stage,' the President was saying, 'let me just reiterate once more what a splendid job he has done. Twenty-five million – I repeat that – 25 *million* rand worth of new sales! Which begs the question, what were the rest of you lazy bastards doing?'

A laugh from the crowd. A shouted objection from a high-pitched voice, and then some theatrical admonishing from various voices.

'My wife doesn't like me to swear,' the President chuckled. 'Well, at least let me say that what we are celebrating tonight is bloody marvellous.'

'They're going to make a toast,' Anna whispered, suddenly next to the Colonel's wife somehow, and so close that she could detect the sour wine scent on the woman's warm breath. '*Ag*, you haven't even got a glass. Where have those waiters gone? So lazy, they bugger off the moment they think they can get away with it. Let me go see.'

The Colonel's wife looked around. All evening the waiters had been swift and omnipresent, filling glasses, lifting plates, folding napkins, opening doors. They had functioned like silent gears, moving the party forward, entirely unnoticed. And now they had disappeared, as if they had never existed, although some of the guests held empty glasses, waggling them quizzically, waiting for the inevitable fill-up or a fresh drink.

'Now, Mr Ibrahim,' the President was saying, as the Colonel stepped onto the stage, his hands folded before him like a little boy, rocking excitedly on his heels. 'We don't have too many handsome men in our business, as no doubt the ladies here this evening will have noticed.' The audience laughed again.

'I'll find someone for you,' Anna whispered and walked away with quick, efficient steps.

The Colonel's wife felt isolated, visible. Naturally, people were turning to her and smiling, anticipating that she was enjoying this moment, that she was filled with pride. But something was troubling her. Anna was right – where had the waiters gone? It seemed like a sign. Something as serious as a barometer suddenly dropping and the sky growing dark and still. A sign that, in this room, only she could read. From the back of the room, she could hear some sort of exclamation.

'Oh, hush,' a man near her said. 'People can be so rude.'

'So when we find an agent that's handsome and good at his job,' the President was saying, 'of course we want to immortalize him.' At this, the Colonel laughed uproariously, the President joining in also, and then pausing slightly, only vaguely aware of some disturbance below, the ripples of which were now moving through the crowd, reaching the Colonel's wife. She had the sensation of standing on a shore, the water lapping at her toes, nudging her slightly backwards, disrupting her centre of gravity.

'And I must say,' the President continued, a tone of uncertainty still in his voice, 'when I saw what the girls in the office had arranged for this gift, I thought, why not me? But then, I'm just the President of this company, not its best salesman!'

The Colonel's wife turned on her heels and moved through the guests, heading for the back of the room where Anna had gone, to the swinging doors that led to the kitchen, ignoring the confused whispers around her. Behind her, the crowd was laughing again, and the President was continuing, emboldened by the response.

'As a sign of our appreciation, we present this portrait of you, Mr Ibrahim, to be hung in our main Gold Lion office, to always speak of your fantastic achievement!' At this, the red-haired girl ripped away the brown paper to reveal a picture of the Colonel. In it, only his face was visible, large and looming, though it had no colour. It had been sketched with pencils on a mauve background. The toast rose up from the guests, and camera flashes popped around them. A great applause broke out. The Colonel stared at the portrait, blinking.

If she had been there to see it, she might have mused on how little it looked like the Colonel, how clearly it had been created by a person who had never seen the Colonel in the flesh. But the Colonel's wife was by then at the door of the kitchen, peeping through it like a child, watching on a television screen around which the waiters had paused to gather at the sight of a riot breaking out in the street, the image of John Vorster Square surrounded by flames, of bodies at strange angles – laying where they had fallen, she thought, though she could not be sure – on the pavement in front of the building.

Beneath the stage, the crowd was still clapping enthusiastically. In the midst of all this, the little boy had danced away from Elizabeth's hands. He had only known one type of applause in his life, and that was when his father had held him aloft at rallies, his eyes burning from stadium lights, the roar of approaching tanks distant, ever-nearing. It was much like now, as he stood alone before his grandfather: the crowd going wild, the sound of cameras, a panic latent beneath the joyous swell of noise. In the space between the Colonel and the guests, Riyaz appeared a solitary figure on two strong little legs, and lifted a fist up in salute. *'Amandla!'* he shouted, and then paused, giddily proud, looking around at the multitude of faces that stared at him, as though he quite enjoyed the stunned and confused silence that he had, all on his own, been the cause of.

FT Kola was born in South Africa, grew up in Australia, and lived in London and New York City before pursuing an MFA at the Michener Center for Writers at the University of Texas, Austin, where she is a fellow in fiction. 'A Party For The Colonel' is her first published story, which appeared first in *One Story* (One Story inc, New York, 2014)..

Space

Masande Ntshanga

I guess you won't believe him, either, but this is what CK tells us, this morning. He says there's a grey man living in the shed behind Ma Thano's spaza shop on Miya Street, a man who isn't a man, one sent down to Earth from a distant place.

Where we are is the local, the name our parents give to the local primary school they pack us off to each morning here in Bisho, and the way CK is saying this, it's the last day of school and the four of us – that's him, Thando, Thobela and me – we're slouching at the back of our Afrikaans classroom, again, our bodies turning to slushed ice from the promise of having failed yet another take-home test in die taal.

CK keeps talking.

He says how this man, behind Ma Thano's spaza shop, he isn't the same as any other man he's ever seen before. CK leans forward and tells us that this guy, whatever he is, he's just something we have to set our own eyes on.

I nod, but all this time CK's whispering, all this time he's writing us notes about this grey man, what I'm doing is watching Mrs Siviwe, our teacher, watching how she's sitting at the front end of our classroom with her head down, and watching how she's scratching red lines in each exercise book that passes under her pen.

She flips open another exercise book.

CK keeps talking.

From where he's sitting on my left side, he leans back on his chair and tells me to tell him which of us is in. He turns his head to the side and to the seat behind him to repeat it to the other guys. Thobela and Thando just nod to him in response.

I go back to Mrs Siviwe and, as I'm watching her, the minute hand on her clock slows down to a stop. Mrs Siviwe has the clock hung above her calendar, a glossy flip-over that shouts "92!' in the school's powder-blue colours, and, when that clock freezes, her pen grows even louder on the page, and, from where I'm sitting, I can hear it scraping the paper like tyres skidding across concrete.

'I'm in,' Thobela says, watching the skid marks filling up in his exercise book.

'I'm in,' Thando says, without looking up from his pencil case.

I turn around and look through the nearest window.

From where I'm sitting, the grass in our playground looks green and symmetrical, as if the field had been pressed down and ironed by a solid bar of the day's heat.

It's a really peaceful place.

I spend a few seconds imagining myself stretching out and unloading myself out there.

When I got promoted to standard three, last year, I did well, and when my mother heard of my results she drove home with a sponge cake for us to eat for dessert – we even sat, the three of us, me, Mama, and Nana, around the long dining-room table we never used for meals. This was in 1991, and it wasn't long until the spirit had taken us over and we brought out the old balloons and streamers we'd used the previous year for New Year's as well as Nelson Mandela's release from his island prison. After Ma cut us a piece of the cake each, she announced that she'd received a promotion at work and told us how, with the way things were taking their course, it was possible I could be taken out of the local and enrolled in a model c as soon as the start of my standard-five year.

When I look back up, again, I find Mrs Siviwe glaring at me.

She has my exercise book open in her hands.

When she shuts it and places it on top of the pile on her right, all the while shaking her head, I look down and write a note to my friends.

I tell them I'm in and CK says, 'Good.'

He says, 'Tomorrow it is, then.'

The three of us nod at him together.

We say, 'Tomorrow it is, then.'

***

Thobela's been named our group leader for the rest of this year. We've decided to crown him because he holds the highest number of stolen goods bagged by a member of our gang. It isn't that close to the end of the year, to be fair, but CK and I tapered off quite early, this time around – we tapped out as early as May, in fact, and as far as Thando goes, ever since his father, the Bishop, drove his Mazda back into their garage and his mother's life, the guy's been extra careful about drumming up the sort of trouble you can fall into for stuffing chocolates and action-hero figurines under your balls.

CK and I have always been small time, anyway.

There's really no loss to be had, here.

The first time we did it, we stole trips into the town, but grew too used to the stone lionesses overlooking the parliament square, the grown-up world of loud pink bricks, hooting cars, typing machines and slippery fried sausages.

My mother had banned video games at my house, citing a collective stink that storm-clouded over a pile of our report cards, but even the homeland soldiers no longer excited anything in us, their jaws and manners just as rigid as the statues that kept vigil over the suits who worked in Parliament Hill.

I mean, they never shot their guns.

So we shoplifted at the local OK Bazaars, which stood just across the street from the Amatola Sun Hotel, where the glass turnstiles were inviting but often kept us from slinking in and walking past the casino, our bare feet moving us from the cold white marble and onto the lush red carpet, then through to the back where – just before the swimming pool where we saw the first white woman in our lives – they had a new Street Fighter machine glowing in the corner for only five bob a game.

At OK, during our short career there, I managed to nab a Bruce Lee poster and a Spider Man figurine; CK scored himself two twin sliver revolver BB guns. Then, one cold Saturday in the middle of April, one guy who wasn't in our gang, this chubby laaitie who didn't go to school with us down at the local, got caught and carried wailing into a dark room at the back of the supermarket. I don't need to tell you which idiot's parents were there. CK and I dropped everything we'd stuffed on ourselves and walked out slowly. We'd heard about the bald security guards who waited in that back room with their batons and shell-toe boots. They'd been put on the Earth to sort out precisely guys like us.

With Thobela, of course, it's a different story. First of all, the guy's better than any of us could ever dream of becoming, and secondly, he only steals panties.

It's true.

In a good week, Thobela tallies up to five pairs, easily, and he keeps them everywhere: in his bag, in his pockets, in his pencil case, and he gets thanked a lot by the guys at the local.

So when my lift bails on me after Afrikaans, that's who I go to.

Thobela.

I walk back from my corner on Siwane Avenue and find him leaning up against the walls at the entrance to our school.

He's got this hatter's grin plastered across his folded, sweaty face and he looks like he's just been standing there, keeping the building up on its feet or something.

Thobela's a stocky guy, too, a bit on the shorter side, and

he's got a deep widow's peak with hair that grows out its longest at the back.

I tell him my problem and he says to me how that isn't a problem.

We take his contract van down from the local's gates and swerve down into Circular Drive. I usually hitch my rides with my driver, Petros, a guy who covers my neighbourhood all the way up to just one block before CK's, and never with Thobela, since out of our entire gang, he's the one who lives farthest from of us up in the north.

We settle into the back of the van as Thabo, Thobela's driver, turns his leather-sheathed wheel and tunes in a jam by Sipho Hotstix. We swerve to the right and roll down Independence Avenue, which has no speed humps and allows Thabo to shift the stick up.

Thobela grins and says to me he has something to show me.

I look and it's his latest pair: a sky-blue number with a small bow knitted at the front of it. It's got a faded yellow stain down the centre where the girl must've crossed her legs and wrinkled the cotton.

I guess that's a period stain.

My first one.

At the back of the van, Thobela's thumb rubs around the patch of off-white with a careful, admiring stroke. He pulls his backpack up and we give the cloth our devotion. The fabric has been scrubbed as thin as the pages of a Gideon Bible.

'She can have babies, now,' Thobela explains to me.

I watch him fold the pair back into his satchel.

The contract drops me off at the bottom of Rharhabe Road, a good five-minute walk up from my house, and Thabo, who's driven us this whole way, tells me I don't need to collect a two rand for him on Monday for the ride – I should count it as a favour to my mother: 'All three for us are oomkhaya, remember, we share a clan name,' he says.

Thobela has another ten minutes or so at the back of the van and so I wave him off. Then I start the walk up to my place.

When I get home, I notice I've broken out in a light sweat, the moisture griming up my collar even more, and our stop-nonsense, more than a few months in need of a shape up now, has toppled over and spread my family's instability into our new neighbour's yard.

Though I guess Mr Sithengi isn't that new, any more.

He's offered to put up a face-brick fence with a red finish that complements our garage for upwards of a year now, but Ma has declined his generosity each time.

'I don't need a handout,' I once hear her say in Nana's room.

Right now, I can see into their green lawn from our porch. A tractor tyre has been carved into a garden swing and it sways languidly under an oak. It looks like a magazine picture. The yard of a happy family.

I unlock the padlock on the burglar, let myself in, and lock again.

In the bathroom, I masturbate twice to whichever girl comes to my mind before I wash my hands and prepare tea for Nana.

'How was school?' she asks me, when I bring her tray rattling into the room.

Nana likes to talk in the moment it takes for her tea to cool down. Afterwards, I mix in her sugar and she lets me have the first sip.

'It was okay,' I say to her.

***

The next day I wake up early from a wet dream and a nightmare I've had about the grey man. The way it happens is that it's a Saturday and even inside my room, with the curtains drawn, I can feel the day's heat, its long fingers circling around my neck and taking my sleep.

Since Ma gives me all my chores the previous night, I know what to do when the morning arrives. She likes to take her rest on Saturdays and Nana always makes sure that I give her enough of it.

The first thing I do when I get out of bed is reach into my bag. I take out my Afrikaans exercise book and push it under my mattress. Sometimes Ma likes to check to see if I've been eating my packed lunches. She has awful days, sometimes, migraine days, when I just let the stuff pile up in my knapsack.

I peel off my briefs for another pair in the drawer, and after I hide my test, I step into the hallway, as quiet as sleep, and make my way into the humming kitchen.

Once there, I take our big pot first.

I empty out the water I poured on it to soak the crust from the pap we ate last night. Then I do the rest of the dishes and sweep. I fill up a plastic bucket with water and Sunlight and mop up the kitchen floor.

Then I take down a box of oats and three bowls for myself, my mother and Nana, and as the water heats up, I step out of the kitchen door and into the morning. The dew on the grass wets me between my toes and I itch. I take a big breath and watch the sky as it turns from pink to white. Then, after a while, I wipe my feet and walk back inside.

I cook and serve myself a bowl of oats.

Then I boil another pot of water and pour it into a vaskom which I take with me to wash inside my room. When I'm done, I lather myself in Vaseline and get dressed in a black shirt and red shorts before I take another look at that stinking test.

I barely scraped over, this time.

I stick it back under the mattress and write a note to my mother about how I've gone playing with Thobela and the rest of the guys. Then I walk out and sit on my front stoep to wait for our leader.

The concrete feels cool beneath my thighs.

I lie on my back and watch the sky change from white to blue.

* * *

Thobela lumbers up to my stoep a few minutes later. He's had to walk it all the way down from eBhalasi, a township just north of our suburbs, bordered by a squatter camp our adults often tell us mocking and warning stories about.

Thobela's dad owns a two-room up there, and where they live is just three blocks down from the landfill that starts off the squatter camp, a place where we kick around plastic bags and scour the pit for toys long lost from the white children who come to sleep at the Amatola Sun during Christmastime.

Thobela plonks himself down next to me and takes out a plastic Rambo knife: his latest find.

'Hey, check it, out,' he says.

I do.

It's a decent piece. I stand and crouch, gouging the air a few times with it like a commando.

Then I hand it back and sit down.

We're quiet for a while.

Two cars pass us by, both of them Toyotas, before I ask Thobela if he passed. He says he didn't and I turn to look at him.

'It's fine,' he says, sharpening the knife's plastic blade on the edge of my stoep. 'I'm not repeating the standard. I'm not going to white school next year. I'll start high school eBhalasi.'

I don't say anything.

'What about you?'

'I passed by one mark.'

I look over the fence, to where Thando's family stays. You can see his place from mine. I guess he's sort of my neighbour, this way.

'Your marks were good last year,' Thobela says.

He's right about that, but I give him a look that tells him to stop.

Thobela laughs.

'I wouldn't want to go to white school either,' he says.

'Do you think it's real?' I ask him.

'CK?'

'I had a dream about it.'

'He's lying,' Thobela says.

He goes back to sharpening the knife.

'I only came out here because I hate Bhalasi.'

I think about my grades and the grey man as we walk over to Thando's house.

***

The sun almost overpowers us. Its light makes our shadows criss-cross the way the world doubles up whenever we squint through Nomalanga's keyhole.

Nomalanga is my friend Thando's sister.

From where I'm standing, I can see her hanging panties and bleached dishcloths on a sagging clothesline. She stands in the shade under the line, a lime wall cordoning their backyard from the eyes of strangers like us. Like always, she ignores the both of us.

When I turn around, I find Thobela leaning over Thando.

Where we are is Thando's driveway, which means we're on cement, very hot cement, and at places we've had to skip over molten tar just to get here. The way it's getting hot is that when you go without shoes, you can't. You have to stand on the sides of your soles and everywhere on your face there's sweat trying to tickle you, sticky rivulets that try to sting our eyes shut.

In front of Thobela, in his check shirt and brown shorts, Thando's sitting on the driveway with both his knees held up to his face. He isn't looking at either one of us, but between his knees and below his face, Thando's hands are busy squashing ants.

They're both grazed and bleeding.

He dips his thumbs in the blood and squashes ants between his feet and everywhere around him, there's blood thumb prints with these little black dots of dead ants in the centre.

He says we can't go inside his house, today.

Thando says we can't do it tomorrow, either.

One time, about two weeks after the Bishop's return, it was me, Thando and Thobela, and we were out on the driveway playing cars with the garden bricks. I don't remember what happened, but Thando opened his thumb against something and screamed. He said it was Thobela's fault, but he wasn't sure. Then he said it was my fault. Then Thando bled and said the both of us, Thobela and I, we'd collected sins. He wouldn't stop saying that, again and again, and then he walked through his front door and disappeared.

We'd collected sins.

'Not ever,' he says, now, about his house.

I ask him, why?

He doesn't look up.

First, and maybe for eight seconds, he stays quiet. Then, looking up with this clot of dead ants stuck to the blood on his thumbs, he squints up at me and says: 'My mother's been possessed by demons.'

He laughs and says they came through the kitchen sink.

We leave Thando in his driveway and walk up to CK's. CK lives on the edge of the neighbourhood, a few blocks up from Rharhabe, and shares a Wendy flat with his aunt in the shebeen district. Often, he lets us go behind their backroom where we break his aunt's beer bottles into weapons, gemstones and dagga pipes, before she wakes up and lets us in for a plate of eggs in the early evening.

When this happens, the three of us chew in silence and I always find myself looking sideways, watching the evening colour the windows the same shade as the perfume bottles trembling on the dresser.

Today, CK meets us halfway down the street. He tells us he's on his way to buy his aunt a beer and that we came right on time.

Thobela reminds him that we came to him.

'What if we missed you?' I ask.

CK laughs, blowing us off.

'You can always find me,' he says.

It's always been difficult to stay angry with him.

CK has a funny face, these big teeth and a voice that sounds like a money man on the radio. He's always twisting his lanky body into a new dance move he's picked up from the shebeens, and, even at the local, he never runs out of a story to tell.

So we shrug and walk with him down Mfelane.

A stray cloud wipes the sun, laying a cover of shade on our path.

'I dreamed about the grey man,' I tell CK.

Thobela plays with his knife and CK laughs into space.

'That's a good sign,' he tells me. 'It's a lucky sign.'

We walk on, before finally turning into Miya.

'It isn't much longer now,' CK confirms.

We can see Ma Thano's spaza from where we are.

CK's face takes the form of a stone as he points it out to us.

He says, 'There.'

He says, 'That wall, there.'

∗∗∗

Thobela and I squeeze ourselves between the walls at the side of Ma Thano's spaza, walking over broken glass and ponds of urine, making steady way to the fence leading to her backyard.

The way Ma Thano's spaza shop works is that when she opens her garage door it doubles up as a tavern.

As we slink past, someone knocks over a quart of beer and froth spews from under the garage door like surf.

Thobela gets himself up on the fence and looks for a dog. Then he flips himself over into the yard.

I follow.

Inside, we look around at the same time. We find a zinc shed built against the cinderblock wall on the far end.

Its door hangs open.

We're still standing when CK sways through the kitchen door lugging a sweating quart of beer.

'Are you ready?' he asks us, in a voice I've never heard from him before. We watch him as he raises the bottle to his mouth, twisting the bottlecap off between his teeth.

'You need a little strength for this,' CK says.

We pass the bottle around until we start to feel our heads lifting off our shoulders. I restrain myself from vomiting each time I taste the beer's bitterness. Thobela sucks on the bottleneck like a pro, taking the brew down in massive gulps. I look at CK, who's grinning and staring at space like an idiot.

'What will your aunt say?' I ask him.

'Nolthando is not my mother,' he says.

I don't say anything else.

I realize we've never asked him about his parents.

A moment passes before CK belches and says, 'Come see.'

So that's what we do.

Thobela passes the quart back to him and we go see.

∗∗∗

The man inside the shed isn't an alien, but he has CK's teeth and the body of an 11-year-old girl. His head sits massive on his small neck, the skin on his face drawn so tight against the bone it looks like it was sprayed on his skull.

Thobela covers his nose the same time as I do.

It smells like the inside of a latrine.

'This is my father,' CK says.

He kneels down next to the man.

'He's like an alien, isn't he?'

Thobela and I say nothing.

CK waves for us to go closer and we inch forward.

'What's wrong with him?' Thobela asks.

'Ma Thano says he got it working in Joburg. No-one really knows what it is.'

CK dribbles a small amount of beer into his palm and pours into the man's mouth. As he gets up, we hear the kitchen door slamming open. Thobela and I throw glances at each other in panic, but CK just stands there. When I reach for him he doesn't move, so Thobela and I run out of the shed without him. We scale the wall just as Ma Thano bursts screaming out of the kitchen.

On the tar, my feet no longer feel the heat, and as we run down Miya Street, Thobela and I, the cloud moves away from the sun and the world seems to change, growing bright and intense like a beam from an alien ship.

Masande Ntshanga is the winner of the 2013 PEN International New Voices Award. He was born in East London in 1986 and grew up between Mdantsane, Zeleni, Bhisho, King William's Town, Estcourt, Pietermaritzburg and Cape Town. He started writing as a teenager, perhaps in response to transition, and published his first story at 18. He graduated with a degree in Film and Media and an Honours degree in English Studies from UCT, where he became a creative writing fellow, completing his Masters in Creative Writing under the Mellon Mays Foundation. He received a Fulbright Award and an NRF Freestanding Masters scholarship. His stories have appeared in *Laugh It Off*, *itch*, *Imago* and *Habitat*. He has also written for *Rolling Stone* magazine. His debut novel, *The Reactive*, was published in 2014 by Penguin Random House. 'Space' was frist published in *Twenty in 20* (Time Media, South Africa, 2014).

The Sack

Namwali Serpell

There's a sack.

A sack?

A sack.

Hmm. A sack. Big?

Yes. Grey. Like old *kwacha*. Marks on the outside. No. Shadows. That's how I know it is moving.

Something is moving inside it?

The whole sack is moving. Down a dirt road with a ditch on the side, with grass and yellow flowers. There are trees above.

Is it dark?

Yes, but light is coming. It is morning. There are some small birds talking, moving. The sack is dragging on the ground. There is a man pulling it behind him.

Who is this man?

I can't see his face. He is tallish. His shirt has stains on the back. No socks. Businessman shoes. His hands are wet.

Does he see you?

I don't know. I'm tired now. Close the curtains.

Yes, *bwana*.

J. left the bedroom and went to the kitchen. The wooden door was open but the metal security gate was closed. The sky looked bruised. The insects would be coming soon. They had already begun their electric clicking in the garden. He thought of the man in the bedroom, hating him in that tender way he had cultivated over the years. J. washed the plates from lunch. He swept. A chicken outside made a popping sound. J. sucked his teeth and went to see what was wrong.

The *isabi* boy was standing outside the security gate. The boy held the bucket handle with both hands, the insides of his elbows splayed taut. His legs were streaked white and grey.

How do you expect me to know you are here if you are quiet? J. asked as he opened the gate. The boy shrugged, a smile dancing upwards and then receding into the settled indifference of his face. J. told the boy to take off his *patapatas* and reached for the bucket. Groaning with its weight, J. heaved the unwieldy thing into the sink. He could just make out the shape of the bream, flush against the inside of the bucket, its fin protruding. J. felt the water shift as the fish turned uneasily.

A big one today, eh? J. turned and smiled.

The boy still stood by the door, his hands clasped in front of him. His legs were reflected in the parquet floor, making him seem taller.

Do you want something to eat?

The boy assented with a diagonal nod.

You should eat the fish you catch. It is the only way to survive, J. said.

I told him about the first dream but I did not tell him about the second. In the second dream, I am inside the sack. The cloth of it is pressing right down on my eyes. I turn one way, then the other. All I can see is grey cloth. There is no pain but I can feel the ground against my bones. I am curled up. I hear the sound of the sack, sweeping like a slow broom. I have been paying him long enough – paying down his debt – that he should treat me like a real *bwana*. He does his duties, yes. But he lacks deference. His politics would not admit this, but I have known this man since we were children. I know what the colour of my skin means to someone of our generation. His eyes have changed. I think he is going to kill me. I think that is what these dreams are telling me. Naila. I cannot remember your hands.

They lifted the bream out of the bucket together, the boy's hands holding the tail, J.'s hands gripping the head. The fish swung in and out of the curve of its own body, its gills pumping with mechanical panic. They flipped it on to the wooden board. Its side was a jerking plane of silver, drops of water magnifying its precise scaling. The chicken outside made a serrated sound.

Iwe, hold it down!

The boy placed his hands on either end of the body. J. slid a knife beneath the locking, unlocking gills. Blood eased over their hands. The fish bucked once, twice. Stopped.

I needed your help, J. smiled.

He deboned and gutted the fish. The boy wiped the chopping board, hypnotized by his own hand tracking thin loops of purple and yellow entrails across it. J. fried the fish in cooking oil with salt and onions and tomatoes. He served a piece of it to the boy, setting the plate on the floor. He set a portion of the fish aside for himself and took a plate with the rest of it to the man in the bedroom.

The room was dark but for an orange patch on the wall from the street lamp.

Who is here?

The *isabi* boy. J. put the plate on the side table and turned on the lamp.

The man began to cough, the phlegm in his chest rattling as he heaved and hacked. J. helped him sit up and rubbed his back until the fit ceased. When it was done, the man was tired.

Why is the fish boy still here? Did you not pay him?

I gave him supper.

As if I have food to spare, the man grunted. He took the plate on to his lap and began eating.

In the first dream, the sack is full and it is being dragged. In the second dream, I am inside it. What will the third dream reveal? You laugh. You say that dreams move forwards, not back. That I am imagining things. But that is why you chose me, Naila. Or at least that is what I fancied then. Now I am not so sure. Some days, I think you loved me for my hands. Other days, I think you threw stones to decide.

The plate on the kitchen floor was empty. The boy was gone. A tongue cleaned that plate, J. thought as he went to the doorway. The security gate was scaly with insects now, some so heavy their bodies chimed against the hollow metal bars. J. opened it and descended the short set of steps outside. He squatted to open the thatched door of the coop. He could hear the creaking, purring sound of the birds. Light from the house slivered the dark. J. inched along, his hipbone clicking as he went from one chicken to the next. They pivoted their heads and puffed their feathers. The last chicken sat upright on its nest but it wasn't moving. J. heard a shudder and scanned the wall. The boy. Crouching in the corner, light-mottled.

    J. turned back to the chicken and inched closer, reaching for it. The feathers were strung with light brittle spines. The bird fell limp in his hand. Then he saw them, hordes of them, spilling down the chicken's body, rolling around its neck, massing from its beak. J. started back. The chicken caved in as a flood of ants washed over it. J. stood, hitting his head on the thatched roof. The chickens were yelping and flapping, feathers rising from the ground. The ants snipped at his skin. As he hunched his way out of the coop, a chicken beat its way past his ribs and loped across the yard, head at full piston. Methodically, J. brushed his body off. Then he reached back and pulled the shaking child from the shadows.

My chest is full of cracked glass. That is how it feels when I cough. But the glass never shatters – there is not even that relief of complete pain. I am sick, Naila. Working for me has only made him stronger. Why does he bother? I thought at first that it was the money. But now I think he has been waiting. I wonder at the dwindling of our cares. We began with the widest compass, a society of the people, we said. But somehow we narrowed until it was just us three. Jacob, Joseph, Naila. You replaced yourself with the baby you birthed. So there were still three. But then your family took our son away. And now there are only two. Every day this sickness bites into my body and soon there will be only one. In the dream that just woke me, I am on the ground. It is night. The man kneels at my side. The face is melted but his hairline has washed back with a froth of white hair and he has those same strong arms. His hands are wet. He is tugging the mouth of the sack up over my thighs. This must be when he puts my body into it. We are in the garden. I woke to the smell of smoke.

J. burned the coop. The four chickens left – one had disappeared in the night, snatched by a lucky dog – huddled in a makeshift corral. The fire smelled good; the dead chicken was practically fresh-cooked. From the kitchen doorway, J. watched the last of the smoke coiling up to join the clouds above. The sun took its time. His saliva was bitter and when he spat in the sink, he saw that it was grey. The boy was sleeping on a blanket on the kitchen floor. J. leaned against the counter, watching the boy's chest catch and release. His skinny legs were clean now, greased with Vaseline. J. had hosed the ants off him and anointed the rash of bites. J. made a cup of tea – Five Roses, milk, no sugar – and balanced it on a tray.

The bedroom was ripe with the metallic smell of dried blood. A copper dawn lit the window: *Kwacha! Ngwee...*

The man looked up when J. entered the room. What was that fire?

I burned the chicken coop.

Why?

J. put the tray on the side table and began to leave the room.

Do not walk away from me. The man spat.

J. wiped the spit from the floor with his sleeve. White ants, he said.

Bloody superstitions. The man sucked his teeth. Is that bloody fish boy still here? I don't like people coming here. They find out who I am and ask for money.

He doesn't know who you are. He's too young. This boy has no family, J. said. We could use the help.

The man lifted his cup, his hand trembling. He sipped the hot tea and winced with pleasure.

The boy goes. I can't afford such things.

The light had gone from copper to white gold, the day spending itself freely. J. squatted on the stoop outside, shelling groundnuts to cook a dish of pumpkin leaves. Students in pale-blue uniforms flirted in the dirt road. J. watched them with fond pity as he pressed the knuckle of his thumb to the belly of a shell. He hadn't tasted *chibwabwa ne'ntwilo* in 20 years. Naila's favourite. When he returned to the kitchen, he could hear voices in the living room. J. looked through the gap between the door and the frame. The man was leaning against the far wall, his pyjamas low on his hips. J.'s eyes narrowed: the man hadn't left his bed in weeks. He was shouting at the boy, who stood with his back to J.

Isa kuno, the man said sternly. Come here! Are you deaf?

The boy moved hesitantly over to him and the man's hand fell trembling on to the bony shoulder. He used the boy as a crutch, levering himself to the sofa. His breathing rasped, shaving bits of silence off the air. In the dull light of the living room, the boy's skin was the colour of a tarnished coin.

There, the man pointed at a picture frame face down on the floor near the sofa. What is that?

J. opened the door. Leave him, he said.

The boy rushed to J.'s side.

He broke it, the man snarled, picking up the framed photograph.

He doesn't know, J. said, looking down at the boy leaning against his leg.

I don't want him here, the man panted.

I owe it to him, J. said.

The man gaped, a laugh catching in his throat. The only debt you owe is to me, old man.

J. pushed the boy ahead of him into the kitchen.

I did not think I would walk again. These dreams give me strength. Not enough. I only got halfway to the kitchen, to the knives in the drawer. They wait like a flat bouquet: their thick wooden stems, their large silver petals. I will gather them up in my tired hands and I will hold them out to you. Naila. Look at you. There is a crack over your face because that bastard boy dropped the picture. But you are lovely in your green *salwar kameez*. Why do you look down? I never noticed before. Your eyelids are like smooth stones in this picture. I am a fool beside you. We reek of arrogance, all of us, J. with his Nehru shirt. How far he has fallen, sweeping and cooking for me like I'm a *musungu*. This picture must have been taken before the Kalingalinga rally, the one that led to the riot. Do you remember? We were so hopeful. So very young.

J. stood above the sleeping man. He watched him for a moment then slapped his hand against the wall to wake him. A gecko in the corner shimmied upwards, its eyes a black colon punched in its face. The man's head fell forwards and he began coughing himself awake. When the phlegm had settled, he blinked.

Supper, J. said, placing a hand under the man's armpit to help him up. The man swept his weight against J. like a curtain falling from its rails. J. guided him back towards the bedroom but the man raised his hand.

No. I'll eat in there, he nodded his head at the kitchen door. J. shrugged and they proceeded slowly in the other direction. J. kicked the door to the kitchen open and, as the *isabi* boy watched warily, he lowered the man into a chair by a small table.

Fish again? the man smiled at the boy.

J. placed a plate of food before the man and a bowl for the boy on the floor. The man stared at his plate. The fish was in pieces, its skin a crimped silver, its eye a button. When J. went to sit on the stoop, the man complained: Join me, he said.

My dream in the living room was short. A man is holding an ankle in each hand on either side of his hips. He drags the body towards the empty sack. It leaves a dark irregular trail on the ground. J. was standing over me when I woke up. You would say that these visions are an old man's nonsense. That no man dreams backwards. Can you see us sitting across from each other now? He eats in silence. The boy on the floor hums a rally song. J. must have taught him that. They are trying to confuse me. I know this boy is not my son but I have to concentrate to keep it in mind. I insisted on this last supper. I am resigned to it. You laugh: you know I am resigned to nothing. You escaped my wilfulness only by dying. I will see this out. We will wrestle like Jacob and the angel.

I do not want the eye, the man said. J. reached for the plate.

Am I a child that you must cut my food?

J. stood and wiped his hand on his trousers. He walked around the boy on the floor who was already burrowing into his *nsima*, humming a song in loops, and opened a drawer and took out a short knife with a wooden handle.

Yes, that one, the sharp one, the man said.

J. sat back down, watching the man insert the point of the knife into the cavity in the fish's head and cut the eye out carefully, tipping it on to the edge of the plate. He put the knife on the table and began to eat in that slow noisy way of his.

So, the man said, picking at his teeth with his fingernail. J. was at the sink, rinsing pots. What will we do about that broken picture?

I can get it fixed. We are still comrades, that glass cutter and me, J. said.

Comrades? He sucked his teeth.

J. leaned against the counter, his arms, damp from dishwater, folded across his chest. What word would you prefer? Friend?

What do you know about that word? The man sucked his teeth again. The boy looked up at them, his cheeks dotted with white bits of *nsima*.

Yes, *bwana*. I know nothing of friendship, J. said.

The man looked at him. Rage beat across the air between them. Eating across from each other at a table again had kindled something.

I did not take her from you. J. released the words one at a time.

I've been having dreams, the man whispered.

No. I will not listen to your dreams. I have had dreams, *friend*. J. spat. He paced the room with the easy vigour of an animal, flaunting his vitality. His words cut through the smell of fish and illness, through the boy's whimpering hum.

I dream of her cunt, J. said. The English word was steely in his mouth. I pull a baby from her cunt. The baby's stomach is round and full and I can see through the skin, I see another baby inside it, five fingers pressed strong against the inside. I look at her face, sweating from labour, and I say, How is this possible? She laughs. Then I know that this is what happens when you use a woman with a used cunt.

The man looked away first. J. strode to the sink and spat in it. The boy was gone, his bowl upside down like an eye on the floor. J. stooped to pick it up and looked back at his boss. The man's eyes were closed, his hands under the table.

We should not talk about that woman.

She is gone.

She has been gone a long time.

And the boy?

The boy is gone too.

The man turned on to his side, gingerly hitching up his knees. J. looked down at him. J. had long ago decided to hate that woman: a feeling which had clarity and could accommodate the appetite he had once felt for her body. But he knew that the man still loved her, that he scratched invisible messages to her in the sheets. J. was sorry for his old friend. But to say sorry would be preface to leaving and he would not leave until it was done. The sick man hiccupped in his sleep like a drunk or a child. J. switched off the lamp and left the room.

When the door clicked shut, the man's eyes opened. He reached under his pillow and the blade snipped him. The tiny pain in his thumb pulsed inside the throng of pain in his body, a whining in the midst of a howling. The man sucked the blood from his thumb and carefully nestled his hand back under the pillow to grasp the knife handle. He could not slow the reversed momentum of these dreams, but he would not succumb like a dog. He kept his eyes open as long as he could.

A man shuffles through the dark, carrying a body over his shoulder. The legs dangle down the man's front and bounce as he moves unsteadily down a corridor. He faces forwards but steps backwards. He turns and fumbles with a door knob. The bedroom door opens with a sucking sound. He bends slowly and lays the body on the bed. It tumbles down piecemeal, buttocks, then torso, then arms. The man stands and looks at it for a long time. All of a sudden, he pitches over the body. He seems grappled to it. A moan lifts and trips and falls into a scream cut short.

Which comes first? The knife handle abrading his palm? Or the wide agony in his chest? The man's eyes open, he gasps. J.'s face floats above as if he had exhaled him: flat as day, dark as night. His fist is pressed hard to his own chest, his palm around the knife's handle. J.'s fingers are wrapped around his, their hands a bolus of flesh and bone, wood and blade. Together, they wrench the knife free of its home. Blood washes over him, its temperature perfect.

The boy stood in the doorway of the kitchen, looking out. It was night. His *bwana* was at the bottom of the garden, busy with a black lump and a grey sack. The boy's mind was empty but for a handful of notions – love, hunger, fear – darting like birds within, crashing into curved walls in a soundless, pitiless fury.

Namwali Serpell was born in Zambia in 1980. Her first published story, 'Muzungu', was selected for the Best American Short Stories 2009 and shortlisted for the 2010 Caine Prize for African Writing. She received a Rona Jaffe Foundation Writers Award in 2011. In 2014, she was selected as one of the most promising African writers for the Africa 39 Anthology, a project of the Hay Festival. Her writing has appeared in *Tin House*, *The Believer*, *n + 1*, *McSweeney's* (forthcoming), *Bidoun*, *Callaloo*, *The San Francisco Chronicle*, *The LA Review of Books* and *The Guardian*. She is an associate professor in the English department of the University of California, Berkeley and her first book of literary criticism, *Seven Modes of Uncertainty*, was published in 2014. 'The Sack' was first published in *Africa39* (Bloomsbury, London, 2014).

The Caine Prize
African Writers' Workshop Stories 2015

#Yennenga

Jemila Abdulai

'Why did you do it?'

'Why did I… kill him?' Yennenga's voice was barely audible above the din of the old Binatone fan.

'Yes,' the bald-headed interrogator responded, both surprised and relieved that she found this question worthy of a response, after ignoring all the others.

Yennenga looked up, and a cascade of braids fell down her back, freeing themselves from the tired, worn-out elastic band that had, until then, held them captive. Her dark brown lips curved into a smile as she ran her tongue across their coarse, desiccated skin. She hadn't had a sip of water in hours. Tilting her head back, she fixed her kohl-lined, almond eyes on the stout man standing before her. Beads of sweat furrowed across his brow, as though congregating to plot the next move. Threats, platitudes, reverse psychology – he'd tried them all. Her gaze travelled languorously to his bushy, unkempt brow; his short, stubby eyelashes; and finally, to his beady, black eyes.

She leaned forward, placing her manicured fingers at the edge of the wooden table. Her skin glistened under the sharp light. The interrogator shifted uncomfortably, unnerved by the full force of her attention.

'I killed him because that son of a bitch deserved it.'

A deep throaty laugh escaped her lips as she slid back against the weight of the metal chair. It was the first time she'd shown any real emotion.

***

There was a media frenzy. Not so much because there had been a murder but rather because it was one committed by Yennenga, the popular television host and tall, striking media mogul with luxurious, butter-fed skin.

And so, despite the fact that the Africa Cup of Nations semi-final was on that night, over 100 million viewers tuned into the often-forgotten 'Justice' channel. Everybody wanted a glimpse of the stunning celebrity gone criminal. A video of her arrest found its way online and the bystander-turned-citizen reporter-turned-social media hotshot began receiving invitations to speak on 'Breaking the news' and 'How to be at the right time at the right place.'

Yennenga's interrogation was broadcast live across Ghana, including former territories of the ancient Mossi kingdoms. It even made a cameo in key news outlets across the continent. The Nigerian-Chinese psychiatrist appointed to her case, Africa's best, deemed her too unstable to be sent to the Nsawam medium-security prison. No, that wouldn't do at all. 'She should be placed in the Weija women's reform facility instead,' he recommended.

Completed in 2015, five years prior, remands and convicts at the relatively upscale facility were referred to as 'ladies' and 'temporarily misguided social deviants'. The acceptable languages of payment for a bed or a room were the renminbi and the dollar. In special cases, the eco, which had finally been adopted in 2017, was tolerated. All five doctors who cross-examined the suspect backed him squarely.

'The 29-year-old Muslim woman is just too dangerous,' they said.

***

Yennenga rubbed her wrists, still sore from the handcuffs that had dug into her flesh. She watched as the 50-something-year-old warder patted down and searched the five others she had arrived with in the minibus. The old, shrivelled female officer with two diamond-like incisions, one on each cheek, and a constant sneer on her face, kept muttering, 'You won't be needing this,' as she turned out pockets and ripped away handbags and purses. She emptied their contents onto a cheap plastic table: a strip of condoms; shea butter wrapped tightly in a black polythene bag; 200,000 Ghanaian cedis; a baby's pacifier and an endless array of mobile phones.

Not bad, Yennenga thought as the women reluctantly handed over their valuables. She always found it impressive how women could hold onto things, even when they had outlived their usefulness.

'You, over there! Step forward, take off your clothes!' the warder barked. Bending down, Yennenga unfastened the wooden wedges she had bought years ago at the Brick Lane Saturday flea market in London on a stopover from a business trip. She straightened up and set the shoes down. Next, she reached for her collar and undid the black bow, pulling first one end, then the other. Her white ruffled tuxedo shirt with its pristine buttons – a priceless find at the Kantamanto bend-down boutique – and her dark blue denims quickly followed. Just as Yennenga was reaching for her bra, she heard the door open.

'That won't be necessary. Give her the overalls,' a rich, baritone voice said.

'B-But... the underwire... it needs to be taken out,' the warder protested, making her way around the table towards him. They exchanged angry words in hushed tones.

Yennenga didn't need to turn around to know who had spoken. She stared at the whitewashed wall, imagining how much better it would look with some colour, any colour really. The cold breeze from the air conditioner wafted its arms around her semi-naked form in a welcome embrace, pinching her chocolate skin into a zillion goose bumps. It reminded her of Adil, how he'd coax the smoothness back with feather-light kisses and envelope her within his burly arms. It always worked; she'd felt safe with him.

'Officer, don't question me. I gave you a command.'

'Yes, sah!'

Yennenga imagined the older woman's creased thighs pressed tightly together, her left hand stiffly by her side, while her right hand stretched stiffly against her temple: the universal gesture of respect. Even as a prisoner, Yennenga wielded power. There was always a superior and an inferior. The door opened, and she and the warder were alone again.

'Put this on.'

The five-foot-three woman grabbed a pair of oversized ash-green polyester overalls and dirty-looking tennis shoes from under the table and threw them at Yennenga. The overbearing smell of multiple layers of sweat roped its way into her nostrils. Ignoring the stench and the yellowed armpits and collar, she put the large one-piece on and slid her bare feet into the shoes. Those fitted perfectly. The warden gestured at a corner of the room. A few moments later, two uniformed guards entered, their muscled biceps taut against the short sleeves of their shirts. There was something about rippling muscles that got Yennenga's juices flowing.

Clench, unclench, clench, unclench.

To distract herself, she focused on acclimatizing her eyes to the yellow fluorescent lights as they marched her through the hallways. Each side of the long corridor had cells, some with a single woman or bed, others with three or five.

It was past lockdown, most of the inmates were asleep. Those who weren't made their wakefulness known:

'Hey sugar, come to mama!'

'Ɔdɔ, me feeli wo. Bra yenkasa!'

They stopped at a thick, silver metal door. One of the guards pressed an unmarked grey card against a black panel. The light flickered from red to green and the metal door swung open, its heaviness echoing down the hall.

The trio walked on. One. Two. Three. Four.

Yennenga counted as they passed by. The rooms alternated on each side, snaking across the walls like the zigzag corn rolls rappers from the late Nineties wore under black du-rags.

'Bitch!'

'Ei you! Me get some punani e-ya!'

Six.

'678. This is you.' The guards unlocked the door and flung Yennenga inside like a crushed flower that no longer served its purpose.

A loud thud, followed by the clanking of a brass ring against the large iron frame signalled their departure. Yennenga listened as the sound of their army-like boots on the linoleum floor receded. Each step a nail hammered into a coffin, heralding her fate. She curled herself into a tight ball, as she had often seen millipedes do, and wept.

***

Outside her cocooned world, the rumours ran wild. Yennenga's case had driven admirers and critics alike half-mad.

How? When? What? Who? *Why?*

The newspapers; radio stations; hashtag universe with its #FreeYennenga and #DeathToYennenga battle; even her own colleagues at the TV station couldn't miss out on the action. They theorized about her motivations. It was as though they had never heard Yennenga's curt response to that all-important question. Some claimed she was a sweetheart, your average girl next door, forever helpful and smiling. Others countered, saying she was anti-social and full of herself, she'd probably killed him in a jealous fit. Even more still blamed it on 'that American culture', all those trips to New York City. He must have done quite a number on her, some of her classmates said, remembering how smitten the two were on their occasional visits. In her hometown people would point to the school, the shea-processing centre, the library: 'Our Yennenga built those.'

And Yennenga?

Well, that was the last anyone heard from her on the issue. She simply would not speak. She had long exited this complex world, even before the interrogator began his endless questioning. She'd just happened to 'return' for something she'd forgotten, tucked away in the deepest vestiges of her mind, when the beady-eyed man had asked that question.

Why did she do it?

It didn't matter. Not to her anyway. Her job here was done. But for everyone else – the unfortunate ones who would be left behind – this episode would be yet another conundrum with which to warm their cold hearts; a nuisance of an itch that defiantly remains regardless of how furious the scratch; a constant reassurance that they were, at the very least, better than someone.

✳✳✳

Yennenga – a social climber who wormed her way into corridors of influence. Diff here? She's bn caught where others haven't. #DeathToYennenga
– @JewelsAGirlsBestFren

When a soul is about to enter the world, God calls it before His Throne. There, with all the angels watching, He tells the soul everything that will happen. The food it will like; the people it will love; the qualities, things it will strive for but never have; how it will allow the ego to bring about its downfall; the reasons it will do everything it does and the lessons it will learn along its path. In telling a soul its purpose, God shares his divine plan, and just as the soul is on the precipice of descending to the human world, the Creator announces when the soul will return to its Maker. But souls never hear that last bit and forget much of the rest. That's what makes the quest for a soul's purpose all the more enthralling: the delicious ambiguity of death, the inevitable encounter with the unknown.

I have always known I would die young. That I would never have wrinkles dancing at the corners of my eyes; paper-fragile skin, soft and rough to touch; or grandchildren to swaddle in my wisdom. For one thing, I don't laugh much. For another, well, I always just knew.

How did I get here?

In my innocent days, I galloped through the grass. My nights, filled with the great stories of my people. Bathed in moonlight, my cousins and I, our shadows, bringing our history back to life. My mother says they chose my name well. Yennenga, mother and protector of the land. For, even before I could toddle, I was drawn to the earth.

Like many other children, I was brought to Accra for school and for grooming by my aunt, a successful trader at the Medina market. Never mind the fact that Mm'Adiza had her own children to look after, or that the meagre wage she made from selling waakye was barely enough. She was living in the capital, so she was successful. My own mother had little say in the matter. What could she say when the land hardened itself against the hoes and machetes it was all too familiar with; a silent rebellion against the many years it had been denied the opportunity to lie fallow and regain its nutrients? When my father's old-school black-and-white TV showed the opulence of Accra folk through Ghanaian films like *Beyoncé, the President's Daughter.* When, by all indications, the grass had to be greener on the other side. For two years my mother resisted, no, fought sending me. She used my thin, frail body as an excuse for why I was unwell and too sick to be subjected to the hard labour my peers had already been introduced to. For two years that excuse worked.

The yield had been bountiful ever since my birth, but in my seventh year, it all changed. Gathered around the large cotton tree as they normally did every morning, the village women chattered amongst themselves.

'So-so-and-so's husband is about to take on another wife.'

'These junior wives have no respect, none whatsoever, for us first wives.'

The state of the village farm cut their gossip short. Under the shroud of the night, a swarm of locusts had laid the farm bare. My mother knew then that she would lose her only child.

The morning of my departure was a bittersweet one. My mother, stoic face, fought back tears. My father, silent as he led me away. I on the other hand, couldn't have been happier. Not because I was going to the big city where the schools were better and children wore clothes shipped straight from America, but because my blue chale wote had been bought especially for this occasion. They were my first slippers.

✳ ✳ ✳

'What did they get you for?'

A woman with a bright duku stood over Yennenga, her overalls pinched tightly at the waist. The ugly-looking head wrap was perched defiantly on her head in jarring contrast to the grim mood of the common room. It had been a week since Yennenga's arrival at the facility and the ladies had placed a bet on who could make the woman with a faraway look in her eyes speak.

She, Lamisi Abang-Ba, intended to win.

She could already feel her soaked labia brushing against the soft surface of the *Always* sanitary pad. The cement paper didn't hold blood well and always left her with pus-filled warts, her vagina singing its sorrow at the double onslaught. Yes, she, Lamisi would win that pack of pads.

'Hey, woman! I'm talking to you! Show some respect.'

Yennenga looked up absentmindedly from her newspaper. She'd been daydreaming again. The older woman had her legs akimbo; hands perched on her wide, cloth-clad hips. Her mouth was twisted up in annoyance.

'Murder. She killed someone,' another voice said.

Lamisi spun on her heel to face the intruder who had just

interrupted her. Eyes twinkling in anticipation, Yennenga stretched out her long legs on a nearby coffee table, making herself comfortable. All that was missing was corn and kube to chew on.

'Who asked you, eh?' Lamisi hissed under her breath, her large eyes angrily throwing daggers at her challenger. Somewhere in the distance, the rustling of a walkie-talkie could be heard, 'We have a 504, Common Room.' The other women noticed what was happening and inched their way forward cautiously. They lived for confrontations.

Ignoring Lamisi's question, the imposter forged on: 'I saw it on the TV, the news. She killed that Minister, the one who has the colonial moustache and likes small girls. What's his name koraa?... Ah-ha! Adil Aminu. Everybody is talking about her!'

You could feel, more than hear, the collective intake of breath.

The mention of his name sent Yennenga spiralling back to Bali, a sore ache tugging at her heart.

It was the morning after. Yennenga stretched her lithe, spent form luxuriously, and life seeped back slowly, as though unsure it was truly over. They'd gone four times, each different, her meeting him thrust for thrust. He'd licked his way to discovery, saying how her rich skin reminded him of the earth. They were alike, she and he. In their lovemaking as in their convictions. They did not capitulate easily. That was both her flaw and saving grace. Slipping on her white and gold chiffon, she stepped outside, careful not to wake him.

The place where you are right now, God circled on a map for you... Our Beloved has bowed there knowing you were coming.

She whispered her favourite verse from the Sufi poet Hafiz, as she dragged a stick behind her, salty breeze dancing, waves lapping gently at her feet. Once done, she stepped back to admire her handiwork.

'You're quite the artist, aren't you?' Adil said gruffly, blowing hot air against her neck as his hands explored her curves. Giggling, Yennenga faced him. She was within the circle, he outside, both barefoot.

'Tell me about your hometown once more, the grassy plains where you played and napped as a child,' he stepped within the circle and pulled her against his chest. Solid. Safe and content, that's how she felt with him. And so, she did.

'Is it true?' squeaked a tiny woman with big afro, breaking the reverie.

Yennenga scanned the sea of women before her. Behind their futile attempts at not gawking, she saw something else: the look of new-found respect.

'Break it up, ladies. Take two steps back. Two. Steps. Back. You know the rules.' A busty guard walked into the room with a long baton.

By the time the women's grumbling had subsided, it was lunchtime. On a regular day, Yennenga would ignore the haphazardly stacked plastic bowls of corn porridge, weevil-infested oil rice, or sludge of God-knows-what, opting instead for fruit, Hausa koko or Lipton tea. But today was Wednesday. And on Wednesday, the familiar smell of camphor greeted her at the door, took her hand, and skipped her over to a stool in a corner. There, she would eat her waakye, one grain of rice or black-eyed beans at a time, while she reminisced about home.

✳✳✳

'678 to the Visitor Lounge. Booth 5. 678, Visitor Lounge, Booth 5,' the loudspeaker hummed mechanically.

Who could it be? Yennenga wondered, chewing on her bottom lip. Mr Obiri? No. Cardinal Berkson? Heck no, he wouldn't dare show his face here; too many questions. Frank the engineer? Hmm. Possible. He seemed to have enjoyed himself the other day. Mr Schneider? She smiled, remembering their last encounter.

Many women think you have to be butt-naked in order to hold a man's interest. Quite the contrary. It's the subtleties: the arc of your neck; the moistness of your lips; the gracefulness of your hands as you mistakenly brush your fingers against him. He was literally panting with desire by the time we had finished reviewing the land-reform bill over dinner at Fabiano's.

Yes, it must be... a lawyer. *Her* by-force lawyer. Mr Akwasi Beaumont.

Yennenga rolled her eyes and picked up the receiver, sitting in partial cross leg on the hard chair at the counter.

'You look well. Are they treating you okay? Do you like your room? David asked me to make sure you are, y'know, comfortable.'

He wrinkled his nose in disgust as he looked around. Yennenga raised her left heel onto the stretcher of her chair, then placed her left elbow on her knee in a pose Adil often teased her about as being 'unladylike'. She reached for the nearest braid and twisted it around her finger.

At 40, Mr Beaumont was one of the country's best lawyers, a single man who weighed 100 kilograms but had no problem running his mouth, especially when it came to his clients. He actually cared. It was cute, but in a tragic kind of way. Indifference had snaked its way into every nook and cranny of the country to the point where anything else was heralded as novelty, praised as visionary, put on a pedestal. It was worrying. Yennenga felt her lunch pushing its way back up her oesophagus. She swallowed hard.

'We only have ten minutes,' he said, glancing at his phone. 'The investigation is still ongoing, but if things go quickly, we should have a court date by the end of next week.'

Yennenga cocked her eyebrow sceptically. There were women in remand for up to three years, waiting on the ever-elusive court date. The facility and its quirky inhabitants were beginning to grow on her. But that was the problem:

getting comfortable, complacent. She didn't belong here. She was meant to sprint with the wind, hair wild with abandon, watching the sun dip beneath the plains. Yes, she would go home. Even if it meant being hanged, a lethal injection, or the electric chair.

Yennenga looked over at Mr Beaumont. His expression was serious.

'I think we could build a strong case to justify a reduced charge or at least make sure you're not handed the death sentence. You are a celebrity and, despite your current stint as a royal pain in my ass, it seems you have some real supporters out there. Look.' He pressed his Samsung mobile phone against the window:

> *'Yennenga Ntenga saved me, my children, five years ago.*
> *She's a hero not a murderer!'*
> *single mother claims. Full story tonight* #FreeYennenga
> *– @*CTVGhana

A #FreeYennenga hashtag. How amusing. The internet gods and goddesses had gotten more insistent with their virtual campaigns in the last two years, especially after the devastating failure of #BringBackOurGirls to return all 270 + Chibok girls who were abducted by Boko Haram six years ago. Digital activists had joined forces with grassroots activists and various human rights organizations. Together, they were taking one giant step away from the computer screen and two steps towards real solutions on the ground – their own words. Of course, they had to create a specific hashtag for that as well: #TheDigiRealityPact. Even the United States President had endorsed it with the usual celebrities in tow. This #FreeYennenga campaign, what if…?

A flutter of hope unfurled itself within Yennenga, turning as one does when waking momentarily from a deep sleep.

No!

No what ifs. That's how disappointment begins.

I remember the single mother. We stood next to each other at Jummah prayers once. I had been a bad, bad girl that week, so I stayed behind a little longer. 'The most excellent worship is dua.' Apparently, that's what the Prophet Muhammed (Peace Be Upon Him) had said. And so I supplicated long and hard until the already-dark skin on my knees was burning black from the constant friction of my abaya against the plastic mat. I had just come up for air after spending 15 minutes in prostration when I heard her.

'Ya Allah, you know me as I know not myself. You understand my needs before I am even aware of it. You protect me from that which I cannot see. You do all these and I will forever give you thanks. You provide for the birds when they ask not. Rent is due. I have no money, no food left. For the sake of my three children, I come to you this day.' Her voice broke.

It wasn't until I felt a splash between the webs of my fingers that I realized that I too had been crying. It was the most sincere prayer I had ever heard. I sat there contemplating it and feeling like a fraud for my half-hearted attempts at communing with God. She made me want to try harder. After she had regained composure, she got up and started rolling up her prayer mat, while I pretended to massage the life back into my sore knees.

Five. Six. Seven.

That's how many steps she took before turning back. 'I think you mistakenly dropped this in my bag,' she said shyly, gesturing to the thick white envelope in her left hand. I reached out towards her right hand, she obliged, and we shook one another, observing the practice of the Prophet.

'May Allah accept our prayer,' I said before walking away.

'Amin,' she responded with tears in her eyes.

***

So this cow is out here preaching importance of keeping girls

from prostitution, when she's a 1st class hoe? Fuck that sh*t!
#DeathToYenanga
– @PurveyorOfTheTruth233

The big city is no place for a decent lady. That's what everyone says. It was also my aunt Mm'Adiza's mantra: 'No decent lady is out after six o'clock.' But that's just it. Everyone says so, including the paedophile, criminal, sex trafficker, pimp. Like a cat trying to clean its facial fur, we shield our eyes from the obvious: the danger is everywhere.

I had just turned 16. Sweet 16. Mm'Adiza pffed at my request for a party. 'There are better things to spend money on. Like items for your marital home.' She gestured at the row of aluminium bowls that stood obediently on her dresser. Painted white, awash in colour, symbols, and the owner's initials, they were a fixture in every northern household. Mm'Adiza would not eat tuo zaafi in any other container; she said it wouldn't taste the same.

'Yennenga, chɛm daa ti da zim tima.'

'Aargh, not again!' I must have said it out louder than I intended because the next thing I knew, Mm'Adiza was behind me, breathing raggedly in my ear, 'What did you say?'

'Kashɛli,' I responded, my face burning with shame.

I untied and redid my red-and-blue wrapper, a gift from my mother. Picking my blue slippers, I set off, shouting greetings to our neighbours as I exited the seven-family compound house. The Medina market was particularly packed, Tuesday being market day. The small mill at the centre was already chugging away, black fumes up in the air, its machines spewing out the freshly ground maize flour we would stir into our evening meal. With the noon sun beating heavily on my exposed neck, I wove through a maze of bodies, animals, provisions, cars and motorbikes, hopping swiftly across the choked gutters. Feet tapping impatiently, my gaze drifted to the trɔtrɔ station. That's when I saw them. Fifty metres away, crushed between two run-down kiosks in a dark, narrow alley, a muscular man with bloodshot eyes was dragging a flailing girl behind him. My pores flushed with adrenaline, I froze. Something was wrong.

The miller's questions broke my trance. I ignored him and hurried in their direction; the congested market parted like the Red Sea. Minutes later, I was staring in wide disbelief at the blackest pair of buttocks I had ever seen. They thrust back and forth, stiff then relaxed, stiff then relaxed. He grunted like a horse, his shirtless torso shaking with exertion. Where was the little girl? I looked around frantically. Her gut-wrenching scream was my response. Her weightless body was pinned under the man's mass. The love scenes I had stolen glances at on TV always seemed airy with butterfly kisses and soft caresses. This? This was barbaric!

I ran back into the market, shouting for help. My cries drowned in the braying of livestock, car horns and vendors calling enticingly to would-be clients. Nobody heard me. I returned to the kiosks: he was gone and she lay bleeding on a slab of stone. I eventually got the attention of a passer-by, a church sister, and with the help of a few strangers, the girl's lifeless body was loaded into a taxi and rushed to the clinic. My 30-minute errand had stretched into an hour.

Too ashamed to recount the ordeal, I told my aunt my pocket had been picked and endured the whipping. We ate kenkey that night.

I found out the next day that the girl died on arrival. Vagina torn apart beyond repair, the four-year old had bled out on the backseat of the taxi. A promising light, our country's future, snuffed out before its time.

That was the day I learned about rape. The day I made a personal vow. The day that led me to David and everything else.

'I will always be the virgin-prostitute, the perverse angel, the two-faced sinister and saintly woman.' – Anaïs Nin #Woman
– @YennengaNtenga

She'd been restless, filled with angst and itching for a moment alone. And now, here she was, safe behind the giant iron door. Yennenga reached into her over-sized ash-green polyester overalls and felt her way to her bra. Her breath quickened, it had been so long. She slipped her fingers underneath the satin royal-blue material with its spattering of white daisies and French lace trimmings. She'd always had expensive taste when it came to lingerie. Her fingertips grazed her left nipple, and she inhaled sharply. The familiar swirl of passion pooled towards her belly as she let out an involuntary moan.

A few seconds later, she found what she was looking for: pages from her journal, the essence of her soul.

Talkative Mr Beaumont could be quite resourceful. With this small gesture he had sent her on the first-class express to heaven and back: 'I found the box at your apartment. David had mentioned you write. I've also heard writing and speaking are quite similar... Anyway, I thought you might like it.'

Yennenga smoothed out the wads of crumbled brown, lined paper. The messy cursive of her 17-year-old headstrong self stared back at her. An entry from the day she'd taken control of her life:

I let him in.

What only days earlier had been an invasion of the highest order, was now an invitation.

To allow this man, this 'silminga', white man – a foreigner to all intents and purposes – to be wrapped up within me, my muskiness, my story. Some would say my very soul.

I am not married. We are not married. I am Muslim, he – who knows? Who cares? Taboos broken. And yet, I let him in.

As the sun dipped behind the large fronds overlooking the kiosk, he dipped into my warmth. And then, he moved. I clenched my eyes shut; bit on my lower lip as the vestiges of pain receded. Until now, I'd only heard about this tearing apart.

The separation of child from woman, the spurting of this hill where a plain used to lie.

I'd also heard about how the man's family, his sisters, would come in the next morning to ensure that the new bride had kept her honour for the special night.

But I am no newly wed. There wasn't a wedding. He's not even my boyfriend, as is the rave right now. We met mere weeks ago, at the local market. He was buying a coconut to quench his thirst. I was watching, sizing him up, as a lioness does her prey.

Yes, I let him in.

But more importantly, I was not coerced, not taken advantage of. I chose to let him in. That makes all the difference.

✳✳✳

Yennenga's trial for murder begins today. Are you team #FreeYennenga *or team* #DeathToYennenga? *FF live via* justice.tv & tweet at us!
– @JusticeTV

It's 10 o'clock and the judge has yet to arrive.

The prosecutor is sifting through paperwork at the other end of the aisle, while Mr Beaumont sits next to me. He seems nervous. We came early to avoid the circus, but it's already inside. Glancing at the jury box, I do a quick headcount.

Five.

Six.

Seven.

They are the true stars of the show, y'know, for after these two months in and out of court, they will decide how I die. In one corner, the stenographer clanks furiously away at her typewriter, her forehead creased in concentration. In another, the crew from 'Justice', laying cables and setting up mics, their large Sony F900 already beaming images worldwide.

The smell of sweat and bloodlust hangs over the packed

courtroom. The scavengers are seated on the far end of the gallery. There's Oriaku, my closest work colleague. She thinks I slept my way to the top. Not surprising. Many others probably think so too. From the moment we met, I knew she couldn't be trusted. How can you trust someone who hides behind layers of fake eyelashes? Anyway, now that I'm indisposed, she'll be making a run for my TV show, that is, if she hasn't already.

There's a slight commotion at the main entrance. Seconds later, a grey head of cotton emerges. Mr Schneider, team neutral. I knew he couldn't stay away for long.

Lamisi. Relentless Lamisi and her rainbow of a headwrap float to mind. I stifle a giggle. Where would she sit if she were here?

Anyway, seated behind Mr Schneider is my dedicated, loving family.

They've been at every one of my court appearances since the testimonies started a month ago. Each time, at least two of them, never all, holding down the fort. Until today. Today, everyone is here, convinced all this is a setup. If only they knew. Mercifully, my old mother is blind. She doesn't need to see what will become of her only child. My father? He died five years ago, while I was finishing my university degree abroad. My aunt followed a year later.

Mr Beaumont nudges me. 'He's here.'

David. My rock through the ages.

It's been 12 years since our little tryst in the kiosk near my house. It had seemed fitting, a reclamation of feminine power where innocence had brutally been taken. We never had sex again, David and I. He'd been aghast at finding out I was under age.

'Are you trying to get me thrown in jail?' he'd said.

I had laughed in response, remarking how incompetent and corrupt the Ghanaian police and legal systems were.

'But I'm a British diplomat,' he'd responded simply.

'Diplomat? What does that mean?'

That's how we became friends. He helped cover my education expenses and indulged my sapiosexual fantasies. Together, we explored our alternate, overlapping worlds – intellectually, spiritually and emotionally. I was addicted. Through him, I learned about politics, economics and governance, and this catapulted me to a coveted journalism stint at one of the world's leading media agencies. He would often ask me to join him at many of the diplomatic events and parties he was invited to across the globe, even after he quit the service. That's how I discovered the powers of networking and of suggestion. I met other women, from various cultures, who knew the art of seduction. This, too, I ate up voraciously.

When I finally moved back to Ghana, fresh with pan-African fervour, I knew what I would become: a modern-day Veronica Franco. In chambers. That's where I would influence my country's policies. I toiled night and day until I won a contract for my own TV show. It gave me the excuse, the access I needed to circumvent unspoken rules, the ones that divide the powerful from the rest of us. With that, I sowed my precious seeds. I was prepared to use sex as an instrument. It turned out I didn't need to. So rare was my kind that the old men and boys who run the country's affairs were content to simply be with me. Either that, or I tired them out with an endless string of words, usually about sustainable farming, my favourite topic.

And then, along came Adil.

Six foot tall, smart, the Minister of Trade, *and* a Muslim? It was as though time rewound itself to the moment I had decided I would never get married, giving me a chance to choose anew. I fell in love and with the fall, I wanted it all. My ecstatic mother ignored my protests; she chose names for her 'soon to come' grandchildren anyway. Ours was a whirlwind romance, with trips to London, Paris, and a magical getaway to Bali. That night, underneath the twinkling stars, God, and the entire universe, I dropped the shield. I made love with Adil for the very first time.

The next day, David called from Accra. We joked that we had a soul tie. He got serious after I finished gushing about my new love: 'Both eyes open, darling. Remember, you're not built like the rest.' He was right.

When Adil started eyeing other women, I wasn't bothered. They are just bimbos, I told myself. When he started returning to our shared apartment in the wee hours, I rationalized it as him being busy, Minister of Trade and all. The lingerie in his briefcase, I simply tossed aside. And then I found the papers.

'All rise!'

We remain standing until the Judge arranges himself on the bench.

'Leave the talking to me,' Mr Beaumont whispers.

I roll my eyes. He's probably worried I'll go rogue and say something incriminating. The prosecutor gives his closing arguments, recapping what evidence they have. They think I killed Adil out of jealousy, for the many women he had. Their simplistic minds cannot comprehend that it was for something else entirely. Something more… *considerate*, you could say.

You see, Adil was not the only one keeping secrets. I had mine too.

As had been predicted, China's need for more land grew with its still burgeoning population. They wanted international co-operation, true, but more precisely, they wanted land, more of it, to secure their future. Any- and everywhere, but particularly in Africa's yet-to-be-conquered, vast lands.

I watched. I had my interests too.

I knew exactly what needed to be done when I discovered Adil's impending deal with China's largest corporation; the deal that would strip bare the savannah grasslands of the northern plains, displace my people, despoil our country, shatter the one place where I'd known little suffering, exchange generations of heritage for ships full of junk. Like that black-assed man who had ravaged a four-year old girl to satisfy his lust and pacify his ego, Adil's deal would have ripped out our nation's very hope. Its very soul.

Our land, *this* land, was our birthright. Not simply something to be given, no, *taken* at whim. And so, although it broke my heart, Adil had to go. He had betrayed my people and me.

'Woyooooo-yi!'

A piercing scream. My mother's.

Decided: #DeathToYennenga, execution by firing squad. In three days. First since 1993. Watch live on justice.tv.
– @JusticeTV

✱✱✱

When a baby is born, the community gives it a placeholder. Saando if he is male, and Saanpaga if female. Stranger. A week later, when it is clear it has decided to stay, the beaming parents reveal the baby's real name. On that same day, the soul decides what it will be called. Sometimes the two coincide, other times they don't. This determines a child's fate: whether it will always have to fight to be heard, or if its name will speak on its behalf.

Laila Yennenga Ntenga.

Chosen by community and soul alike. Her first, because she was born in the middle of the night. Her second, after her ancestor. Princess Yennenga, pearl of the kingdom, legendary horsewoman, skilled warrior, hunter. Mother and protector of the land.

'Can you believe these people? They going to show Yennenga's execution live. How heartless can one be?' The woman pointed to the scrolling text at the bottom of the screen.

The ladies were gathered in the common room, the mood more solemn than usual. They pretended to watch a debate on the humanity of shooting someone to death, but were really there out of solidarity with the woman who never spoke. It was what they did whenever one of their own left the facility.

Yennenga was seated in her room, musing. Her final wish had been simple: waakye. She had wanted to taste the swirl of camphor and pepper on her tongue one final time. David made sure they got the best, straight from Yendi. Swimming in memories of her happy childhood, she had devoured it, one grain of rice and black-eyed beans at a time.

She heard the familiar clanking of brass ring against iron. It was time.

Yennenga looked straight ahead, her crown of braids held high as the trio walked down the dimly lit corridor. Just as they reached the doorway, she stopped. Looking over her shoulder, she searched the ash-green sea for sharp hues of red, gold and purple. Her khol-lined eyes finally found Lamisi's.

'I really like your duku,' Yennenga said calmly. With that, she entered the van, headfirst, wrists clasped together, feet bare against the land.

A moment later, she was gone.

Jemila Abdulai is the founder and editor of the award-winning website Circumspecte, an online platform dedicated to meaningful insights, interaction and creative action. An economist by training and a self-proclaimed wordsmith, she has been writing since the age of 10 and uses digital technologies to explore the nuances and interactions between African culture, development and philosophy. Alongside features on Al-Jazeera, the BBC and Thought Catalog, she has written for Devex and the LSE Africa Blog and helps spur meaningful dialogue on her home country Ghana and African development through Circumspecte's Google Hangout conversation series.

The Road Workers of Chalbi

Dalle Abraham

He walked into the village one evening with a human head on a pike. He held the blood-caked spear high with a smile on his face. Elderly men, waiting for evening prayer as they played Ajua under the village acacia, looked up from their game but none moved. Children watched from afar, huddled in small, eager groups. Women wailed and their frantic tearing at their headscarves died the moment they saw the murderer trouncing around with a human head as a trophy.

The villagers gathered around Ali, eyes glued to the head with its ashen eyes, pain still written in its eternal stare. Elderly men were visibly saddened by the young man whose head lay impaled prostrate by the pike. Ali, tall and stocky, stood head and shoulders above his fellow villagers, imposing like an old camel, repeatedly shouting as if calling a sleepy crowd to attention.

'Atonement!'

'Atonement!'

'Atonement!

His pace and tone sounded like the rhythmic government criers on loudspeaker passing through the village: Attention, attention… polio vaccinations!

'Atonement! Atonement for Indian ghosts in Africa. We finish. Atonement for Arabic djinns. We purge. Penance for suspect cats sent from Mombasa. They become men, you know?'

He continued shouting in a stentorian boom. None dared speak. The madness of his might and insanity of his thoughts forbade questions.

The expedition that followed the blood trail the next day found the remains of a body mauled by hyenas beside a prayer mat and a water bottle. No body to bury. No means of identification. They returned and buried the head in an unmarked grave away from the village cemetery. The dead man was relegated to the periphery of memory.

Women silently whispered prayers asking God to protect their children and keep Ali safe and to give him the strength to always repel prying eyes and protect the village from strangers who preyed on unsuspecting men to feed their egos.

And, as the years passed, Ali effortlessly hauled sacks full of daily household waste and secretly quenched the nightly desires of married women with his reputed performance. He never married. He abhorred the domesticity of men his age. He straddled a world of inchoate desires and inconceivable senses, disappearing for months and returning as suddenly as he had left; unannounced. Like a messiah, his unconventional ways were accepted.

He acquired other titles and became the defender of the village from foreign evils. He hovered around the Church Sisters when they first showed up. He tracked them for any signs of evil and gave up when they invited him to partake in their meals.

When the Kikuyu from Nairobi came prospecting for oil he kept a long vigil around their camp reading their daily actions for signs of trouble. The Kikuyu left him alone. He returned to the village.

***

Many years after Ali entered the village with a human head on his spear, the Chinese arrived in the baking afternoon sun of mid-July. Men with a purpose, they moved into action, in nods, hand gestures and curt words. They worked in setting up their camp as the entire village, all its 250 members and their many children stood there watching. The children were an assorted collection of dusty white feet in well-worn tyre sandals. The tired-looking elders were in patched rags, the playful women in colourful dhiras, the lanky boys in curly afros. Schoolboys in blue tacky shorts and shy girls with defiant boobs stood at a distance watching as the Chinese worked in a co-ordinated way like a column of ants, bolting nuts and tightening screws to walls that defied the winds.

The villagers stood there and collected knowledge of the newcomers like tools that were necessary for shaping their interaction. Mutwiri the tobacco vendor's observation about all the Chinese being left handed was discredited the moment they began working.

'Excellent men of finesse...' said one man reputed for his wide travels. 'At the border of Somalia and Congo, they made a lake in a desert like this!' he said as he made an expansive sweep of his hand. He was a master of non-existent dreams and places.

'Devil worshippers, these Chinese, they create roads never trodden, conjuring dreams not imagined,' said another woman. Others cleared their sinuses and spat dusty phlegm.

The camp, comprising little square rooms like unmarked dominoes, sprung up overnight and stood defiantly in the shifting dunes, a stark contrast to the village a few hundred metres away, which was made up of an impoverished collection of cone-shaped circles. Their ochre-smeared, pock-marked walls were artistically visible as a huddled settlement of circular huts in the desolate vastness of the Chalbi sand dunes. Lonesome acacia trees were scattered across the landscape.

Chalbi, the village and its new appendage of the Chinese camp, was a small and far-off place from the rest of the world and people often came with preconceived notions of the place being very conservative. It was. But, again, its ability to accommodate other ideas, people and things which posed no threat to the general wellbeing of the village made it otherwise. Such that one who came with clean, outstretched hands without any ulterior motives was welcomed. There was a general ease in the air and in the life of the people; they were hospitable, playful and inquisitive in an honest way, forcing newcomers to form a positive opinion of their general likability. This impression forced Mr Chang, the road workers' supervisor, to relax his taut ways and dilute his commanding airs with a very approachable spirit, making it easier for both his workmates and the community to mingle and to socialize – to almost eat from the same plate. The desolateness of the place made it even more necessary for good society to thrive. The nomads went about their business amicably with their visitors and selectively accepted what came from the world through the Chinese. At the water kiosk set up by the camp, women generally joked with Chinese men jovially.

'You marry girl in this village,' said one playful woman.

'Me have one wife at home,' answered Mr Chang, with a smile lighting up his eyes.

'Two girls good for a hard-working man,' said the woman. 'Beautiful daughter I have… you are handsome… I give you… you bring cows,' she added in a very coy, motherly and knowing way, all the time staring at him.

He blushed from the stare more than from her words.

Ali watched all this with a renewed awe. He felt, for the Chinese, a profound respect. Men of infinite abilities. They worked with a fervour, hard wired with an indomitable verve. He observed their adroitness with an animated silence.

Every evening Ali walked back to the village with new information about the unbound capabilities of the Chinese life. He walked from house to house saying: 'Of all things that crawl, it's only the train they don't eat,' he said the day he saw them kill a python for supper.

'Of all things in the air, it is only the planes they don't eat,' he said when they set up traps for little birds.

'Of all water creatures, it is only the ship they don't eat,' the day their suppliers brought dried shrimps.

The Chinese appetite transcended village taboos. They bought dogs and old donkeys from the villagers who watched with frowning disgust. Mr Chang could not find anyone who could skin them. However, Ali covered his mouth and nose in an old Arafat, sharpened his knives and set to work. He got paid in two new thousand-shilling notes.

Mr Chang stood over Ali as he worked one evening and said, 'Ali, too much Chaku in Kenya, too many animals, very few people. In China too many people… very few animals… food is very little.'

Ali repeated the information to the villagers.

'They are starving in China,' he said.

The first time he stayed around their camp to watch them eat the donkey, Mr Chang had in quick gestures beckoned him and in curt words said, 'Ali… Gooda… guda… very gooda,' between mouthfuls of donkey bites.

The Chinese men played with the eager schoolboys who gathered every evening in front of the large camp. The schoolboys arrived with covered tins and clear plastic water bottles with both dead and alive crawly insects, scorpions, rats and frogs. Others killed snakes and carried them in sacks to the camps. They talked and laughed excitedly. They learnt to be fast and very efficient. There were no fixed rates for all their catch and the Chinese men, as if to tickle the boys' fancy, bought whatever came to their camp. They soaked the scorpions and drank the water. They were dramatic.

The village acquired a chaotic night life. Chinese men strayed from their camp at night and walked into dark smoky huts. The camp bustled with more people. Road workers and young men in search of dreams. New women, talkative ones, came from Marsabit. Perfumed and henna-decorated, the women sold miraa and openly joked and flirted with the young road workers. The Chinese men wooed young girls and old men sank into the nostalgia of their youthful days.

The small village and its single street became too small for all the gossip. For the new blood that ran through its old veins. A whole street came into being, a collection of sparkly, shiny iron sheets, and a wines and spirits shop became the very heart of the village, tucked between a roadside kiosk and the barber shed. The street declared its temporary ambition from afar. The barber shed only had a borrowed chair and a small mirror fixed on a large carton. Two seedy food joints with makeshift tables fixed to the ground and old blocks for chairs faced each other, competing to serve watery meals to fulfil the ravenous appetites of the men who worked on the new road. A butchery that operated once a week and a phone-charging kiosk became the face of new dreams.

Outside the village, everything else seemed dead for the Chinese. Endless stretches of the land, sand, dust and the sweltering heat of the sun made a day's toil unbearable. It was a lonely road with very few vehicles, people and events. Occasionally a herder would materialize out of nowhere and ask for water with his silent sheep, their gazes fixed to the ground, adding to the general melancholia of the vast space that made one long for the playful village and its people.

For Mr Chang, the camp and the village were like two places representing different times of his life. He missed his home city in China and, when observing the pastoralists' ways, he remembered the stories of his Tibetan mother and uncles. However much he tried distancing himself and tried to forget his nomadic ancestry and his uncles' strong attachments to livestock, in Chalbi it tugged at his heart.

Mr Chang came to the sudden realization that, at his age, it was in simple ways that life acquired a disturbing clarity. Like a walk in the evening through the village, with the cover of darkness when small wick lamps and their weak lights brought to mind whole worlds away. Tibetan temples he had visited as a young man with many candle lights fluttering in the night like flowers in the wind. The sight of village boys tugging at the ropes around the neck of goats that were far stronger than they were, brought to mind his uncle and the stories of growing up in the Ngari prefecture. Now, though, he rejected these memories. Only occasionally allowing himself to soak into nostalgic reminiscences of a long-lost dream. But the world of memories had a destructive influence and he sought to balance the attraction of the pastoral lures by locking himself into his office and working for hours. It was in one of his deeper immersions into the office and camp affairs, filling books of accounts and signing off expense cheques, that he heard the distant call of his name; it came from afar, coming closer and louder.

'Mr Chang... Mr Chang...'

As the voice came closer Mr Chang noted the impatience in Ali's tone.

'Mr Chang... Mr Chang... Mr. Chang...'

This loud summons disrupted the silence of the whole camp. Camp workers stopped and looked at Ali. He continued shouting into the vast openness. The camp guards kept away.

'Mr Chang... come out now...'

Tiny eyes looked at Ali from the square rooms. Topless Chinese men in colourful boxers walked out of their rooms and stared at the unfolding drama.

Mr Chang came out of his office and stood in the doorway. He saw Ali and a little procession behind him. The local Chief, a Church Sister, Madam Teacher, a young girl and two Administration Police officers following at a steady pace.

Ali stormed like a loaded gun ready to sweep away anything standing in his way. Mr Chang, openly alarmed, managed to put on his most civil and disarming face and welcomed the team into his office. He listened to the Chief in silence with a worried frown on his face. Ali was angry. The delegation would not allow him to speak. He sat seething in silence.

Mr Chang, who was sweating profusely, summoned two of his aides and, after a few seconds of back-and-forth whispering, they sounded the bugle and, like schoolchildren in an assembly ground, the Chinese workers stood in line in the middle of the camp. Those heading out for work stopped and returned to camp, leaving vehicle engines running and water flowing from taps. Naps were cut short. Cigarettes crushed after only a few puffs.

Mr Chang, with spittle drops raining out of his quivering lips, shouted in short bursts the accusations labelled by the village delegation. The road workers stood in deathly silence either in fear of Mr Chang or in deep shame at the atrocious act. Mr Chang stood like a stern teacher in front of his misbehaving class waiting for an unforthcoming confession. He stepped backwards and whispered to the Chief, who whispered to the Sister, who whispered to the Teacher and the Nurse. The Teacher, Nurse and the Sister walked briskly, their heads cocked high, into the office and came out with the little girl walking unsteadily between them. Teacher and Nurse were by her side with their hands resting softly on her shoulder while the Sister in her nun's clothes walked behind the girl. The trio led the girl in solemn silence. A murmur, like a leaf fluttering in the wind, swept through the assembled Chinese men. Gasps of disbelief at how young the girl was.

Every gaze was fixed on her unsteady steps. She was like a president inspecting a guard of honour except for her downcast and painful steps. This was a search for a monster. She walked from one end of the line to the other, her gaze fixed on the feet of the men before her. She stopped briefly and stared up at the face of each man. She could not tell one from the other and the Sister gently nudged her to turn back with whispers of encouragement. The girl looked at each face, now trying hard to remember details that had evaded her – the height of the man or his hairstyle – but nothing came to mind. And she looked at the Teacher with the eyes of a pleading child. Confusion caving out hollowness in eyes that were once bright and playful, now windows into a vacated home. The Church Sister held her to herself and the girl crumbled into a silent sob.

Mr Chang whispered to the Chief then turned to the assembled men and in curt commands asked them to leave. The boys dispersed and the camp, like a paused TV programme, came back to life.

Inside the office, he sat with the Nurse, Teacher, Church Sister, Chief and Ali as the two Administration Police officers stood outside waiting.

'This is problem… This is worry for me, for workers and for the girl,' he said, pointing at himself and those outside.

The Chief nodded.

'This is very wrong…. but me Mr. Chang cannot do anything… the girl only can do something… she needs to say the man and we…' he said, pointing to each of them. 'We can then do something…'

The Chief looked at the others and sank even deeper into the leather sofa.

'But for hospital… I give this,' said Mr Chang, and from his wallet drew two new notes of one thousand shillings and pushed them to the Chief across the table.

The Chief looked at the others. Like a man in search of help to know what to do or say. Reading from the Chief's indecision and seeming to forget the rest of the people inside the room, Mr Chang stood up and in a dismissive way walked over to the Chief's chair saying, 'Bwana Chief, take back the girl and we shall talk in the evening.'

Chang picked up the two shiny notes lying on the table and gently dropped them on the little girl's lap.

'For hospital…'

That was when, like a possessed man, Ali shot up and quickly drove into Mr Chang and rammed him against the wall. With one huge crash and like a crumbling glass wall, Mr Chang sank to the floor. Ali grabbed the money and tore it into pieces. Like a man bequeathing flowers over a grave, he sprinkled the pieces of torn money on Mr Chang's head. Mr Chang, in shocked disbelief, leaned against the wall and sat still.

The two women shrieked and ran out, leaving the Chief begging Ali to stop. Chinese boys who had their ears plugged with Beats-by-Dre headphones only reacted once they saw their boss being dragged by the collar in the sand. No-one had the courage to come any closer to Ali. His reputation was well known by everyone, Chinese and police alike.

***

When the bugle went off in the Chinese camp, the villagers were awakened by a gossipy cadence. The miraa-selling women and idle men began their speculative stories that soon grew into a very dangerous rumour. That was how the news reached most of the villagers of a young girl raped and tied up by the Chinese. Everyone modified the story to suit their needs. Tired old men who viewed the Chinese's heavy trucks as noisy things tormenting their old age, masked their anger in the poor girl's story. Weak men secretly whispered to each other about how the road workers preyed on their wives. Young men, who sat idle on their verandahs, accused the Chinese of not employing enough locals. Noisy women spoke about the new risks to their daughters. They tied old kangas around their waists and shouted angry words until large veins stood erect on their foreheads. Uncompensated men from the village and other camp workers, who had over the past months suffered from small accidents and machine malfunctions, collected themselves in the narrow streets like wrecked vehicles and began crafting ways of getting their revenge. They assembled their exaggerated miseries in very dramatic ways. Limping, groaning and wincing at old pains. All these masked anger and sharp words burst out like raw sewage. Like a small cloud growing into a storm, they gathered in the narrow street and retold their stories.

It was Amino, the drama queen, two-time divorcee, village feminist, mother and widow who came screaming, holding a torn dress to her bosom.

'Lala lala lala... diro lala... alaa lala,' she said, holding up the dress of a young girl.

'Look, look, look.... look... my people look... see for yourselves what...' Her voice quivered and died in her throat. She held the dress to her heaving chest and broke into a sob. Other women joined her wail and tore off their headscarves. The street became like a sheep pen that had been attacked by a hyena.

'Let's go and teach them a lesson,' said one boy through clenched jaws, a thick vein filling out on his neck.

Like men possessed, they stoked up the wanton chaos. Schoolkids ran amongst their parents chanting, 'Chinese must go... Chinese must go!'

The camp guards left the huge gate and ran back to inform Mr Chang.

Like a chorus of doom, the chants entered the camp. The crowd suddenly stopped. Teary women, boys with clubs, the excited schoolchildren and the men all stood silent.

They saw Ali dragging Mr Chang by his shirt collar through the sand, leaving a trail behind him. He deposited Mr Chang like a bag of dirt in the sand, daring any of the Chinese to come closer. The Chief and APs watched silently. Mr Chang lay at Ali's feet, blood flowing from his head.

'From today. Stay away from our village,' he said, like a king passing a decree.

'We shall kill you... I promise... I will kill you...' he kept repeating, like a man who meant what he said.

Ali, it was generally agreed, had a mouth like a camel's. It dealt with the soft leaves and sharp thorns of the acacia with equal relish. He could speak gently and harshly in the same breath. And today, his lips quivered with the message of death.

He turned away and walked back. The people who had come chanting moved away. Disappointed that they wouldn't be allowed to do any damage and to calm their mob anger down they talked animatedly the whole time about what they could have done to teach the Chinese a lesson.

'Even the British colonizers were forced to leave… Who do the Chinese think they are?' they said.

***

The Chinese stayed in their camp and the villagers in their homes but gallons of petrol and diesel were stolen. Bags of cement disappeared from camp stores. The isolated villagers brimmed with an awakened need to exploit, to steal. The young prospered on thievery and conceit. Every day, there were squabbles over men, over unpaid credit for miraa or heated debate on how to divide camp spoils.

The Chinese workers quarrelled with elderly women who queued with their yellow jerricans for water. The villagers sought reasons to fight the Chinese. Innocent actions were treated as great hostilities. One elderly man, dressed in elaborate traditional regalia that brought out an ancient glory, marched slowly out of the village one evening. Excited, and forgetting the new tensions, one Chinese man innocently got out his camera and was in the search of the best shot when the elderly man walked up to him and, without any warning, crashed his herding stick into his head. Kids going home from the school beyond the camp stopped and laughed until tears came to their eyes. The Chinese man, stung by shame, clenched his fists into a ball like a karate instructor. The kids stopped laughing. Breaths were held and heartbeats quickened. They watched in silence. The old man stood regarding the Chinese man in front of him approaching with kicks and fist pumps. He lifted his long stick and thrashed like a maddened herder. Thrash and thwack. He slashed and smacked in quick successions. The long stick rammed into the Chinese man's side, shoulders and legs. There wasn't any chance of saving face. He stopped and ran like a mad goat. The schoolkids ran after him like dogs.

Newly married women and young girls made it their concern to often mock the Chinese workers, holding out their pinkies, the sexual smirk very clear, when they came across Mr Chang or any Chinese workers along the road. Mr Chang stopped going into the village, staying away from anything that was beyond the camp's perimeter.

Dalle Abraham is a Kenyan writer. He was part of the 2014 Kwani? Writers' Workshop. He has been published in *Chimurenga*, *Jalada* and *Kwani?* He is currently working on a collection of short stories and a novel.

Wahala Lizard

Nkiacha Atemnkeng

The King Airlines flight, TI 237, a Boeing 747-800 plane to Addis Ababa, had been pretty eventless until a boy rose from seat 23L and tumbled into the aisle. Every passenger who saw the boy fall backwards tilted their heads in his direction, on the walkway. A white American guy in 24L, directly behind the boy's seat, made a futile attempt to grip him.

'Are you okay?' he asked. The boy shook his head.

'What's wrong?' asked a light-skinned black woman to the boy's right, sitting in 25M. The boy opened his mouth to talk but suddenly contorted and disgorged a rivulet of vomit on the aisle rug. The lady in seat 25M moved her feet quickly in an effort to dodge the rancid mess but part of it landed on her legs. 24L had not been in the path of the puke, but he moved his right leg anyway and took out a Kleenex. He held it out to the boy and pushed the call button. A flight attendant came rushing to the scene.

'Sir, are you all right?' the flight attendant asked the sick boy. His mouth was agape. His breathing was less rhythmic. He finally spoke in a whisper.

'No, I am not. I have nausea. I hope it is not Ebola.'

Immediately 25M heard the word 'Ebola', she sprang forward.

'What? Did you say Ebola? The boy has Ebola, oh! And he has vomited on my legs. Oh my God! Who sent me to this seat? I am dead. Please move, let me keep away from the vomit.'

'Madame, please don't touch me, he has vomited on your legs, don't infect me with your Ebola vomit,' a burly light-skinned Ethiopian man in 25N warned.

25M started shedding tears. The flight attendant stooped, examining the patient. He raised his head slowly. His eyes had gone red and he was sweating profusely. He also had a high fever. Vomiting, sweating and fever were all Ebola symptoms, though nothing had been confirmed in the boy's case. Another approaching flight attendant stopped, right next to Flight Attendant 1.

'I'm not from Liberia,' the ill traveller said slowly. 'I don't even know where Guinea or Sierra Leone are. I don't have Ebola!'

'Did you fill in any health form before boarding this flight?' Flight Attendant 1 asked.

'No.'

'Did any medical personnel check your temperature before you boarded the plane?'

'No. Passenger temperature measurement is not done at the Douala Airport in my country.' The flight attendants exchanged glances.

Flight Attendant 1 stayed with the weeping 25M, consoling her. Flight Attendant 2, who was also the flight purser, walked towards the cockpit door, picked up the wired device and spoke on the PA system.

'Captain!'

'Go ahead for the captain!' His voice was gruff.

'We have an emergency. A passenger just fell down in the aisle and is vomiting!'

'Okay, implement targeted clean-up and infection-control measures. Then let me know how he is doing.'

'Copy!'

Flight Attendant 1 made her way towards the cockpit area to put on a face mask, protective clothing and to get cleaning equipment.

Most of the passengers had begun fidgeting. 25M continued weeping theatrically. Commercial air travel could be a potential vector for spreading global pandemics, especially airborne ones like the eradicated SARS.

The sick traveller lay in the aisle, heaving. 24L shook his head.

'I'm really puzzled by the lady's exaggerated dramatics,' he said.

'Well, this is the type of reaction that happens when your Western media creates an issue and then whips everybody into a hysterical frenzy,' 25N retorted.

'What do you mean? He sparked all of this. Why did he mention Ebola when he started vomiting? It's no different from saying, "maybe I have a gun in my purse" while you're on board a plane. It can cause panic,' said 25M.

'He didn't say he has Ebola. He just raised some concerns about Ebola,' an Arab man in seat 26N pointed out.

'There is no reported case of Ebola in Cameroon, so why should he suggest it? Ebola is surely going to be a hot word aboard a plane or in any airport terminal now,' said 24L.

'He's got Ebola symptoms, for God's sake. How did it develop in the affected countries? Was it not from a first case like this?' 25N asked.

'I think it's the lady who blew things out of proportion. What he said was that he had nausea, not Ebola. I was travelling to the UK in 2005 after the London bombings and was narrating a teenage drinking incident to my wife. I used the phrase, "being drunk was the bomb". Another passenger thought I said I had a bomb on board and informed the crew. I almost got into trouble because of that. It taught me that one has to be careful about using certain words in certain places,' said the Arab man.

'I didn't blow anything out of proportion. Why don't you let him vomit on your feet, too,' said 25M.

'The Western media needs to stop scaring the public. They should state the facts about Ebola and how to prevent it. Instead of perennially pounding us with gory images of scrawny and helpless Ebola-infected people and corpses and skyrocketing infection figures,' 25N said.

'You have a point there. I think this Ebola is the world's

next AIDS,' said the Arab man.

The purser returned to the sick boy, watching him breathe.

'Ebola is worse than AIDS, oh! And now I have it,' 25M claimed.

'Ma'am, please don't talk like that. He may just have regular fever. We will clean your feet with alcohol and if there are any Ebola viruses in the vomit droplets, they will die,' the purser said.

Flight Attendant 1 returned. The purser put on gloves and took a bottle of alcohol and tissue paper from her, which she used to clean the feet of 25M. The woman looked a little relieved after the cleaning.

Flight Attendant 1 scrubbed off the mess on the patient's body with disinfectant. He held his face in a grimace and rolled over. When she finished cleaning him up, she gave him an air-sickness bag to use, in case he vomited again. Then she helped him to an empty seat, near the lavatory. It was quite a distance from the last passenger. His head slumped but the flight attendant held him up again and lowered him to his seat. He continued breathing deeply.

Some of the passengers changed seats and moved towards the middle part of the cabin. The flight attendant restricted the use of that lavatory to the ill traveller only. She proceeded to clean the vomit mess on the aisle thoroughly, which she put in disposable plastic bags. Last, she sterilized the target area with alcohol, took off her gloves in the toilet, disposed of them in a plastic bag and washed her hands.

'It seems people now need to wear an extra layer of clothes, disposable gloves and masks even to travel!' a Chinese female passenger in seat 24N said.

'That sounds ridiculous. The risk of a person catching Ebola on a plane is very low, like an aircraft crashing after being struck by a meteorite,' said 24L.

'I would rather look ridiculous and be safe than regret!' the Chinese woman said.

'Uh huh, like some Asian passengers I saw at the airport

wearing face masks and gloves to prevent catching the virus, as if the Ebola virus is now airborne,' 25N teased.

'I disagree with you all. Bitter kola can kill that virus. Eat a lot of bitter kola, drink lots of salt water and the virus will die!' a Nigerian guy in 23K said.

'Hilarious! Kola does not kill the Ebola virus. Is it because the virus is shaped like a worm that you believe salt water can kill it? Just like it dehydrates and kills earthworms? That's absolutely not correct,' 24L said, in a burst of laughter.

'Ban all flights from Africa,' the Chinese woman shouted.

'Why? Ebola is only in three African countries! Ban flights from those countries instead. Not all of Africa!' reasoned the Arab man.

'*A mon avis, Ebola n'existe pas. Ce que vous appelez Ebola n'est qu'une invention des Blancs pour semer la peur à travers le monde,*' a francophone Cameroonian man in 24K said.

'*Moi, connait, ça existe!*' the Chinese lady said, in what she believed was good French.

'That thing exists but it was created by the white people in their labs to reduce the growing African population,' 25N said.

'That's rubbish!' 24L snapped.

'They say it has no cure. Yet they fly infected American citizens from Africa back home and treat them. But the infected ones in the affected countries are dying every day. It doesn't make much sense,' 25N said.

'I think that's why Kofi Annan called it a poor man's disease,' said the bitter kola guy.

'The experimental drug Z-mapp can treat it but it's in limited supply,' 24L explained.

'That's a lie!' said the bitter kola guy.

The lively debate continued as the purser communicated with the captain on the PA system about the condition of the ill traveller. He had stopped vomiting and his condition was stable, though he still had a fever. But he wasn't coughing.

After a couple of minutes, the purser announced lunch.

Four flight attendants rolled out two trolleys packed with food and drink. They began to serve the passengers on the front seats, handing them trays full of rice, chicken or beef sauce, vegan food, cake, bread, cheese, soft drinks, beer and wine. Some of the passengers ate with ravenous appetites, while others toyed with their food, chewing slowly and distorting their faces, in a manner that portrayed that they didn't particularly like what they were eating but had no choice anyway.

25M had stopped weeping and somewhat recovered from her Ebola infection shock by the time lunch was being served. Flight Attendant 4 halted in front of her with an open food trolley. She gave a warm look and smiled before asking, 'Are you okay now, ma'am?'

'Yes.'

'Would you like chicken or beef for lunch?'

'Em…'

25M instinctively turned and glanced at the food trolley, before making her choice. She stared at the food trolley in a manner that no passenger had ever looked at a food trolley before. Flight Attendant 4 repeated her question, watching her keenly.

'Ma'am, would you like chicken or beef?'

'Lizard!' 25M suddenly screamed.

Flight Attendant 4 widened her eyes and furrows immediately appeared on her forehead.

'What?' she snapped, not making sense of the woman's choice.

'Lizard! Lizard! Lizard!' 25M screeched again, placing the most bizarre food order Flight Attendant 4 had ever heard in her entire six years working for the airline.

'Em, we, we, don't, serve… lizards for lunch ma'am, I'm sorry, please stop screaming.'

'There is a lizard in your food trolleeeey!' she shrieked, pointing at the interior of the trolley and jerking from right to left like she had been bitten by a driver ant.

'What?'

Flight Attendant 4 turned to look at the trolley, but didn't see anything at first. And at that moment, turbulence struck and she lost balance. The plane dipped and that uncomfortable feeling of weightlessness came upon them. It was like the plane was going straight back down, as it made its balancing trajectories, quavering and staggering like a drunk.

The turbulence had caught them unawares. When the second dip occurred, Flight Attendant 4 held a seat. All of a sudden, a big red-and-blue lizard with an orange head jumped out towards her. When she saw it, she bent over, towards a passenger's food tray, to get out of the way. She hit the tray and soiled her uniform in the process, but didn't scream. The lizard brushed against her left shoulder and bounced on seat 25M.

'Get away,' she yelled.

The lizard fell straight on the right breast of 25M and gripped her dress right on her boob to gain balance. She held both hands upwards, Moses style, and shuddered. But the reptile nodded thrice, like the big male Agama lizard that it was, and did not budge.

She then released the outburst. It was a tumultuous fit of deafening sounds, which emerged from her mouth like fine grains of sand, and scattered through the cold winds of the whole pressurized cabin.

'Haaaaaaaaaaaaaaaaaah!Arrrrrrrrrrrrrrrrgh!'

Quite a scream! But she finally plucked the courage to flick the lizard away with her right hand and the creature glided in the air. The two annoying incidents had the woman swearing,

'Useless airline! You let people vomit on my legs. You let lizards jump on my breasts and it's a lizard you serve me for lunch. This is too much. I will sue you people! Useless airline.'

Most of the children had now taken over the screaming

and passengers were fidgeting too. Some were moving about left, right and centre in utter confusion.

'*Un lézard à bord! C'est de la folie. Impossible. Je n'ai jamais vécu une telle chose, même pas dans les romans de Mongo Beti, je n'ai jamais lu quelque chose comme ça,*' 24K expostulated.

'Kill that ugly lizard!' 25N ordered erratically, pointing as it dashed towards his sandals. He tried to raise his legs to his seat but the space was so small his feet hung in the air.

The awful smell from his toes pricked 25M's nose. She sniffed the air like a police dog and lashed out, 'Jeez, put down your smelly feet!'

25N quickly lowered his feet, with a frown on his face.

The lizard took off in the opposite direction.

25N shouted again, 'Kill that lizard!'

'No, that's against animal rights. It's not a poisonous lizard. I can use it for scientific research. I need to know how it got on this plane in the first place,' 24L said.

'Damn it, kill it,' 25N said.

'How can a big, strong guy like you be scared of lizards? This one is harmless,' 24L laughed.

'Kill that devilish creature! How can it jump on my breast?' 25M said.

'Kill the lizard. It's a delicacy in some cultures,' the Chinese woman said.

'No, please don't. Lizards have souls, no matter how small they are. They have a right to live, just like human beings,' the Arab man protested.

'*Tuez cet animal ! Le lézard est en train de semer la panique. Pas d'animaux à bord – tuez le,*' 24K said.

'The rule is no live animals on board. If it's running around and scaring people, then we just have to kill it. You can't carry a lizard in your carry-on luggage,' said 25N.

'Then catch it alive,' suggested the Arab man.

'Who wan catch that fast ting wey don cause this wahala so?' the bitter kola guy asked.

'Then kill it,' 25N ordered.

'Kill it yourself, scared big man,' urged 25M.

The captain had heard the noise and asked the purser on the PA what was happening in the cabin. The purser informed him that the panic was caused by a lizard that had emerged from one of the food trolleys. The captain exclaimed and asked her to make sure it was caught, as soon as possible.

The lizard pecked at a piece of vegan food on the rug, which a passenger had thrown due to the chaos. It bustled around, through people's restless feet, in an effort to disappear from their view. The flight attendants moved about looking for it thoroughly. The lizard slowed down, crawled and hid under a piece of tissue paper. Not for long though, for a foot kicked it out and it rose out of the paper. Two flight attendants pursued it along the aisle and it whizzed across as fast as it could, dodging some kicking feet. Other passengers shot disposable spoons and knives at it. But it kept running towards the cockpit and hid there.

Some minutes later, the cockpit door partially opened and the co-pilot peeped out. He asked the purser, 'Has it been caught?'

'Not yet.'

'Where is it?'

'It hid somewhere around here. We are still looking for it.'

The co-pilot glanced around to catch a glimpse of the reptile but he couldn't.

'I want to use the restroom,' he said.

'Okay.'

He opened the cockpit door completely and walked out. As he began closing it with his left hand, the orange head of the reptile shot out of its hiding place and made for the cockpit door. The co-pilot gasped when he saw it running towards the open door and flung his left leg to kick it away. The reptile wheeled to his right and he missed completely.

'Oh, no!' the purser exclaimed, as it entered the cockpit.

The captain was drinking a cup of coffee and didn't see it when it crawled in. But he immediately turned in its direction, when he heard the missed kick and scurrying movement. He paused with his cup right before his lips and muttered, 'Damn it, the lizard!'

He lowered the cup as the co-pilot turned at the door.

'Be careful, the lizard just crawled into the cockpit.'

'Yes, I saw it.'

The captain threw his disposable spoon at the lizard but it crawled forward. The spoon hit it on the head and it ran around haphazardly. It got so close to the captain's feet that he freaked out and spilled coffee on himself. The lizard moved leftwards, the liquid dropped rightwards. The captain moved upwards, swaying from side to side.

'Goddamn it! Who put a lizard on my plane? I'm a pilot not a fucking zoo keeper!' he barked, moving his right hand back and forth. 'Get off my cockpit!'

'Be careful, captain!' the co-pilot cautioned.

'Yes. Can you get away from the door?'

'All right.'

The co-pilot moved. The captain rolled a piece of tissue paper into a ball shape and shot it at the lizard. It scampered around in the cockpit, trying to find its way out. The captain climbed on his seat, looking around. When he saw it, he brought down a leg and gave it a gentle kick. The lizard skated out of the cockpit, landed and took off again.

A little girl on one of the front seats screamed. Her younger brother didn't shout, though. He asked their mother, 'Mummy, was the lizard flying the plane?'

'No, why would you think that?' their mother retorted.

The lizard kept crawling quickly. A bold man succeeded in grabbing its red-and-blue tail. But it pulled itself so vigorously away from the man's grip that its skin broke loose and its tail gave way. It got off his hands and fell on its back. The man flung the wriggling tail away. The lizard tossed and turned, landed and balanced on its claws. Freedom again! It skipped right across the walkway, as passengers yelled. Its speed was slowing down considerably though, as fatigue set in.

After zigzagging through the legs of some passengers, it arrived at the rear end of the plane, halted and did three push-ups: a remarkable show of its male ego. It crawled to one corner, where there were empty seats, and lay prostrate. But there was someone there, watching it keenly. The ill traveller, who was sleeping in a bedlike position on two seats, stretched out his right hand quickly and covered it with his air-sickness bag. The lizard jumped and hit the plastic covering from all angles. Yet there was no way out.

'I've caught the lizard!' he said slowly and held up the air-sickness bag. The lizard squirmed inside the bag. Some passengers rejoiced.

'Ah, na so! Finally! After yi don chakara place soté,' the bitter kola guy celebrated.

'Now kill the lizard,' 25N said.

'How can a sick boy catch a lizard and a big, strong man like you be scared of lizards?' 25M asked 25N.

'Maybe he's allergic to lizards,' the bitter kola guy said.

'I've never seen anything like this before. It's like a movie,' 24L said.

'*C'est du jamais vu. Cette histoire mérite une page dans les journaux,*' 24K said.

'Let me think of a suitable title for the newspaper article: "Lizard on a plane"', suggested the Arab man.

'Lounge lizard!' proposed 24L.

'Wahala lizard,' the bitter kola guy chipped in. Some people laughed.

When Flight TI 237 finally landed at the Bole International Airport in Addis Ababa, all the passengers disembarked from the plane except the ill traveller and the lizard. The boy was transferred to a health unit in an ambulance and quarantined to be tested for Ebola. The lizard was transferred to the station manager's office at King Airlines and put in an empty plastic container. The station manager took a good look at it and shook his head.

'Ugly Douala lizard! Look at the little thing that could

potentially bring down a plane.' He took pictures of it and transferred them to his laptop. He sent some emails with photos of the lizard attached. He made lots of phone calls too, wondering aloud to himself all the time, 'How did this thing get on board? How did they allow a sick person to travel?'

The next day, the station manager received some emails. The first one had the ill traveller's Ebola test result. The next was a report explaining how the lizard got on board the plane.

Some days later, 25M received an email.

Dear Customer

We are writing to apologize for the unfortunate incidents that happened to you on King Airlines flight TI 237. We affirm to you now that we have investigated the matter. First and foremost, the ill traveller tested negative for Ebola. He was only suffering from a bout of malaria. Also, video-surveillance cameras at the Douala International Airport captured images showing how the lizard got into the food trolley. It happened in the airport catering department. One of the food trolleys hadn't been closed properly, so the lizard crawled into it.

We assure you that we have tightened up security at our catering company and check-in desks so that such incidents will not happen again. To fully express our apology, we have granted you a free return ticket to any country of your choice that we fly to when next you travel on King Airlines. We regret any pain the incident may have caused you and promise to deliver the impeccable service that King Airlines has been known for as *The African Airline with a Difference*.

Kind regards
Mr Et-puis Koi
King Airlines Representative

Nkiacha Atemnkeng was born in Cameroon and is based in Douala, where he works for Swissport at the airport. He is passionate about aviation fiction and comedy. His illustrated story book for children, *The Golden Baobab Tree*, was published by Aalvent Books in 2014. His work has also been published in the 2014 Writivism anthology, *Fabafriq* magazine, *Munyori* and some other literary websites. His insights can be found on his personal blog, nkiachaatemnkeng. blogspot.com

Nehushtan

Diane Awerbuck

Wherever he went, the procession of ghosts tugged at his clammy high-vis vest, whispering endearments and threats. Malan wondered if he could stop taking the malaria pills, if the sweats and the sickness would be worse than the spirits.

It must be the meds, he told himself. He swallowed a sympathetic mouthful of beer. The vaccinations two weeks ago were a couple of three-in-ones at the Fish Hoek clinic, for diseases that belonged in the desperate, helpless Middle Ages – typhoid, cholera, diphtheria.

But there was only so much modern medicine could do. For real heart-sickness there was no cure. Malan knew it first-hand: he had been a familiar face at the clinic over the last year. If he had to look at the plaque at the door once more – a leering serpent, red on bronze, curled around a stick – he really would lose his mind. 'Don't call these sessions grief counselling,' the doctor kept telling Linda and Malan. 'Call it family therapy.'

Except that I don't have a family now, Malan thought, for the thousandth time since the hit-and-run. Just a wife who won't cry, and a small boy's shoes still in the cupboard, paired like Noah's creatures in their march to the imprisonment in the ark that was also their survival. Sometimes, in the wakeful starless night, he heard the shoes pattering in the passage.

He knew that Linda lay wide-eyed beside him, her body turned bony and unfamiliar with sorrow. It's not just you, Malan wanted to tell her. Danny was my child too, my only son, my last link to the human community. What else is there? He imagined reaching out and making a warm bridge of flesh in the dark with her but it was impossible. She hated the smell of liquor on him. The doctor at the clinic back home said that 80 per cent of parents who lost a child ended up getting divorced. It stood between them, a chasm, while above them the waterfall of misfortune roared and crashed.

When Nokya Construction had called for civil engineers for the new dams in the eastern highlands, everyone had told Malan it was a sign, until he had believed it too. He had little choice. No local company would hire him. He started out with good intentions, but by the end of the week he would be roaring drunk, blacking out, pissing his pants, as if his penis cried for him because his eyes could not.

Now he sat a whole other country away from Linda, in the site compound's empty bar. There was a fish-woman painted above the door, her face turned sulkily away, fading into the evening, a single pearl earring like a misplaced tooth. MERMAID'S TAVEN, someone had lettered. Malan wanted to correct the spelling, but it would spoil the painting.

He tried to ignore the mistake while he waited for the engineer, who was leaving the unfinished site in the morning. Tonight was Khumalo's send-off: he had given up on the project. 'Bad concrete,' he had told Malan earlier in the day, his spit like confetti. 'Too many injuries. Too many delays. And then this thing with Elias drowning. These guys are desperate for work, and they lie when you ask them if they can swim. Now our boys don't even want to finish. I wish you good luck with these lazy ones, my friend, because you will need it.'

The lake was already dammed at the narrow neck of the valley. There would be two smaller dams built downstream, clean water channelled in aqueducts to 10,000 square kilometres of newly irrigable land. Nokya Construction would redraw the map of the entire country, and be handsomely paid by its international donors. Malan thought that if you could get up high enough, you would see the area growing green as algae instead of the parched brown of the empty breadbasket of Africa. They were playing liquid God.

But all dams – embankment, gravity, buttress and arch: Malan had seen them all – needed maintenance as they aged, so that they were able to carry a realistic load, resisted deformation and collapse. It happened every few years, even in the First World. Spillways clogged, concrete cracked, tectonic plates shifted under the earth. The contention walls imploded for reasons that didn't matter in the end, not if you were in the water's path. Flash floods destroy a dam, no matter how much planning we do, Malan thought. It just breaks under the strain. And if it happens to a dam, why not a person? When he looked at his own clay core he saw only neglected channels, diversions, leaks. This job was his last chance. Malan stared at the way his hands seemed distant, elongated and wavering. To make steady contact with another human being, he raised his palm. The bartender bowed and poured him another expert Zambezi, the head frothing just over the lip of the glass so that Malan had to inhale the bubbles or wet his weak hands. Concentrate, he told himself. Only beer: no spirits. One more, and that's it. Don't fuck this up.

He watched the bartender as he wiped the counter, refilled the water jug, ticked something on a clipboard. The man was young, his life still unmapped. He wore the same amulet on a thong that everyone in the doomed village did: a small snake carved from greenish soapstone. Maybe I should wear one, Malan thought. Except no talisman would protect the downstream villages from the deluge when they filled the dams.

He drank, but the beer tasted flat. Maybe that was the malaria tablets too. They were hard to swallow, powdery and bitter, and there was some justice in that. The jitters and the nausea he could handle. He was used to his own nerveless hands in the migrained morning after, when the bottle by the bed was his clue to the night before. That and his splitting skull, and Linda's dull disapproval. 'The demon drink,' she said with sarcasm, as if he had chosen to be possessed.

But the tablets in their blister pack refused him the deep black death of the bottle. They gave him the opposite – dreams that he fought throughout the night, his throat aching and his legs tingling with dread. Malan wasn't a fool. He knew that the driver who had killed his son had also taken his peace of mind. Sleep was for the ignorant, the happy, the clear of conscience. But, now that he was over the border, the pills had made everything worse: the light brighter, the trees deep green, surreal. He couldn't trust himself, couldn't decide whether the currents he had seen in the reservoir this morning were real, or if the workers' reluctance was infectious, another sub-tropical disease. Maybe he could ask Khumalo, if he ever showed up.

Malan felt in his pants pocket for the little package he kept there. Still safe. He swallowed half his flat beer and was glad that his wife couldn't see him. He wondered what Linda was doing, if she was buried in one of her shiny romance novels, just as he was lost in the rough landscape of the site. At least the pay was unarguably in dollars. Earlier in the day he had realized how hard he would have to work to earn it. Malan found himself perched not on a palanquin but a rust-flecked piledriver, riding high as the workers leaned on their picks and spades, squinting up at him. One foot in the grave, thought Malan, and the other on the necks of my fellows. They were local men, silent and resentful, their real lives hidden. Malan understood that he would be lonelier here than he had ever been back in the wide, bland streets of Fish Hoek. Only the land spoke to him, in sighs and whispers. Overhead, birds of prey kept circling, as if he had travelled back into some more vivid and dangerous past, where an eagle might pluck him from a river bank and flay him, mid-air.

It was not difficult to see why the workers were dragging their feet. Soon the land would be cleared, the village given back to the floodplain, ancient as the Nile, the buildings only briefly manifest as houses and clinics and schools. The people would be settled somewhere higher and drier to languish on government pensions, their gone-befores left behind, lying submerged by the brown water of progress that pressed them flat on their ancestral backs. Malan could not bring himself to ask the men how it felt to take a pay cheque to turn their own home into a ghost town.

Now that Malan had given up waiting, Khumalo appeared, picking up in mid-sentence. 'As I was saying, they did not want to go.' He shrugged and heaved himself onto his bar stool like a seal until it squeaked under the careless weight. 'You can't blame them. Who would want to leave everything they know, even if it's a shitty existence? And the stories. These are not city people.' He wiggled his fingers and spoke in a grandmother's nagging quaver: 'The people under the water are unhappy. That is why the worker drowned. Now he will come back to take revenge.'

'You mean like water spirits?' asked Malan. 'Like nyami-nyami?'

'I mean like mermaids,' Khumalo said, and laughed. 'Do you not know that they always need more citizens for their underwater towns? There is a whole country under the sea. And the sea begins high up in the mountains; it must be protected on its journey. Even the smallest spring has its guardian. And each river has its own village under the surface.'

'Huh. An entire village.'

'A mirror village: houses, people, cattle – everything. Our Lord Himself said: as above, so below. In the early morning you will hear the bells as the boys drive their cattle along the river bed.'

'Do you really believe that?'

'I am a born-again Christian.'

'But not one of those snake cults,' Malan joked. He secretly fingered the serviette folded in his pocket.

'Ha. People believe what they believe. You know, Moses healed the Israelites with his brazen serpent, Nehushtan. Who knows why these things work?'

'But you asked the n'anga to come and perform the rites here. That's not Christian.'

'To deny these things is to deny yourself.'

'But what do *you* think is going on?'

Khumalo stared at Malan, and he hoped that the other man was not looking too hard at the broken veins in his cheeks, his drinker's nose, his lack of purpose.

'Okay. I will tell you what I tell the workers. There must be a suction underneath the reservoir which creates a hole and the water will actually be swirling so violently that if you fall in you will not come out. Even if you have an oxygen mask. That's what happened to Elias. Or maybe they are remembering 30, 40 years ago, when the comrades who died for Independence were thrown into the lake.'

'But that was long ago. Their fathers' time. It's over.'

'Is injustice ever over?' Khumalo had stopped joking.

Malan thought of the water sprites in the old stories, the ondines and naginis of the wellsprings, the voracious mermaids toothy as eels, all the wriggling dreamcreatures that would make their way towards him in the facebrick compound where he tried to sleep. The single bed was made of the same bricks as the walls, like lego, or a crematorium. He winced and thought of his dead child, how Linda had tried to pack his toys into his coffin before they abandoned him to his fiery afterlife. I could not protect my boy, and he depended on me, Malan thought. In his life and in his death.

He stood up. 'I think it is time for me to go to bed.'

'Don't forget to say your prayers,' said Khumalo. 'And don't worry. It's usually only the big dams like Kariba.'

Malan undressed in his tiny room that smelled of fresh concrete and graveyard earth. He felt in his pants pocket for the serviette he carried with him, and he unrolled it. He tried not to handle it much, but the temptation was always too great, to touch this relic of his only child.

The sour worm fell out, eager for the light, and rolled on his palm. The sugar from the worm was almost rubbed off. Malan knew that if he got it wet it would dissolve entirely. The gelatine in the sweet was rubbery but not resilient: it came, after all, from hooves and marrow bones, the remains of creatures spirited into something else.

Danny had loved sour worms. He would have eaten whole tubs of them at a sitting if his parents had let him. This final one Malan had found under his pillow, half yellow, half green, furred with hair and lint like a centipede. Danny had howled when Malan had tried to take it away. 'Look at it! This is disgusting, my boy. And you want to put it in your mouth?' His son had wept and wept, beyond what the sweet was worth, hiccupping as Malan held him on his lap, thinking, I need a drink. Danny had fallen asleep half an hour later, after his father had sung the lullaby 12 times, the remnant of some faded folk song:

> *Dance to your daddy, my little laddie.*
> *Dance to your daddy, my little one.*
> *You shall have a fishy in a little dishie.*
> *You shall have a fishy when the boats come in.*

Now Malan set the sour worm in his metal cup beside the bed, and lay down, defeated by isolation. No father of his own to hold and guide him; no child of his own to hold and guide. In the warm insomniac dark the familiar pain settled on his chest.

It was useless. His stomach kept clenching like a fist. He could not drink enough to sleep – not on-site, where he was in charge – and the pills were making the room go round.

Malan sat up. Maybe he could go for a walk, check on the shoddy workmanship he had inherited. He knew his way around, and no-one would even have to see him. The workers

– those who were left – would be in their own quarters, playing games with quick counters they carved from wood, or dreaming their impenetrable dreams.

He dressed again and returned the sour worm to his pocket. 'My lucky charm,' he told the worm, and patted its sticky back. The heat from his own body warmed it.

The moonlight was scanty. He picked his way over the powdery soil of the compound until he got to the site, where the bones of the earth arched, exposed in the dry bed. He scrambled down the steep slope to the bottom and went to inspect the fresh contention wall as best he could in the pale light.

It stood smooth and implacable, ten times his height, the border between hundreds of thousands of kilolitres of hoarded water and the patient course below. Its concrete smelled raw and familiar as blood, gritty under his fingers. The seams were neat, though the concrete was taking a long time to dry. He would walk across the bed, letting the wall guide him, then go further up and look at the water itself for signs of disturbance, for the whirlpool he was sure he'd seen. Maybe it was caused by an obstacle under the surface, like the skeleton trees that still stood, their branches like serpents. The valley had not been cleared before it was filled with water: 'Too expensive,' Khumalo had said. 'We are already behind schedule.' Everything living there had been submerged and left to decompose.

Malan was almost at the other side of the river bed when he blundered against a thin branch. It hooked his pants pocket. He felt the scratch, and then the blood reversing through the cloth, seeping black in the moonlight. Not a branch – a staff, jammed waist-high in the ground. The breeze was making the little hairs on the back of his neck try to stand up. He rubbed his hip and sucked the blood off his fingers.

At the top of the stick was tied a raggedy washcloth that the wind moved gently, and Malan thought of scarecrows and flags. Was this what Khumalo was doing when Malan was waiting for him in the bar? Or was another worker trying to sabotage construction?

He felt a sudden hot rush of annoyance. This was the kind of crap that stopped this country moving forward, that made his workers delay a project that would send clean water to thousands of their countryfolk, that would spare little girls the endless hours they spent walking up and down, balancing tubs of water on heads too heavy for the tender stems of their necks.

And more than that: if he didn't complete the dams, Nokya would never hire him again.

He grabbed the rag and ripped it from the staff. The thing tore easily, and Malan realized it was not made of cloth. He rubbed it between his fingers and thumb. It rustled like wax paper.

Snakeskin.

This again. What had Khumalo called it? Nehushtan. Why did thinking people believe that touching the skin of a snake would heal them of their afflictions? Children, especially, were always being sent with offerings for the snake-man, who secretly milked the poison from his hissing exhibit and publicly survived the bite. They fell for it every time. Everyone wants magic, Malan told himself, a miracle that would prove that the Lord holds the universe in His cupped and ineffable hands, that there is some clear and special purpose for each of us. But I will not believe that my boy had to die because it was God's plan.

Malan shivered. He flung the skin away, and the wind picked it up. Like a winged creature it was spirited upwards, climbing so high that Malan had to crane his neck to see it in the night sky among the stingy stars.

Then the wind dropped and he lost sight of the snakeskin. The damn thing had probably landed in the water. If the men saw it floating there in the morning they would use it as an excuse to go even slower. Malan clicked his tongue in annoyance. He couldn't reach it without immersing himself in the murderous water of the reservoir. They had never recovered Elias's body, had they? Better to leave the snakeskin, and get rid of the stick altogether.

He began to yank the staff out of the ground. As he wiggled it free – the stick had been shoved in with such force that it penetrated the bedrock – he heard the tinkling sounds behind him. He must have felt it all along and assumed it was the wind, but now he was listening properly. The agreeable breeze on his arms was gone. His stomach churned and there was a faint ringing in his skull, the blood dashing and frantic in his ears, the way the air pressure changed before a storm. He checked over his shoulder at the contention wall.

In the moonlight the seams in the concrete were shadowy. Were they darkening? How was it possible that there was already a leak?

The sound of the bells grew louder.

Over the wall of the reservoir came the little boys with their cattle, whistling and waving sticks, each with his own snake wrapped around it. The serpents were handsome: long, slim fellows with yellow eyes. Behind them trooped the denizens of the underwater village, who had inherited the drowned animals of the valley, tidy pigs and goats and a multitude of chickens. They drifted, ordinary and determined, feet and hooves not touching the dry bed, snakes winding around their thin legs as they went. Then came the dead comrades from the Struggle, their fists raised, one woman who wore a beret and toyi-toyied a metre off the ground. The man right at the back must be Elias, thought Malan in a daze. He knew him by his high-vis vest. On either side of the procession drifted the eternal mermaids, who sing but cannot cry. They wore their snakes draped around their throats like necklaces. The moon glinted on the women's pointed teeth as they warbled and hissed:

> Dance to your daddy, my little laddie.
> Dance to your daddy, my little one.

You shall have a fishy in a little dishie.
You shall have a fishy when the boats come in.

Malan covered his ears. He knew who he would see next. He bent over, ready to expel the hot vomit that he was sure would rush up as his stomach rejected the beers from the bar.

Nothing came: he would not be relieved of his suffering.

Malan was afraid to look. The gone-befores and their herds kept streaming by him, the snakes flicking their tongues, turning the air cold where they touched.

And then Danny stood before him, whole and unburned, as he had been in life. He said nothing, but he held out his small hand, splayed like a starfish in the moonlight. Malan clapped his own hand over his pocket.

'Please,' he said. 'Don't make me. It's all I have left of you.'

His boy turned to point behind him and Malan saw that the snakes had not stopped pouring over the contention wall. They were a wave of snakes, and still he could not move out of their path.

Then there were no longer snakes, but only roiling brown waves, and the wall finally gave, as it had been trying to do for all the days since it had been built, dissolving the false boundary between the sterile water of the reservoir and the natural watercourses that the earth had designed itself.

It hit Malan in the chest and he heard one of his ribs crack, a door that had slammed too hard somewhere in his chest. He toppled over backwards and the frothing water carried him with it, rushing downhill to the village, as it had always intended. Malan was buffeted against the bank and his head thumped against the scabbed rocks there. He went limp, acquiescent, and tried to close his eyes.

The boyish ghostly fingers plucked at his pocket, and Malan felt the sour worm being extracted from the interior cloth of its shrine. He began to weep real tears, and his jagged rib nudged sharply at his soft organs so that he was sure something inside him had burst, flooding him with misery.

The fingers would not release him. They kept prodding and pummelling at his body, as the midwife had once laid her hands on Linda to deliver Danny on his long red journey from the underworld to the earth, and as the spirits of the water would do when they ferried his son back to the place of creation.

The brutal hands of the ancestors pushed Malan up the slope of the river bank until he lay panting on the churned earth like the new Adam, the reservoir of sorrow smashed open in his chest, his grief flooding out over the indifferent mud, just as the clean air rushed in to take its place.

Diane Awerbuck wrote *Gardening at Night*, which was awarded the Commonwealth Best First Book Award (Africa and the Caribbean). Her work has been translated into Mandarin, German, Russian and Swedish. Awerbuck's short stories are collected in *Cabin Fever*. Her short story, 'Leatherman', recently won the Short Story Day Africa competition. Awerbuck's latest highbrow-horror novel is *Home Remedies*. Poetry and interviews are at http://aerodrome.co.za/tag/diane-awerbuck/ and her doctorate on trauma and humour is coming soon, right after she finishes her new spec/fic series, as Frank Owen, co-written with Alex Latimer.

Swallowing Ice

Nana Nyarko Boateng

Nobody had time for grief, but I cried anyway. I was told to go wash my face any time someone saw me. Cold water exorcised pain; at least, that was what my family believed. Get your entire face wet and live. But now, only a part of my face felt wet and sticky. It was drool, thick as starch, spread between my left cheek and my pillow. I needed to get out of bed.

Fridays had hurried feet; there was always too much to do. Two hours of reading, a phone call to place at 2.10pm, a cheque to pick up by 4.00pm, get Max's milk and sit in traffic for hours. Max was already up and daydreaming as usual. I wiped my face with the back of my hand and turned the pillow over. Every day, I prayed for two things: talking trees and a sky that changed colours to correspond with the days of the week – red on Mondays, green on Tuesdays, yellow on Wednesdays, blue on Thursdays, purple on Fridays, pink on Saturdays and black on Sundays.

The wall clock said nine past noon but it couldn't be. I woke up at 11.00am every day; my body's internal alarm clock understood this. At 10.56am, I would open my eyes, fall asleep again for four minutes and by 11.00am, I'd be up on my feet heading for the toilet. I made breakfast. One bowl of mashed kenkey, no milk, mine. Another bowl of mashed kenkey, lots of milk, Max's. And a third bowl of milk, which I placed at the foot of the bed. Max and I would sit on the floor and eat. When we were done, we would get back in bed and touch each other till my breath turned heavy and God descended. I'd cry when God came and left.

Max often went out and returned when I was writing. Writing was mostly staring at the mango tree outside my window and wishing I shared a language with it. The cracked mirror that hung by the window held my distorted reflection that eyed me up. I pushed up my left cheek in a mock smile whenever I saw my reflection in the mirror.

There was a vibration in the room. I checked the edges of my bed to see if my phone was trapped in there. It wasn't. The mattress was a bit smaller than the bedstead. Books and other things I put on my bed often slipped into the tiny space between the bedframe and the edges of the mattress. I got on my knees, looked under the bed, and there it lay, flat on its back just as I lay for Max. He would purr with pleasure when I stroked his stomach each afternoon and every night.

Under the bed a 10 pesewa coin, Ama Ata Aidoo's *Changes,* a pen, a box of cigarettes, an empty Mentos chewing-gum pack, and my Vicks inhaler shared space with the phone. I picked up the phone and dragged my body out for fresh air.

'Shit, no!'

My red carpet was doused with milk. I rushed to the kitchen for a napkin. For six years, not once had I knocked over the milk bowl. Waking up an hour and nine minutes late seemed to have ruined everything. There were no napkins in the kitchen. My laundry from last weekend was still up on the line and I wasn't ready to go out yet. Max hadn't finished his food. His beady eyes stared at me with displeasure. Then, he left the room.

The carpet darkened as it soaked up the milk. I pulled off my satin shirt to mop it up. It was useless. I used my blue cotton bed sheet and wiped as hard as I could. There was no saving my bloody carpet. I went back to bed, covered my feet with the milk-stained bed sheet and checked my phone. It was 3.17pm on my phone. It couldn't be. I had just woken up. I checked my wall clock again, it still said nine past noon.

I checked the time on my laptop; it was always set an hour early. It said 4.18pm.

'Shit, shit, fuck!'

I had to get to the office by 4.00pm. We needed the cheque for groceries. I didn't earn much, but my weekly cheque was good enough for Max and me. I was a journalist; a liar, if you want, but I was never late for anything. I wrote freelance for the *Accra Times*. I didn't like being around people much. They stared at me. My pseudonym was 'Vivian Quack'; I made up stories that were presented as actual news. The standards of journalism in Ghana worked perfectly in my favour. People took whatever they read in the papers as facts; other newspapers just copied my stories without acknowledging me or verifying the details. I liked my editor; he knew I made most of my stories up, but it sold his paper. If journalism's first obligation is to tell the truth, without fear or favour, then we were fearless in manufacturing the news. I got one-word responses in capital letters for every email I sent to him: 'OKAY,' 'CHANGE,' 'GOOD,' 'IDEAS?' I wrote three stories every week. I asked for 100 cedis for each, he paid 60. He always paid me on time; 180 cedis, every Friday. I would call in at 2.10pm to check if my cheque was signed and pick it up at 4.00pm.

The last story I wrote made the front page:

Gayism at KIA – Two Arrested!
By Vivian Quack

Two persons have been arrested for allegedly committing lesbian acts at Kotoka International Airport. The accused persons are Miss Serwaa Boadu, 29, an architect, and Miss Jane Owusu, 27, a photographer and dance instructor.

The alleged incident occurred on the evening of 17 May 2013, a few minutes after Miss Boadu's plane landed at KIA from the US. As soon as Miss Boadu got to the arrival hall, Miss Owusu ran and went to embrace her, after which they were seen French kissing, much to the shock and disgust of the crowd, who had gathered at the arrival hall. This led to a commotion where the crowd set upon the accused persons with the intent to lynch them. Immigration officials and policemen at the KIA intervened, and the two women were handed over to the police, who arrested them.

They will be arraigned before the circuit court this morning and prosecuted. Our sources indicate that both accused persons are highly connected members of society. Miss Owusu is the executive director of Girl Child Foundation, an organization set up by the accused to offer free art courses for young girls, while Miss Boadu, prior to her sojourn in the US to study, was a top-level manager at a renowned architectural firm based in Accra. There have been speculations that Miss Owusu uses her foundation to recruit young girls into lesbianism.

Lawyers contacted are torn about whether or not the accused persons can be properly charged and convicted for unnatural carnal knowledge. While some criminal lawyers opined that lesbianism was unnatural, contrary to Ghana's customary and criminal laws as well as its Constitution, others were of the view that the criminal code did not specifically prohibit lesbian acts.

Friends of both women have expressed shock, saying that they little expected either of them to conduct themselves in this manner since they are both decent Christian ladies. Indeed, while Miss Owusu is said to have been a strong member of the Pentecostal Church, Miss Boadu is said to be a faithful member of the Methodist Church. Meanwhile, their pastors, and other men of God contacted so far, have stated that this incident is an indication of how close we are to the end of times and as such would advise all Ghanaians to pray and be vigilant.

It was 3.23pm. I dressed up and left the house.

***

When I got back home, it was 7.42pm. I couldn't decide what to make for dinner. A cabbage and a bottle of water were all I had left in the fridge. Max hadn't returned. It was unlike him to stay out for so long. His breakfast was still on the floor. I took a whiff of it and ate it. The security light flickered. I went outside to see if Max was there. He wasn't. The light winked at me again. I stood there barefooted, not sure what to do.

For six years my life had been my own creation. Everything was pre-set and recurrent – wake-up time, the food we ate for breakfast, sex, the language Max and I spoke, and the songs my doorbell rang – Christmas carols all year through.

On Fridays, Max stayed at home alone and I went out to pick up the cheque. On Saturdays Max would sit by me as I did the laundry in the backyard. We would burn the toilet papers after doing the laundry. I would whistle tunes from the Catholic hymnal the whole time and he would stare at me like I was doing something wrong. Our favourite place was in bed, we did everything in a hurry just to get back in bed. Sundays were the only days my doorbell rang; 'Jingle Bells' and 'We Wish You a Merry Christmas' played consecutively. I'd only open the door on the second ring of 'Jingle Bells.' And they would be there in their thick glasses and plastic smiles – the Jehovah's Witnesses, a man and his wife. The man in his well-tailored white shirt and dull-looking tie, the wife in her kaba and slit attire with a handbag caught in her armpit.

'Beautiful afternoon, Brema.'

I'd smile. Every Sunday afternoon was beautiful to them. They'd have one each of their booklets for me, *Awake* and *Watchtower*.

'Can we come in for a brief discussion?'

'Oh busy today, next week.'

Every week, I said the same thing to them and they smiled, they didn't ask any questions, they just handed over the booklets and left. I preferred '*Watch Tower*' to '*Awake*', so I read that first. The couple were my first Sunday guests and I looked forward to seeing them every week. I'd turn on my stereo when they left and increase the volume until my walls began to vibrate. It was a call for my next Sunday guest, my landlady; she spoke softly, always had complaints, never wore a smile. 'We Wish You A Merry Christmas...' I'd open the door and she'd be in a Gino tomato sauce branded T-shirt and a long black skirt which had a cover cloth wrapped over it. She squinted. Her eyes had rheum in them all the time.

'My young lady, how are you? Can you turn down the music?'

'Yes please, I can, do you want me to?'

'Of course, and your backyard needs sweeping. You live in this flat with people, nobody knows when you are at home, nobody knows when you are not, what if something happens to you? And I have told you not to burn your toilet papers at the backyard, put them in a polythene bag and drop them in the bin, the ashes fly around when you burn them. We have asthmatics in this building; the smoke is not good for them...'

'Uhm, yeah, sorry, I'll sweep. Thanks for stopping by, Aunty Korkor.'

When she left, I would lock my door and light the same brand of cigarette that came with a minty taste and a bad headache the next day. Max, the Jehovah's Witnesses and my landlady were the only people who didn't make me nervous. I loved having them in my life.

It was 8.27pm. My apartment began to feel oddly cold. I turned the bedroom lights on and noticed the cobwebs up in the corners of my room. It felt like the walls had moved three steps closer. My drawers seemed darker than they had been. Max had still not returned. Something was wrong. I noticed the dead mosquitoes on my wall. They were sitting in blood like women on their periods. I went into the living room and looked outside the window. I wanted to take a walk but I wasn't sure where to go. I just wanted Max to come back home. I sat down on my couch and woke up on it the next morning.

It looked like it was going to rain. The rain clouds were a darker shade of pink instead of the usual darker shade of grey. Max wasn't up in bed when I went to the bedroom to check. My box of cigarettes had fallen under the bed again. As I drew in and puffed out, I tried to hold back my tears. I knew Max had left me. Go and wash your face, a voice in my head said. Lauryn Hill's brittle voice, *'I find it hard to say'*, accentuated my pain. I turned the volume up to the highest my speakers could contain and 'Jingle Bells', my doorbell rang.

'My young lady, how are you? Can you turn down the music? Your clothes have taken up all the space on the lines, please go and remove them so other people can dry theirs. Look up at the sky, if you don't remove them today, it will get soaked by the rain. And, oh, your cat has been lying in my backyard since yesterday, I think it is dead.'

I was panting when I got to her backyard. Max's mouth had foamed and flies were hovering over his body. I held him to my chest and we went to our bedroom.

Six years ago, when I found him under the mango tree outside my door, his right hind leg was broken. I carried him in and tended to him. One day, we were sleeping when he started licking my fingers; I liked how his tongue felt on my skin, coarse. From then, I would dip my index finger into milk and wet different parts of my body with it – my clitoris and my nipples. Max would lick off the milk and I would dip my fingers back into the milk bowl. I'd pull him up to my stomach and tickle his ears after my body shook, and tears would fall on the sides of my face.

* * *

As it drizzled outside my window, I felt the tiny drops of rain in the insides of my stomach. Max lay on my chest, stiff, with all four legs raised. When I closed my eyes, the raindrops turned into snakes crawling up my window to bite me. When I opened my eyes, my head was buried in a toilet bowl and I was eating faeces. A throbbing pain resided in one half of my head.

It was cold and getting dark. Max's body grew putrid. He began to smell like sweet cheap incense and meat that had gone off. I wrapped him up with the milk-stained bed sheet and put him on the right side of our queen-size bed. I couldn't fall asleep without wondering if maybe, I didn't feed him enough. Maybe, I didn't love him enough. Maybe he was going to wake up and walk, like a king in his grey coat of fur and his soft ears. I couldn't fall asleep so I went online and googled 'how to resurrect a cat'.

✳✳✳

'Jingle Bells,' my doorbell rang and woke me up. The sun's heat filled my room. It was a beautiful day, at least to the Jehovah's Witnesses, but I was in no mood for platitudes. I stayed in bed, eyes closed with Max lying alongside my right arm. His body was cold. I wanted the Witnesses to break open my door and enter my bedroom with miracles in one hand and breakfast in the other.

'Jingle Bells, We Wish you a Merry Christmas, Jingle Bells, We Wish you a Merry Christmas, Jingle Bells…' My headache worsened and I decided if they rang my doorbell one more time, I'd go outside and scream at them. 'Jingle Bells.' I hoisted my body up and contemplated carrying Max along. If Max was going to wake, I wanted to be there when it happened. But he looked too peaceful, too far gone, so I left him to sleep. I went to take a wee and the doorbell stopped ringing. I didn't really want them to leave, but Jehovah's word needed spreading, I supposed, and there was no time to waste on closed doors.

I held my breath on the fourth day. The stench of Max's stiff body overpowered every smell in the room. I was running out of reasons to live. I googled 'how to prevent a cat from decomposing,' and opened several blogs dedicated to cat love, cat resuscitation, cat burials, cat allergies, cat cremations; it was a never-ending cat world of prescriptions, experiments, luck and failures.

'Boil it, microwave it, wrap it in a towel and bury it, refrigerate it, mummify it,' cat people suggested on comment threads. One comment which had 538 thumbs down on my favourite cat blog, 'Cat Lovers', threw my heart into a race that intensified with each word the fool had written.

'It will decompose because you cannot outsmart Jah, the alpha and omega. Your cat is at stage omega, DEAD, you can never alpha that shit up, loser. The only thing you can save is the bones but pray the dogs don't find them, haha! All you privileged-ass rich folks, instead of focusing on cats, why don't you focus on your kids? Babylon!' – Messiah Son.

'I don't have kids, you asshole, and I most certainly hope you don't have any kids. It will be a tragedy to have your stupid genes passed down to anybody. What the fuck are you doing on Cat Lovers if you hate cats? I hope you die a miserable death, I hope nobody ever loves you. Fuck you, Messiah Son, fuck you in your nose!'

Every three minutes I refreshed the 'Cat Lovers' page to see if Messiah Son had responded to my comment. Nobody responded to my comment.

I heard footsteps coming towards my front door and so waited for the ring but 'Jingle Bells' only rang in my head. When I went out to check if anybody was there, a big black polythene bag was leaning by my door. I opened it; it was my laundry from last week, shirts and napkins hugging each other. The mango tree leaves swayed to the wind; I filled up my lungs with the fresh air and walked back into the stench.

'Max, Max, please wake up.'

Small insects crawled uncomfortably in my stomach. I wanted to puke; the smell belittled Max's eternity. So I lifted him up into the freezer for the ice to keep him and my hopes afloat. The next day, it had wrapped around his body, ending every warmth we shared, but Max was still mine, and I, his. Each morning, I'd open the freezer, look at him, and scrape some ice into my palm – that became my breakfast.

Nana Nyarko Boateng is a writer and editor. She is the CEO of Gird Center, a writing, editorial and training services company based in Accra. Her poetry and fiction has appeared in *Reflections: An Anthology of New Work by African Women Poets*, Lynne Rienner; *Summoning the Rain: An Anthology by African Women Writers*, Femrite Publications Limited; *Fusion: Libations*, Prairie Schooner; *Look where you have gone to sit: An Anthology by New Ghanaian Poets*, Wolei Publishers; *Defiled Sacredness: An anthology about the ravages of rape*, Mensa Press; *We are one from one place: An anthology about schism in the human family*, Mensa Press; and in the *New Legon Observer*, University Press. Nana writes to celebrate the human spirit and to promote our bottomless capacity for change.

Lusaka Punk

Efemia Chela

Fuzigish. The Velvet Underground. Sleater-Kinney. Bikini Kill. The Sex Pistols. Sonic Youth. PolyStyrene. The Ramones. The Dead Kennedys. Minor Threat. Joy Division. Screaming Foetus. WITCH. Blondie.

I'd fallen asleep on my laptop again after another night of watching YouTube skits. My music player was open and on so loud I couldn't fathom how my body had blocked the noise out for a full 10 hours. Maybe it was getting used to this year of nothing. 17. After A-levels and before university there was that rotting long drop in Lusaka. There weren't that many universities in Zambia and the ones we had were extremely overcrowded. During open days, I had felt campuses seethe like marketplaces. There was a mandatory year out for school-leavers in the hope that by 2014 the institutions would be a little emptier. Then we could get in and clog the system back up again. It was a sedentary year and was beginning to seem like an endless summer.

The olds thought we had a great deal: 'In our day there was National Service. That is how the head of the Reserve Bank lost two fingers. She played with the wrong end of a gun during army training.'

But the heat was oppressive and there are only so many naps you can take. I thought hard about it sometimes. Perhaps we were never part of anything. Being part of nothing brought on a creeping dread. 'You're not going on a gap year,' my father insisted. 'Do you think you are white? Just help out around the house.'

My naïve mother smiled and her hands unclenched as if they were looking forward to a break. They didn't know their son was going to spend most of his time outside the spiky brown gate of our home. My nights were for Leicester Street, its dive bars and half-forgotten conversations on the pavement with the other punks. My days were unmade beds and visiting friends' houses. Whoever's pool was the cleanest automatically had their house turned into HQ. Other assets were the lack of parental units, if smoking was permitted indoors and extra phone chargers. Our new phones were smart enough to do everything apart from keeping charged for more than five hours. We couldn't complain more. At least I was going out tonight.

I had no idea who she was. She was deep in the stage of a tribute band called Brunette. The bassist, I think. She thought she was a backup singer but her mike looked turned off. No red light. Or at the very least it was turned down to the lowest.

I sang-shouted along to 'Dreaming' with everyone else: 'When I met you in the restaurant, you could tell I was no debutante!'

And Xanthia, the lead, shook her shock of blonde hair over her face and leaned into the crowd. On the tips of her purple Docs she sweated, dripped into the crowd's embrace and dropped off her bra. The Turin Shroud of the pit: it was passed around so everyone could touch that sacred instant relic. Absorb the power of the Cs that used to rest inside. The frenetic heart that used to batter against the underwires to the pulse of punk rock.

A couple of chords and cheers later it was the time of night when the air inside DOG was going sour from sweat and sulphuric with farts. This former internet café, now dank hell, covered not even in band posters but warped printouts from Google Images, prompted a stream of people to wade out for a smoke.

I was at a loose end, having lost my mates in the crowd,

so I thought again about picking up smoking. It gave you something to do. It was a way to pick up girls committed to dying before their time. Anyway, for now I was leaning on a Flame of the Forest tree while trying to look cool. So cool that I had to be alone, you know.

'I'm Lottie,' she said after asking for a light. She hollowed her cheeks, taking in the smoke. 'Thanks'.

I waited.

'Mbongwe,' I offered.

'You don't sound very sure of that.'

She laughed, tossing her braids into her upraised left hand, then with the other one she fanned the back of her neck.

'No, I'm sure,' I said. Almost immediately after I thought that somehow saying that made me sound even more unconvincing. I began to feel hot with embarrassment instead of cool. That may have had to do, though, with my leather jacket and red stretch pleather trousers and the 30-degree heat.

'What's your favourite Blondie song?'

'Ummm.'

'Come on, you're in Brunette. You should have it like that,' I said.

'Well, it's one we never play,'

'*Accidents Never Happen*?' I asked

'That's a goodie. We've always said that we'd play it if we ever got an encore. Or played for more than an hour. I mean I think we should. Though Xanth says punk shows should be quick and dirty,' Lottie said.

'Like sex in a public toilet?'

'Yeah. Exactly.'

'What about *The Hardest Part*?'

'We did it last Wednesday. It's tricky. I like the ska vibe of *Die Young, Stay Pretty* but I guess I probably like *Picture This* best.'

'You guys never play that, huh?'

'Nah. Not that popular with the others. Debbie Harry predicts the rise of computers though.'

'So it's completely awesome!' I said.

'I know, right. Super underrated song. Aren't you in a band too? Isn't everyone? I feel like I know you already.'

I was in a shitty band called D O P E, one of those non-bands where everyone calls themselves a producer. Our musical output was mainly efforts on Minimoog synthesizers and hopscotching on the tiles of expensive music-making machines. We took a lot of elevator muzak samples and rigged them to play backwards but really it was all about the beats. We cooked it all up while stoned in someone's step-mother's townhouse. It was kind of chilled hip-hop influenced post-punk stuff for people to half head bop and awkwardly sway to. I was in charge of the undertow of menacing beats that dragged people in. White Lusakasites liked it the most because they had no rhythm, no reason to be unhappy and this was the perfect score for their lives. They liked to thug out a bit to it, pretending to be tougher and more hustle-ridden than they were. Our EP, 'F O L L Y' (fuck, I was so against all the spacing) filled lulls in conversations pretty well and DOG liked it to close down the night in the last few hours of the party. By 2am we wouldn't admit our feet were hurting, our ears were done with sawing guitar assaults and, even though punk would never die, we needed to wind down. That was D O P E's niche.

Cryptic Palace was our hit track and despite the catchy mainstream appeal I had created in it, Lottie still said, 'I was kind of cool' and 'I should meet her tomorrow.'

∗∗∗

The next afternoon was fucking hot. It was always fucking hot but for some reason today's burn in particular seemed punitive. We were near the roundabout that was given to us as a Gift From The Japanese People. It was by far the most interesting and imposing roundabout in the city.

'Is this climate change?' I panted.

'It's bloody cruel and unusual torture, Mbongwe,' she said. 'Fuck nature! I'm going to New York. Apparently you can't see the sun for the concrete.'

'It could be on purpose. International donors coming to visit and...'

'And we're sweating more aid money out of them. Yeah. Probably. Look, there are no fucking herbs here. I'm going to get shat on when I get home,' said Lottie.

'Your rabbits eat herbs??? No way. Bullshit.'

'Of course. They're presidents.'

I looked at her blankly. Was I heatstroking out?

'Kaunda, Chiluba, Sata. Guy Scott...'

'He's only been a Vice President.'

'He speaks Klingon. Extra points.'

'Fair play. I approve. Actually. No, I don't. Do you think you are white? They should just eat grass.'

We had no idea why the Japanese had sent over 'The Chicken' in 1996 and when they came to Lusaka to build the roundabout they wouldn't tell anyone why. The details were hazy. Maybe they couldn't tell anyone. Maybe the builders didn't speak English. They just built it, surrounded it with African Violets, a grey pebble ring and grass and left. Its weird shadow was a backdrop for our collecting. Everyone had always kept bunnies in Lusaka. Rabbits were fluffy distractions. While they lived, they could be fed on the odds and ends of greens and once dead, their meat was succulent and delicious.

We both needed to collect bunny food today. My mother had said that one of our future dinners was pregnant and I had to bring back more Shoprite bags of grass than usual. I'd brought a scythe but Lottie was pulling something she thought was mint out of the ground and getting green juice under her nails.

'You see when you feed them only herbs, they radiate the smell. Chiluba's minty, Kaunda's a zesty coriander, Sata's basil and Guy White's...'

'Just grow a damn herb garden at home then!' I shouted.

'Hey, that's true. Though I don't know if they'll survive in our wasteland.'

She sat down in the grass and took out her phone. Where she was sitting was dry now but I suspected the sewage that sometimes deviated here and fertilized it well, making it so long and an almost nuclear bright green. The next time I turned my sweaty back she was smoking.

'Do you want to be in another band?' she asked.

I thought woefully of D O P E and its lack of instrumentation.

'Like a real band?'

'Yeah,' she said.

'Might as well. We've got more months of doing shit like this.'

'What?'

'Mundane crap,' I explained. 'It's three months since school ended and way before 12 months from now all the cool stuff we're up to will be so boring we'll pick suicide over doing it. Drinking, smoking, wandering, keeping cool. Playing video games with one hand and eating dry cereal with the other. Sexting, watching potholes fill up with rain, making music, breaking into places, the internet.'

'Then let's go to my place,' she said.

✳✳✳

Her house was hermetically sealed. She prised open the door like a stiff jar to let us in and then closed it so quickly there was a strange selfishness about it. I felt privy to a place that nearly no-one knew existed. A theoretical place in a Philosophy paper. If a house is alone in a forest etc. Discuss for 20 marks.

It was incredibly dusty. I'd been there 15 minutes, standing around talking to Lottie when I looked down. My white tee was browning and the glass of Mazoe I hadn't really touched was forming a skin. A real skin, I suppose, since dust is mainly skin cells, isn't it?

Christ on a bike, the dust. The dust. I always hated how houses had that tacky green net over the windows. It was to prevent female mosquitoes sucking the blood out of us and leaving malaria behind. We'd all had it a couple of times. Mostly when we were younger.

Maybe I'd known Lottie from primary. Maybe visited her in a hot sweaty room and held her hand, limp and deaf to the touch. She'd have been squirming like a split worm, feeling each blood cell break in her body. Malaria was that way. They'd have closed all the curtains and windows and swathed her like a mummy in mosquito nets. It was a bit late then. She was already a sunken-eyed diarrhoea machine. I'd have put a cold bit of chocolate in her dry mouth quickly before I was lifted away too early to see her reaction.

All the diamonds of the netting were glutted with dust. I bounced my fingers against it and blew hard. It couldn't be dislodged. She ran up the stairs and I choked. She came down again, leaving a roadrunner trail in her wake.

'Sorry, yeah, we put in carpets because we kept slipping on the dust on the tiles after my mum...'

I remembered hearing about her mother passing from someone. It was an awkward and unexpected death. Plastic surgery, I think was what did her in.

They had terrible taste in carpets and had brought back the 70s *sans* any of the era's glamour. There was no desk in here, just books relying on the walls and gravity to stay up in tall stacks. Papers wedged between books to keep them from drifting away. Photos, bills, files and anything too.

Just as she threw down a notebook, ZESCO took away the power.

'The Lord giveth and the Lord taketh away,' I mocked.

'Awwww FUCK!! It will take a couple of minutes for the generator to kick in,' Lottie complained.

The notebook had the usual toothache-twee Paris cover marketed to people who had never travelled but had a nonsensical religious fervour for big Western cities. She'd black-markered most of the stuff out. The Eiffel Tower had a forcefield condom hovering around its steel phallus and the slogan was now I <3 Kariba.

'Read it and tell me it's bad. Just so I'm sure,' she shouted, plugging her ears and swivelling away. Just then the generator grunted and the power was back.

I spent too long looking at the shredded low-hanging strips of black, half-heartedly on her back. It was all right there, the DIY punk spirit I loved. Everything was emotion – ruined, haggard and homemade. Dodgy romance that raced at the speed of young lives. It was us and we were right.

Our parents wilfully mistook it for teenage angst because there were parenting books and apps for that. And we'd help them download them but punk was something rougher and darker than they thought. It took ugliness, noise and chaos to beautiful ends that seemed illogical to anyone outside the scene. Lusaka punk didn't have the hollow emptiness nor the cold breeze through the soul of discontent. It wasn't the noxious hypnotic drowse of listlessness. It was a freedom through anger and setting ourselves so distinctly apart. Liberty through control loss. Passion kicking holes in the quotidian. We fucked up the status quo and broke down idols other people had made. As we sped off into the future, people could look through the rip in our shirts and the rip in time and think 'What the fuck was that?'

Why did you put cyanide in our cigarettes?
Why did you put cyanide in our cigarettes?
Don't you know that after the show?
It's all we've got

Why is there Uranium in our cigarettes?
(MARIE CURIE!)
Why is there Uranium in our cigarettes?
(MARIE CURIE!)
Don't you know that after the show?

It's all we've got.

Why did you put tar in our cigarettes?
Why did you put tar in our cigarettes?
Don't you know, we can't afford blow?
Tar the fucking roads! It's all we've got.

'We can scream it over guitars and a three-piece drum set,' I concluded.

I high-fived her. We had a winner.

***

Xanthia snarled, 'Denis, Denniiiiiii.'

Brunette were in the house again. Xan was staring at her boyfriend. I couldn't tell whether she loved him or hated him. Probably both. He was in the crowd. Now if I could just see him. She was channelling Courtney Love. Swooping her guitar, her head sideways, inches away from missing the mike but just catching her voice hard into the song. Her boyfriend Chilufya looked as pale as a black man can and was holding her three drinks. It wasn't so much a settler and reacher relationship as a hunter-prey deal. Yes, deal. No-one was in a relationship they really didn't want to be in. There were always options. Choices. No-one said being a punk existentialist was easy. Being an existentialist was saying yes to having your penis eaten by a German. It was roofieing yourself with eyedrops when you couldn't afford booze. It was my white mohawk and the damaged relaxed hair being held together by gel.

They'd found a better use for Lottie. As the only one who could sing some decent French she'd been given co-lead vox on *Denis*. She went wild in the spotlight of the single bulb on stage. She danced free, like she was all alone. The crowd stopped clapping their hands automatically like they were bored in church and dared to move to this song that wasn't even really that punk. To quote Tom, the editor of *Vomit* (the scene's best zine) who had an Asperger's-like precision for music genres, *Denis* was:

Blondie s sad foray into the new-wave label they had been given. Eating it up and blowing out a bubble of sickly sweet gummy pop. Like most imported products, it was only cool because the wrapper was in another language.

We looked up at her heart-shaped face and pit-black lips making foreign shapes and stretches. Talk-singing and a little off key, she rocked on. I was teacher proud. She took the song all the way to the end, stamping her feet, showing off her black and red chitenge dress with the unravelling hem that made you think it had once been much longer. She jumped off side stage before Brunette's set was over.

'Lottie, you were the raddest thing alive but Xanthia looked pissed. Fuck, you were shit hot!' I screamed.

'Thanks! Couldn't've done it without you. How pissed was she? Was it all over her shoes?' she asked.

'Yeah, but who cares?'

She told me how they had fought backstage about the dictatorship Xanthia'd turned the band into. Mumba, the drummer, had started crying during the argument. Lweendo, the keyboardist, had stormed out around the time...

'Then I said,' Lottie reported. '"Punk is musical freedom. It's saying, doing, and playing what you want." Then she said. "Don't fucking quote Kurt Cobain to me." Then I said, "This band is no longer fucking punk. It's just your shit derivative vanity project. I hate you. I'm out."'

We hugged. 'I'm so glad,' I said. 'You're no longer trapped.'

'Look at all the unwanted male attention I'm getting from that last song. I swear Mubanga just looked at me. I think he wants to give me his gonorrhoea. How romantic!'

She flipped him off and we laughed. Like any pack of animals there was an alpha male and female. I didn't know who the female was since I'm not into that kind of thing. I only knew Mubanga was the alpha male because there was always some girl crying black eyeliner in DOG's unisex bathrooms over him.

'Xanthia can go get fucked,' she mumbled, while lighting a smoke. 'I'm done with Brunette. I was only still in it for Debbie Harry.'

We crossed ourselves at the mention of the goddess's name.

'Right. Did you ever get a reply to that email you sent her?'

She gave me a sulky face.

'No. Blondie is still touring together and she's too busy being incredible and stuff. Listen, I'll see you tomorrow. I've got some shit to deal with plus my guitar's still on stage.'

✳✳✳

We had practice at my house obviously. But it wasn't so much practice as a series of sound checks and instrument juggling. We didn't want our sound to be too polished. That wasn't the point of Hologram. I could play the Moog blind and we'd set up a cymbal and a snare next to me. I had a drumstick sticking out of each pocket. Lottie didn't because she had her bass guitar which she'd tuned differently to give us more range of sound. I really wanted her to walk on her guitar at the end of each show just like Kim Gordon did at an Amsterdam gig once.

'I mean you have six guitars. Your dad owns a huge mine on the Copperbelt,' I said.

'Hahaha. True. I will, but only if you wear all of Debbie Harry's outfits when she was in Blondie. I looked in your wardrobe while you were downstairs. Did you make all of these? They look great!'

I felt queasy. She took out the blue jumpsuit and the yellow dress from *Picture This*.

'Come on. I know you're gay. Everyone does. It's completely fine. No-one cares. I mean it's not like you're the bottom of the scene. That's Chanda W.'

I cackled. 'Yeah, everyone and everything has been in Chanda W.'

'His sexual appetite is a little unnerving but I've been part of the protection squad that walks him home so he doesn't get attacked,' said Lottie

'Yeah, he's a cool guy and he does always have poppers.'

'I admire his devotion to free love and the destruction of the gender binary,' Lottie said, hand on her heart.

Suddenly fired up, I said, 'Okay we're doing that too. Fuck the gender binary. I'll wear my Blondie outfits.'

'It will piss Xanthia and the rest of the Brunette sheep off sooo much. I can't wait.'

Apart from her guitar, Lottie had a tambourine anklet to manoeuvre. We'd made it using a lot of rubber cement and stubbornness. There was also that huge kick snare she had to play with her free right foot. We were like two homeless one-man bands who'd decided to make a busking band instead of having a tramp fight. The duo format and multi-instrumentation was tight but I thought we could pull it off. Sex in a public toilet, remember! Hologram had two original songs with one cover, *Picture This*. With any luck the crowd would sing half of the songs. Our songs were words that had already been in their hearts and we'd just put them in our version of choral disorder.

***

I went to Tom's mum's shag pad in Kablonga to make this week's zine.

'Mbongwe, my man!'

'Peeing Tom!'

Tom was a legend at 19 as the city's richest anarchist, street artist, and a general pain in society's ass. He read political theory like a beast and painted in the morning, then wrote our truth in the afternoon. At night, he rocked hard as nails. Recently he'd ordered some exceptionally expensive spray-paint from Amazon which was essentially invisible ink. It could only be seen at night. It was activated by urine and then glowed blue punk slogans like 'Hands Off My Ovaries' and 'Death To Sugar Daddies' around Lusaka. When you saw him sucking up water like an elephant, you knew large-scale rebellion was 45 minutes away.

'Hey! I'm making my mark on the city. Taking it back from the capitalists.'

'Rad! Hey, is the World Bank still renting this place out for Marrrrrge? I thought she stopped working for them ages ago.'

'Yeah, she did. Marrrrge tells my dad she goes to work each day but she just comes here and has sex with some random. Those neoliberal paradigm arseholes pay 10 months' rent in advance so basically you can do whatever you want. They can't and don't take the place back any sooner.'

I saluted. 'Fuck the 9-to-5! Go Marrrrge!! I'm going save that deception for if I'm trapped in a loveless heteronormative marriage in the future.'

'I was going to use it for my Outsider Interference spot in *Vomit* next week.' He added, 'You should tell her how much she inspires you. She's super depressed. She just looks at the wall in the master bedroom when her sex buddy doesn't come over. And the houseboy is completely over getting 10 types of make-up stains off the sheets.'

Tom and I walked into the bar. The floor was covered in papers and magazine cut-outs and collages and manifestos and black and white litho prints. *Rolling Stone Magazine* was run by cunts. We had our own literature: zines we pasted together, photocopied short print runs of and distributed for free. We only made non-punks pay. I had all the issues of *Nervous Gender*, a zine named for the band, that focused on LGBTIQ issues, poetry, support groups, and pictures of imaginary monsters. *21st Century Punk* was mainly politico-steampunk pulp fiction. *Bum-Bum*, I actually contributed to, since it was about punk fashion past and present and the Leicester Street aesthetic.

Vomit was by far the best written. It was known for Tom's scathing critiques of music, local politics and on the other spectrum the glorification of a few Zambian punk bands and overseas punk revival and garage rock like The White Stripes, YeahYeahYeahs and Sistronix. Tom was wasted here. There were no decent art schools in the country. He had applied but realistically was never going to get into Central St Martins in London or Rhode Island School of Design in the States. Or any of the other fancy universities he'd applied to.

That was what this year was for. It was to dream for a couple of months, size up the international competition online and then lower your standards like the tide going out minute by minute. But as Debbie Harry said, 'Dreaming is free'. This year was for promising yourself every night not to be like your parents. It was for ripping off scabs. It was trying to give up your middle-class comforts one by one. It was passing around books the library wouldn't buy if they were recommended to them. Like 'How To Make A Bomb!' or 'A Biography of The Female Orgasm'. The donors only sponsored textbooks.

'Philistine cunts,' I'd called them.

Creating an improved present and an even better future was overwhelming. We tried to spur ourselves on by isolating ourselves from the self-congratulating diplomatic, political and 'development' people. Their parties, their children, their fundraisers, their team-building exercises were circle jerks where they showed off their saviour complexes. They'd swarmed Zambia and were giving a manicure to an amputated arm instead of reattaching it to the body. They walked around with sweatless faces. Glands shrivelled by years of air-conditioning, long meetings and even longer suppers at the Radisson Blu. A film of satisfaction, a soft cataract, had formed over their eyes, preventing them from seeing that their efforts were shallow and they mostly did nothing. The enthusiasm of their first year of being here had mutated into a cultivated smugness.

The older-generation Zambians were pretty much resigned to the status quo and to true freedom kept in a chokehold. Some of them at least had the decency to look sad and defeated but very few. Upstairs, Marrrrge seemed to have figured out the lie of her life. Most adults were annoyingly positive. They wouldn't accept they had been betrayed by independence, democracy and rapaciousness. They dutifully broke their backs making a living during the week and went to church for opiates every Sunday.

Our church was DOG. Punk was our religion. Other people listened to music. We snorted it.

Tom took a huge bong rip then said through the smoke, 'Do you know who I hate the most right now?'

'Who?' I asked.

'Those stupid fucking Americans our age who pay to come here for six weeks and save Africa! Those poverty junkies with their selfies with fly-covered kids.'

'I know! I know! If you type #Zambia on Instagram that's all you see. People have stopped hearting my sick leather jacket I spent hours making. Those fuckers!' I raged.

'You see. Damn shitheads. You can't get a single apprenticeship or internship because it's been sold to them as a zoo experience.'

'What should we call this? Tourism oppression?'

'Hmm, I'll think about it. Just promise me you'll never become a writer,' he said.

I was a little hurt but I agreed. 'So you'll definitely punt me and Lottie's new band – Hologram?'

His eyes bulged. 'Shit, is Brunette breaking up? I thought they were fairly good. They've been around for a couple of months now.'

'I don't know. They might reform. More importantly we have two songs which are amazing and we're playing tomorrow night, so come.'

Of course Tom would come. He was DOG's barfly. He never had to buy his own drinks.

***

Another night on Leicester Street. Or Le-sister Street as we called it now. We'd decolonized it by pronouncing it with a Zambian accent. It was a damp dirt alley by a field, lined with lawless bars that would serve alcohol to crawling babies. There were no IDs, no streetlights, no mainstreamers, just punks.

'I love your jumpsuit,' someone said to me in passing.

'Are you still going to LSE?' Lottie's man-for-now asked me.

I was surprised he was here. He was the rarely spotted Kondwani. Most people didn't even know if he was still a punk. There were rumours he was sucking on the Oxfam teat now. Even Lottie didn't know if that was true. Kondwani was a freelancer romantically, from what I could gather.

I replied, 'Well, you know how it is. Just waiting to see. Focusing on my music now and the cause you know.'

He snorted a line of coke off the back of his hand and his eyes watered a little. 'Yeah, I know what you mean. I'm applying to Harvard for the third time.'

In the face of such pathos, Lottie and I tried to hold our facial features in a nonchalant pose.

We cackled like witches once inside DOG.

I Wanna Be Your Dog by The Stooges was playing really loudly and I suppose that was why I didn't hear the psycho bitch swinging at my head. BOOM! Right in the cheek. I was down on the floor. Jesus. It was ground glass, a mix of spilled drinks, lost safety pins, cigarette ash, dried-up Sprite, globs of spit. There was probably a good deal of semen and blood down there too. The filth stuck to me like molasses. I stumbled up and it looked like Lottie had taken out one of X's teeth. I rammed myself like a bull into her and she crashed on a table and couple suctioned together at the lips. Punks love a fight. Anarchy is an aphrodisiac. I heard Tom screaming, THE AMERICAN NGO PIGLETS ARE HERE!! KILL 'EM!!' Soon the whole crowd was lunging, jumping and running into itself and the intruders. Through a drooping fake eyelash I saw X break Lottie's nose. I ripped out her earring through the flesh. Xanthia's screams were lost amongst everyone else's. I glued myself to Lottie and pushed her into the street.

We looked at each other, covered in bruises, glitter, grit and bright anonymous blood.

'We should play now. We can get to the stage using the back door,' I said.

Lottie hesitated, squeezing her nose with her fingers.

'We can switch the music off there too.'

'You're a genius, Mbongwe. We should play while the blood's still flowing.'

We started running to the back door of DOG. 'I can play really loud static to shut everyone up,' I said.

Hologram was on stage. The instruments and lights were plugged into the generator. Lottie looked up at the lightbulb doubtfully. No-one in the crowd even noticed us up there. The fighting was still thick and people were lubricated by blood, homebrew and instant revenge. I found a paraffin lamp backstage, lighted it and put it a ways behind us just in case. Lottie and I looked at each other knowingly. We were ready so I hit the static. The loud glitching of the Moog forced everyone's attention on the stage. The fighting stopped and the air wobbled with the weight of heavy breaths taken. It looked like concussions and recriminations all round and as if it would all start again in a couple of minutes.

'We're Hologram and we like punk rock!' we shouted.

We launched straight into 'Ike vs Tina'. Everything was sounding incredible. Even the mistakes were making it better. My Moog looked like a butcher's block but I didn't care. Something big was happening here. Then ZESCO cut the power. The lights in the audience went off but we were still on. Very on. A short thank you and we moved on to a screaming version of 'Picture This'. Our punks sang along wrong to the last line: 'Take a pocket computer try to do what you used to do, yeah!'

Lottie and I winked at each other before the big one. It was still dark down below and people started trying to light their patch in the crowd with their lighter up in the air. Lottie was smoking on stage, staggering around while preaching our sermon of the night.

'Are you sick of corruption?

Do you hate it when the Department of Housing builds another mall?

Do you like getting trapped in potholes?

They say "If a white flag means surrender, a black flag represents anarchy."

WE ARE THE BLACK FLAG!'

She threw a lit cigarette into the crowd and said 'Sing along.' We started the pound.

Why did you put tar in our cigarettes?
Why did you put tar in our cigarettes?
Don't you know, we can't afford blow?
Tar the fucking roads! It's all we've got.

Even the freshest, hottest new things on the scene need to piss. The bathroom mirror had once been long and large but now two-thirds of it was shattered. There was torn-up kwacha glued on it and marker scribbles and stickers all over it. We looked into the reflective surface that was left. Lottie and I smiled. We really did look like homeless people. The hardest-rocking, coolest, punkest, homeless people in the world.

Efemia Chela was born in Zambia in 1991, but grew up in England, Ghana, Botswana and South Africa. She studied at Rhodes University, South Africa, and at Institut D'Etudes Politiques in Aix-en-Provence, France. When she grows up she would like to be a better writer and graphic novelist. She enjoys eating pizza, playing croquet and watching black-and-white films. Her first published story, 'Chicken' was nominated for the 2014 Caine Prize For African Writing. She continues to write and publish stories whenever she can find a working pen.

The Writing in the Stars

Jonathan Dotse

The Guardian spurred his horse on to a full gallop through the narrow, winding streets of the old city, followed closely by five companions, leaving behind the chaotic sounds of iron clashing in vain against the thundering fire of the invaders. The four raced towards the outskirts of the city, to the edge of the desert, where they stopped to take a final look at the destruction that was being unleashed upon their beloved city.

The Guardian and his men watched in silence as arcs of fire erupted all across the northern sector of the city, cutting through every line of defence, the shrieks of the wounded rising together in a harrowing chorus of death. The men had no words to express the depth of their anguish. They had spent years preparing for this day; when the last remnants of the once-mighty empire would be crushed by the merciless onslaught of invaders, but to finally witness the inevitable unfolding was driving daggers into their hearts.

The raiders from the north had launched several attacks on the city in recent years, each one more devastating than the last. The defenders had barely managed to repel the onslaught – until now. Their swords and spears, ancient charms and amulets, were useless against the strange sorcery the foreigners possessed. Messengers had been sent to nearby Gao and Djenne, and as far as Agadez and Niani, in urgent requests for assistance from the allies of the empire. The few reinforcements that were promised never materialized. Meanwhile, the city's defences steadily weakened to the point of collapse. Since last moon, most of the population had fled to neighbouring kingdoms in anticipation of this final assault, the Guardian's wife and only child among their number. Those who remained had resigned themselves to the mercy of their new masters.

The Guardian dismounted and stood before the five others, casting his gaze upon each one of his men. They wanted nothing more than to be fighting alongside their brothers in the streets – not to save the city, for the city was already lost, but only to stand in the ranks of their doomed comrades as they faced the unstoppable terror of the invasion; to leave the mark of their blood on the hallowed soil of their ancestors. These six men were bound by the most sacred of oaths to lay down their lives for the empire, but they also had been entrusted with an assignment of the utmost importance; one whose gravity weighed as heavily on their hearts as their desire for martyrdom. The Guardian saw pain written clearly in the eyes of his men but, beyond the surface of their despair, he also saw a wellspring of determination. This unbreakable resilience, shared between them, was the only source of his hope.

'Look!' he said, sweeping a hand over the ruins of the city, 'how the jewel of the desert, the greatest treasure of humankind, is turned to dust. The prophecy of our great Teacher has finally begun to unfold. Fear God and honour the spirits of the ancestors, for we are but grains of sand in the eyes of the Eternal Ones.'

The Guardian knelt down and carefully drew the Seal of the Order in the sand; tracing a wide circle and, within it, three symbols in their sacred language. This was a final reminder to his men of the cause which they had been called to serve from the early days of their youth. He then mounted his horse, drawing the hood of his cloak over his head. His powerful black steed shifted restlessly, perhaps sensing the cloud of impending danger hanging heavy in the air all around them. The Guardian then turned to look at the city one last time.

'For as long as the heavens remain above the earth,' he recited, 'may the sun light our feet and the stars guide our paths.' Then all six chanted in unison: 'And may the God of the universe be with us!'

The men reared their horses and charged off into the unending darkness, charting their course towards the east, beginning the arduous journey to complete their final quest. As the inferno disappeared over the horizon, the Guardian knew in his heart that this was the last time he would see the city of his birth. He whispered a prayer of hope into the night that the hand of God, the Architect of chance and destiny, might rest upon him and his men, to protect them as they embarked on their final mission. For in their hands lay the fate of humankind.

✳✳✳

An alarm was ringing. Sara wouldn't have heard it if Zongo hadn't also been buzzing around her, prodding at her shoulder with its spindly carbon-fibre limbs. She lifted her head from the desk, squinting at the white glow from her computer screen, and brushed away the thin locks of hair that had been pressed to her face.

'What time is it?' she mumbled.

'The time is 3.17am,' Zongo answered, in its androgynous, almost-human voice. 'The date is 17 April 2036, and the temperature outside is 23 degrees Celsius. The weather today will be...'

The words barely registered. It was still dark outside the window of the single-bedroom apartment. The annoying little drone hovered beside her. She folded her head back into her arms.

'Sara, the scan is finished.'

The scan. A vague sensation stirred within her.

'What?'

'You asked me to wake you up when the scan was finished.'

Awareness slowly seeped into her consciousness. The imaging scan was complete. That meant there was only one more thing left to do before she could finish the preliminary report for her doctoral thesis. And, of course, tonight was the final deadline.

She jumped to attention and ran into the living room, which was cluttered from wall to wall with bookshelves, radiographs, scanners, and storage cases filled to overflowing with her personal collection of obscure finds. She retrieved the leather-bound book from the cylindrical white scanner, replacing it in its storage box. She returned to her computer and tapped on the deskpad to bring up the results of the scan. Hundreds of yellowed pages of text were collated and displayed on the screen as small rectangular icons, arranged into a grid layout. She tapped again and the first page was enlarged to fill the screen. Centred on the page was a circle inscribed with three strange symbols.

Sara had discovered the book while reconstructing historical artifacts recovered from a Sufi shrine in the old quarters of Timbuktu city. It was one of several shrines which had been damaged during the insurgency over two decades ago. The book had been found buried deep within the rocky foundation of the shrine, wrapped carefully in a sheepskin pouch. Local tradition held that the shrine was built in the 17th century, a fact which was confirmed by radiocarbon dating of the objects found within it. However, the same radiograph readings indicated that the book was at least a century older, meaning that it had its origins long before the creation of the shrine. That in itself was nothing remarkable. What really puzzled her was that the book was written entirely in a language which at first glance resembled Arabic script, but was composed almost entirely of symbols she had never seen in all her research into the history of language in West Africa.

'Zongo, get Professor Kelechi on the line.'

'Sara, the time is 3.25am. The Professor will most likely be asleep by now. Perhaps you might want to wait until sunrise to make this call.'

'Don't get smart with me, Zongo, just get him on the line.'

Zongo complied without further comment.

Moments later, a gruff voice rasped through Zongo's speakers.

'Sara? What's going on now?'

'Sir, I've just completed the scan of the text; the one I told you about last night. It appears to contain coded information, and I'll need access to the mainframe to attempt a full decryption.'

'Is that why you're calling me at this hour?'

'Yes, Professor, I believe this finding could tell us a lot more about the history of the current excavation site.'

'Sara, I don't see how this has any bearing on your thesis. Your work was meant to focus on the restoration of damaged artifacts. You're already several weeks behind schedule with your report and you know I can't push the deadline back any further.'

'I know, Professor, but this might just turn out to be the most important discovery since the decoding of the Voynich Manuscript. Let me just get to the bottom of this. It won't take more than a few hours.'

'Look, Sara, I know how passionate you still are about your past work, but you also know that the board wants our department to focus more efforts on restoration. That's why you were offered this grant in the first place. You're one of the best researchers in our department and I am generally inclined to trust your intuition, but I'm not going to assist you to ruin your career over this trivial matter. Forget about this unnecessary diversion.'

The line went dead.

'Idiot!' Sara yelled as she slammed a fist on the desk. 'How can he be so narrow-minded?'

'The Professor does make a valid point,' Zongo offered. 'Perhaps, it may be wise to–'

'Oh, shut up, Zongo.'

Sara buried her hands in her locks and suppressed a scream. Before getting her PhD in archaeolinguistics, she had sworn to herself never to return to academia. The first grant from the University of Timbuktu had changed her mind. Now she was within sight of her second doctorate, but her initial apprehensions had begun to resurface. Her research objectives were always dictated by the donors, an inflexible bunch of upper-crusters who were only concerned with whatever field of study was most fashionable at any given time.

But Sara was determined to get to the bottom of the mystery.

'Zongo, get me Farouk. And I mean, like, now.'

'Connecting to Farouk,' Zongo replied and, within an instant, was displaying the dim, grimy-looking interior of the young boy's rented room. A proliferation of display screens and network cabling were strung haphazardly along the walls of his apartment, so it took a while to notice his thin, black form emerging from the shroud of darkness. Farouk had a policy of never disclosing his actual location so, as far as she knew, he might be living next door or on the far side of the moon.

'Long time, Sara,' the boy said, in his French-affected English.

'I need your help, Farouk, and it's really urgent.'

'Straight to business, huh? Okay, what can I do for you?'

'I've got to run a decryption on a coded text from one of the sites I've been working on, but this one is going to take some serious horsepower.'

'Ah, I see. But I think the University mainframe is online, no? Or is there some problem with the Timbuktu grid?'

'No, no, they're just not giving me access. Some bullshit politics with the board.'

'Politics? No problem. I can fix that for you, easy. Real easy.'

The boy immediately went to work, disappearing into the

flora and fauna of his electronic jungle. A few minutes later he reappeared onscreen.

'It's done. I have now set up a secure virtualized super-computer using timeshares from seven different mainframes: one at the Ecole de Kinshasa, two at CERN in Switzerland, another in Novosibirsk, two more at the SKA at Carnarvon, and, of course, the one at your politics university. Is that enough horsepower for you?'

'Farouk, you are a genius!'

'Yah, sure, so you will marry me now? You know money is no problem for me; I can take very good care of you. We will make many beautiful, genius babies together.'

'I do love you, Farouk, but not that much,' she said as she tapped on the deskpad. 'I'm sending you the scans and reference files right now.'

'Receiving. But I think you are considering my offer, yes?'

'Think again. It's business before pleasure, Farouk, not the other way around.'

'Ah, but you are too serious for me, anyway. No fun. No joie de vivre...' he shook his head as he drifted back into his dark world.

Zongo cut the line and descended towards its recharge station as Sara went to pour herself a glass of water. She sat by the dining table, wondering about the potential significance of the text, and the authors of this cryptic language which seemed to have no greater purpose than to obscure information from prying eyes. And they had succeeded: for over 400 years. What secrets were they trying to hide?

When Farouk called back at sunrise, Sara was by her desk, sipping on a double shot of espresso from a vacuum flask as she pored over the scans.

'I don't know what else to say, Sara – I cannot make any sense of this.'

This caught her completely by surprise. It was blasphemy coming from the mouth of one who considered himself a god of the networks, an omnipotent deity within the electronic realm. He was not the type to accept failure, let alone admit it.

'What do you mean? Are you messing with me?'

Farouk remained silent for a few moments before he replied.

'Sara, I don't have 10,000 degrees like you, but I do know my cryptography. You see, the whole point of encryption is to make information appear totally random, and that's what my results are showing; that this text is nothing more than one long string of nonsense. But if there is any meaning to that randomness, as you seem to believe, then I can tell you one thing for sure – there is not enough horsepower on this planet to decode that book.'

***

At first, it was nothing more than a suspicion – an intuition, a subliminal shift in the song of the winds, the sounds of shadows sailing across the dunes – but by the third sunrise of their journey, the Guardian was sure they were being followed. Mid-morning, the men spotted the forms of a dozen riders on the horizon. They were being pursued.

'This can only mean that our temple has been discovered,' the Guardian said to his men. 'They will surely have captured Teacher.'

'We could have protected him,' said Keita, visibly agitated.

'Yes, we might have, but only at the cost of our mission. Did Teacher not tell us that sacrifice will be demanded of every one of us – even himself? In this, too, his words have come to pass.'

'Those savages,' said Musa. 'They are like a plague upon the earth. They do not seek to build, only to destroy. What kind of evil possesses them?'

'There is no evil in humankind, and neither is there any good. There is only the drive to seek happiness and avoid suffering. The invaders are no exception. They only seek to relieve themselves of suffering, even at the cost of inflicting it upon others. They are being driven by forces beyond their control. We have now entered a New Age, when a great change will sweep across the four corners of the earth, leaving no peoples untouched in its wake.'

'What then will be the fate of our own people?' asked Ahmad.

'The same as all humankind – they will rise again. In time, this tragedy will be forgotten. History will be written and rewritten until our memories are erased from existence – until the prophecy of our Teacher comes to pass. We can only pray that the invaders do not discover the location of the Sacred Book.'

The six riders reached the foot of the mountains by noon, proceeding until they found suitable cover within the recess of a cave at the edge of a steep rise. They shared the final, meagre portions of the bread and water they had brought along to sustain themselves. The end was within sight.

By nightfall they were ready to begin the trek up the desolate face of the mountain but they could not allow their pursuers to discover their final destination. Two of them would remain at the cave, to ensure that the others would not be followed.

'I volunteer,' said Keita.

'And I,' said Ibrahim.

'So be it,' said the Guardian to them. 'May the God of the universe be with you.'

'And with you,' they replied.

The two men readied their weapons and released their horses, retreating into the darkness of the cave as the Guardian and his three remaining companions continued into the mountains.

***

After the evening prayers, Sara left her apartment, brushing through the crowded souk as she made her way towards the Medina; the oldest quarter of the city. Unravelling the mystery of the coded book was now the only thing on her mind. Her initial suspicions of its importance had been confirmed beyond doubt. The attempt to decrypt its contents had only raised even more questions about its origins. How was it possible that 16th-century scholars could devise a form of encryption that was indecipherable by the most advanced computing technology of the 21st century? Neither did she think it plausible that anyone in that era would have spent volumes of valuable paper on a nonsensical text. Everything about this book appeared to defy all logic.

She decided to dig deeper – closer to the source. The shrine had been kept by the same household since its creation. She had visited some of the family elders formally to ask for their permission to begin the excavation. Back then they had seemed reticent, almost hostile, at first, but she put this down to the personal nature of their relationship to the shrine. Looking back on those encounters now, she was beginning to suspect that they might have been holding back some information from her.

The house was located close to the entrance of the shrine, where separation barriers were still in place. She was welcomed at the entrance by a young veiled woman, who led her into the courtyard.

'I would like to speak with Mrs Touré – I called the house earlier. Is she around?'

'Yes, she is expecting you.'

Sara sat on a straw mat laid out underneath a date palm growing in the centre of the paved courtyard. An old woman emerged from an arched doorway a few minutes later and seated herself across from her.

'Welcome, Miss. How may I help you today?'

'I have some questions about the shrine; in particular, about a book we uncovered during the excavation. We found it buried beneath the foundation. I'm hoping you can give me some more insight into its origins.'

'Is that so? This is the first I'm hearing of anything under the shrine. Perhaps, if you describe the contents of this book, I might be able to tell you more.'

'That's the problem. You see, the book is written in a strange language – one that has never been documented before, and I can't make any sense out of it. I can show you some of my scans.'

Sara pulled out a screensheet, which displayed images of the first four pages of the book. Mrs Touré reached forward to take the sheet from her. She examined it for several moments, and turned her gaze to Sara, staring at her with an intensity that made her nervous. And then she rose without saying a word, returning into the building. Sara wasn't sure what to make of the woman's reaction, but she waited patiently until she had returned, holding an old picture frame, which she handed to Sara. In it was a faded celluloid photograph of a middle-aged man standing next to a woman in hijab, who held the hand of a young girl. Despite the difference in age, Sara could see a resemblance between the young woman in the photo and the old woman sitting before her.

'That was my grandmother,' Mrs Touré said. 'She used to tell me stories about times gone past, when this small, dusty city was once the centre of the world. Scholars would travel here from all corners of Earth to teach and learn. That all ended when we came under attack from the raiders of the north. Much of our greatest treasure was plundered, and a great deal of learning was lost forever. After that, the city entered its period of decline.'

Sara was well aware of the history of Timbuktu, how the empire of the Songhai – the last great empire in West Africa – had been brought to its knees by the constant raids of the Berber, Tuareg and Moroccan kingdoms, with the help of conscripted European infantry. The arrival of the arquebus, one of the first modern firearms, had changed everything. This was the stuff of textbooks.

'But there was something else she told me,' the old woman continued. 'When I was young, I really believed that it was true, but in my later years I dismissed it as a fabrication. According to the story, the first king of the Mali empire, Sundiata Keita, created a special group of the most learned scholars in the kingdom to serve in his court. They reported directly to him, and were known as the Guardians of the Empire. After the fall of Mali, they continued to serve under the kings of the Songhai empire, which came afterwards. Their activities were always shrouded by a veil of secrecy. This lasted until the fall of Songhai, after which they were never seen nor heard of again. That is where the story always ended, whenever my grandmother told it.'

Sara had never heard of any such legend in all her years of research. She didn't know whether she ought to believe the old woman, but she had no choice but to listen.

'And according to her, our family is descended from the last leader of the Guardians. His name was Abdul Rahman Touré.'

'Do you know if any of this is true?'

The old woman reached underneath her shawl and pulled out a silken cloth, about the size of a handkerchief, and handed it to Sara. Embroidered into the fabric was an unmistakable inscription, almost identical to the one in the book. Sara's heart jumped. She was onto something.

'May I ask how you got this?'

'That is our family crest,' the woman replied. 'It has been used for as long as any of us can remember.'

'And do you have any idea what these symbols might mean?'

'Of course,' the woman answered. 'I never had the opportunity to go beyond secondary school, but even I can tell you what they are. That's the problem with the youth of today: too much knowledge, not enough education. Why, can't you see? The answer is obvious. It is written quite plainly in the stars.'

At first Sara was confused by this remark, but as she examined the symbols more closely, the obvious conclusion struck her with the force of a lightning bolt.

'Thank you!' Sara exclaimed, jumping to her feet, 'thank you so much!'

She knelt down and kissed the hands of the old woman in a spontaneous expression of gratitude. She ran out of the compound, after saying a hasty goodbye, and down the street, towards her apartment in the metropolitan district. She stopped in an open square to look up into the night sky, where she stared at the answer, or at the least the first part of it. She traced the outlines of the three symbols in the stars above. Orion. Phoenix. Kranich. Three constellations, all visible above the Sahara.

Triangulation. They were reference points; directions to a specific location. A message from the dead to the living. Written plainly in the stars.

***

Touré and his men were minutes from their destination when they heard the first shots ringing out across the mountainside. They froze in their tracks as the shots continued sounding in scattered bursts. There was silence. And then one final, solitary shot.

'God rest their souls,' Touré said.

'We three will remain here,' said Abubakar. 'We can slow them down. Not for very long, but long enough.'

'So be it,' Touré replied. 'May the God of the universe be with you.'

'And with you.'

The men drew their bows and took up defensive positions. Not long after parting from them, Touré heard more shots, this time much louder than before. The pursuers were very close behind. He ignored the sound of the approaching threat and scaled the face of a large, rocky plateau which jutted out near the peak of the mountain. The mission was almost complete.

He unhooked his satchel and removed his instruments, and began carving into the rock with all of his strength and skill, as the sounds of the struggle below gradually gave way to a deathly silence. In less than two minutes he had completed the inscription. A wave of peace overcame him. The work was done. The future was now in the hands of God.

Some day, he thought, as he descended from the peak, some day, the Seeker would retrace his footsteps to the peak of the mountain, and uncover the hidden truth. He offered a prayer of thanks to God as he calmly walked towards the sounds of the approaching men.

A moment later, he was staring into the faces of his pursuers: a motley group of mercenaries, most of whom were total strangers to the land. Of the dozen which had been spotted in pursuit, only seven remained, all of them armed, but three were badly injured. This caused Touré to smile. His men had not gone quietly into the afterworld. And neither would he.

'May the God of the universe save us all,' he prayed, drawing his sword for the last time.

✳✳✳

Sara was halfway up the mountain in a rental hovercar, with Zongo driving her up the winding road that snaked high into the Aïr mountains. She had set off as soon as she was able to triangulate that general area. Zongo steered the vehicle off-road, dodging large obstacles and sailing over smaller ones. When they arrived at the destination, Sara climbed out of the vehicle, looking out over the expansive desert.

With Farouk's prodigious knowledge of cryptography, they were able to put together the final pieces of the mystery. Most of the characters in the text were stylized representations of the various constellations, arranged into specific configurations. The reason they were not able to decode the text at first was because they only had half of the equation. The other half was written into the infinite complexity of the heavens; in the relative positions of a multitude of stars to a single, absolute reference point on earth. In effect, the Guardians had harnessed the forces of the entire universe to create a colossal machine, the greatest supercomputer in existence. And so in order for the decryption to work, it had to be calculated with the same computational precision as was used in the encryption. They needed to find the exact location of the reference point from which all of the calculations were based.

'There should be some kind of indicator somewhere around the peak of this mountain,' Sara said. 'Zongo, search for the target symbol.'

The drone detached itself from its harness and flew out over the rocky terrain.

'Sara, this could be a huge discovery,' said Farouk, on the other end of her comlink. 'And not just for university politics, you know? If we are able to unlock this encryption, there is no telling what else we can do with this technology.'

'I suppose, but all I want is to know more about the lives of our ancestors. We can always discover new technology, even if it takes a thousand years. But we can't learn anything about our past without a historical record.'

'Target has been located,' Zongo announced, hovering over a spot some 30 metres away.

Sara ran over to the spot and knelt down, inspecting the faint carving in the rock. It had weathered over the centuries, and was now almost imperceptible, but it was there all right. A few more years, she thought, and it would surely have been erased from existence. But they had arrived in time.

'Have you found it?' Farouk asked.

'Yes, we've got it. I'm sending you the co-ordinates.'

While Farouk fed the data into his network of hijacked supercomputers, Sara traced her fingers across the faint grooves of the inscription. Touré had been at this very spot, 400 years ago. He could not have known with any certainty that someone would eventually uncover the mystery. She wondered what it must have felt like to carry the burden of a secret that might never be revealed. Above all, she wondered what kind of knowledge was possessed by scholars whose intelligence had somehow outpaced modern civilization for centuries. There was only one way to find out.

'You're not going to believe, this, Sara.'

The readout of the transcript began to scroll down Zongo's display, translated into English from the original Arabic script:

> In this Sacred Book lie the Greatest Treasures of Humankind,
> The History and Philosophy of the Architects of Civilization,
> Of the Builders of Pyramids and the Readers of the Heavens,
> The Hidden Keys to Infinite Power in the Light of the Eternal Ones,
> The Rightful Legacy of All Children of the Sun.
>
> These are the Archives of the Guardians of the Empire,
> Keepers of the Lost Knowledge of the Ancients,
> The Ones who Write Secrets in the Stars...

Jonathan Dotse is a technology evangelist, freelance philosopher, and speculative fiction writer living in Accra, Ghana. He is currently working on his debut novel, a cyberpunk mystery/thriller set in the sprawling metropolis of Accra in the middle of the 21st century. He has also contributed articles and short stories to a variety of print and online publications, including Jungle Jim, Acceler8or, and Brave New Now. Jonathan created the AfroCyberPunk blog in 2010, while studying Management Information Systems at Ashesi University.

Burial

Akwaeke Emezi

My mother had this dressing table that was all reddened wood and black velvet with oval mirrors, streaks of metal marring the glass. She told me it had been shipped from London when she and Papa left their flat in Brixton and came to Nigeria because he was tired of the snow. Later, Papa told me that it was second-hand, like the wall unit and the leather sofa set. I asked him what snow looked like and he opened the freezer, scraping soft white off its inside walls and heaping it into my small hands.

'Just like that,' he said. 'Only much more.' He knew how to answer questions in straight lines, never taking a detour just because I was young, never deviating in the name of protecting me. I was 12 when he became sick, so quickly, and bedridden. My mother said we would travel soon because the doctors here were more likely to kill him than save him, but she was talking in corners. He waited till she left their bedroom to let me crawl under the quilt into the damp heat of his skin against the mattress, then told me he was going to die before she could get him on a plane. I didn't believe him – my father was also a storyman, a mouthy trickster for all his straight lines. I let him sleep before I wandered over to the dressing table to smell my mother's lipsticks. I sat on the velvet stool and crayoned a deep burgundy across my mouth, smacking my lips and frowning. My reflection looked like a bundle of pale kola-nuts, rotten blood smeared on my teeth, Papa's eyes looking back at me from inside my face.

He died a week later, just the way he said he would, before

she could get him on a plane, and the family immediately got involved. Aunty Nonye, Papa's younger sister, drove up from the village with her daughter Ify while my mother called Papa's brother in London, Uncle Jachi, who dropped everything and flew home.

On the day of the burial, I sat on the edge of my bed with my hands pressed against the hard foam as I retched and sobbed, refusing to come out. My mother stood outside my door, her voice like a metal ruler.

'Unlock this thing.'

I glared at the small bolt that I'd slid closed, the one Papa had put in for me when I insisted I was old enough to have some privacy, and I screamed my refusal at her. She was meant to be helping me finish my hair; the car was waiting outside and they wanted to soak Papa's body into the thick pale earth before the sun sank. Aunty Nonye had already gone there to oversee things, leaving Ify to come with us. I could hear Uncle Jachi's voice from the corridor, raised and raging at how I was delaying everyone. He used to be my favourite uncle when I was much younger; he always brought me Archie comics and bars of Cadbury chocolate when he came to visit us. My mother also called him her little brother because they were close, she saw him often when she flew through London, but I had seen the way his nostrils flared every time she called him that, just a fraction, just a small muscle betraying him. She would laugh as she said it, as close as she came to a laugh, and touch his arm.

'Gabriele,' my mother said, calmly. 'I don't have time for this. We are not going to be late to the burial.'

There was no way we could be late. It was still morning and the burial wasn't until early in the evening but my mother liked to plan things ahead. Immediately after Papa died, she'd called Uncle Anton, her brother in Cologne. I'd listened in on the conversation, to her voice grating against itself in rapid German, a stray word or two clicking into place in my head. The rest had been an unintelligible guttural thing, a quick rearranging of my life over a piece of static. We were leaving, moving to Cologne before I would start school in Switzerland because I only had a few years left and her brother was paying for it and it was a good place to finish me. Those countries meant nothing to me. My country was the patch of grass in the front of our compound; it was the cactus garden next to the front door, the ridges of corn under swelling avocadoes, the terrorist creepers of sweet potato we could never kill once we planted them. My country's flag was a cocoyam leaf.

'Fuck the burial!' I answered. The first time I'd heard that word was a few years ago when the driver from next door had used it while sitting outside under the water tank, talking to our househelp, Grace. He'd been drinking bottle after bottle of Star beer while she filled up the plastic gallons, water muddying her feet as he complained about his employer roughly. I was watching the fireflies as evening crawled over us, ignoring their conversation until he dropped his Igbo and switched to Pidgin.

'Nna mehn. Fuck Oga sha.'

He waved his beer bottle drowsily as he said this and Grace hissed furiously, snatching it out from his hand as she glanced over at me. 'Shut your detty mouth! Abi you dey craze? You no dey see pikin?' She quickly bustled me back into the house, ordering him to go home and warning me to forget what I just heard. I didn't forget it, that word that upset Grace so much, and I heard it again on TV when Papa had dozed off in his armchair and didn't check what films I was watching. It felt like the right word to convey exactly how much I didn't want to be in a car driving towards the grey flesh they claimed was him.

After I said that, after those words winged out of my mouth, there was a stunned silence outside my door. I clutched my throat, feeling like the air was being sucked away from me into my mother's inhaling rage. I expected her to scream back at me but instead her shoes clicked twice as she stepped away from the door. Her voice was so low that, if not for the shocked and stilled air, I might not have heard her.

'Jachi.' Heavy footsteps thudded on the tile as my uncle walked down the corridor towards us. His weight stopped in front of my door.

'Open her door for me, please.' My mother's voice stayed low and the air was still paralysed. He shattered that, slamming the bulk of his shoulder against my door and breaking it open. The pitiful bolt flew off and I threw my arms up to protect my head from the hurling metal. It clattered harmlessly against my wall and echoed off the floor as I lowered my arms slowly to see my mother standing in front of me, her cheekbones washed with furious red. She'd scraped her blonde hair back from her thin face, winding it into a strict bun on the nape of her neck. Her mouth was a dark burgundy print against her skin, slightly spaced teeth bared between her lips. I stared back up at her with my father's eyes and she cracked a slap across my face, her arm tight. My jaw swung a slow path sideways under the force of her hand, which she then used to smooth down her dress. The black velvet hissed under her touch, a severe sheath that cut off in the middle of her shins.

'Fix your hair and get into the car. We're leaving in five minutes.' She turned and walked out of my room, her heels tapping out a precise beat as she faded down the corridor. I pressed both hands to the side of my face as my blood took fire, hot salt steeping in my eyes. Uncle Jachi reached his hand towards me, surprised at my mother's small violence, but I flinched and he stopped himself. I thought he was gathering air to say something to me but Ify entered the room with a brush and a jar of hair gel.

'You people should hurry up,' he said instead, to us.

'Yes, Uncle.' Her reply was automatic as she dropped the gel and brush on my bed, crouching to hug me. I stared at Jachi over her shoulder, watching him as he backed out of my room. He looked uneasy, the way I wanted him to look. I wanted him to have trouble in his soul forever.

The morning they told me Uncle Jachi had arrived from London, Papa had been dead for five days. I had run into the parlour to greet him, still wearing my nightdress, stumbling to a halt when I saw his face. People used to mistake him and Papa for twins, even though he was a few years younger. My relief at seeing him dissolved into grief and I stood there in numb shock, only sinking down to the sofa when he pulled my arm to sit next to him. I let him envelop me in one of his warm hugs, his palm against my spine in solid reassuring pats.

'It's okay,' he said. 'Don't cry, ehn?' The pats became strokes, long applications of pressure along my back. I felt shrivelled from all the weeping I had done already, dried up.

For my last birthday, Papa had got me a tortoise to add to the small menagerie of animals that we kept: the canary that escaped during a cage cleaning and sang rebelliously from the avocado tree where it settled down, the ungrateful green parrots that pecked everyone who tried to feed them, the endless cats and Heidi, the dog. The tortoise died a few weeks later and we buried it under the guava tree. Papa said that in a few years the flesh would have dried away and we could dig it up and I could keep the shell on my bookshelf. When I heard we would be moving away, I had gone outside and sat by the tree, then sobbed so hard that the turkeys lying in the shade by me stood up and jogged off slowly in alarm.

I didn't want to break inside my uncle's arms, so I started to pull away. That was when I felt his other hand on my chest and my throat seized. It was not a passing brush or a quick squeeze – he cupped his fingers under my left breast and encircled it with his thumb, then slowly pulled down, stroking every inch till his hand was pinching my nipple, then he let go. I jerked back from him, sour swirling up from my stomach and he looked back at me like a lizard, his nostrils slightly flared. Grace walked into the parlour with a tray and my mother came behind her, wrapping herself in a robe.

'Jachi, you landed safe. Thank God,' she was saying. He stood up to hug my mother and I sat there, feeling my pulse shake my skin as my mother wrapped her arms around his neck and put her face in his collarbone.

Papa used to have a thing for insects. He would show me the beetles that grew on the bitterleaf plant and he let them crawl over his hands. We would tie strings around the waists of the bumblebees that buzzed around the mango tree and fly them like kites for a few minutes before Papa would release them.

'You have to let them go,' he explained to me when I threw a little tantrum because I wasn't done playing with them. 'They don't belong to you.'

My favourite insect was a little crawling thing that reminded me of both armour and a mimosa plant. When you poked this little bug, it would curl up into a ball, plates of its exoskeleton locking you out. We called mimosa 'touch-and-die'; if you touched it, the lines of leaves would flutter and fold inwards, against each other, drooping and closing and withering. That was what happened to me that morning when Jachi arrived from London. My mother looked down at me, my hair flattened from sleep, my nightdress rumpled. His arm was around her waist.

'Go put some clothes on, Gabriele,' she said. 'And brush your teeth, we're having breakfast soon.'

I wanted to say something but Grace was pouring tea and asking my uncle how much sugar he took, my throat was crippled and my father was dead. I left the parlour and in the nine long days between his arrival and the burial, I avoided being in the same room as him. It was obvious since many people were paying us condolence visits and we were expected to receive them as a family. As soon as he walked into the room, I would stand up and walk out, making a quick excuse to my mother. It would have been considered rude, but I was a half-orphan and so people assumed I was sick with sorrow.

'It's because Jachi resembles her father,' they said. 'Ei-yah, poor girl.' My mother must have believed this because she never ordered me to stay.

The only person I told about what happened was Ify and her face blanched into dullness when she heard. There was a silence that I cried into and when she spoke, even her voice was blunted.

'He touched me too, a few years ago. When I was around your age.' She didn't look at me.

'Did you tell Aunty Nonye?' Ify nodded slowly.

'She told me to pray for him.'

My mouth fell soft and open. I already knew I wasn't telling my mother, not after she'd just lost Papa. This would break her heart and she'd just blame herself for not protecting me better. I couldn't do that to her, not when she was already so splintered. If I didn't tell her, maybe I could just forget it one day. I didn't want it to scatter the whole family and I didn't want to become the centre of a storm. Forcing back tears, I realized that Jachi had waited until Papa was gone, until Papa couldn't save me. But Ify's mother knew. She knew and she didn't do anything. I stared at my cousin until she shrugged.

'I think he did things to her when she was small.' We sat together, the gentle horror of blood linking us. I reached out and held Ify's hand tightly, in silence.

After Jachi left, I let Ify brush my hair into a puff, slicking it down with gel. We would be wearing matching traditional during the burial ceremony, all my aunts and uncles and cousins, except my mother. I'd been meant to wear black like her but Ify had begged her to let me to wear the wine lace traditional, to be one of them, just for this day, for his sake. My mother had looked at me first, at Papa's black copper eyes, his snub nose and wide mouth living on my face, before she gave her permission.

They sewed me a long dress with a fishtail skirt that made me feel like my back was straight. My mother had always refused to have anything sewn for her, even when Papa was alive. When we all went to functions together, she stood out in her edged dresses and scant jewellery, tightening her jaw and staring everyone down. The aunts resented the way she refused to even try and fit in, the time she spent teaching me how to make waffles from scratch instead of learning how to cook jollof rice. It was only in our house that we understood, that she stayed in this country only out of love, that all of this was just how she looked when compromising, that she spoke English to me because it was the only language she shared with his mouth.

The burial would take place in the village, an hour's drive away, because that's where Papa was born and where his body belonged. I sat in the car and watched my mother stare out of the window, watched her wedding ring collect the sun as we drove off. Cars were packed on the expressway until it branched off into the smaller tarred roads and then again into the compacted white clay. It was still early when we arrived at Aunty Nonye's house, so Ify took my hand and asked if we could go to her room. I looked at my mother, who raised her chin and stared at us with her wet moss eyes before dipping her head in a slight nod. We slid past the adults and barricaded ourselves in her room, where I dropped my bag, unbuckled my sandals, and pressed my soles against the stretches of cold tile. Ify flopped onto the bed, dangling her skull off the edge and watching me. She had threaded her hair into sleek shiny worms lying in neat rows against her scalp and her skin was taut from the corners of her eyes.

'I can't believe she finally let me out of her sight,' I said, spinning morosely on my heel.

'You're the only thing she has remaining.' Ify stretched her arms out over her head and her fingers brushed the floor. I stopped spinning and looked down at the tiles, my mouth heavy. She jumped off the bed and pulled my hairband off, letting my hair burst out into a thick cloud.

'You should wear it like this for the burial,' she said. I twisted a section of it between my fingers, the scent of pink oil wrapping around my nails. I was not allowed to wear it loose.

'Can you do it so that it looks like your own?' I asked shyly, raising my eyes to my cousin's. She held my gaze, locked. We both knew that my mother dictated how I wore my hair, that I needed permission to thread it. It wasn't the sleek gold that poured off her scalp nor was it the iron tight coal of my father's head and neck. It was a watered sanded brown, uncommitted spirals and confused straight pieces, full and soft. Ify touched it.

'Like mine?'

I nodded. At least it wouldn't be loose.

'I think I have remainder thread,' she murmured to herself, before flashing her strong teeth. 'We can do it.'

I clapped my hands as she slid over the bed and dragged open a drawer, pulling out the spools of rubber thread and tossing them on her sheets. I picked one up and turned it in my fingers. Ify glanced at the clock – the burial was starting in three hours.

'We have enough time. Sit down.' She gestured to the floor between her legs as she arranged herself at the foot of the bed and dropped a pillow down. I obediently sat and she switched on the television before parting my hair into small sections.

There was always something about having my hair touched that spun me away from my body and so I let the noise from the TV wash over me, feeling the tug of her hands and the answering wrench at my scalp. I wondered how Papa would have felt to see me with threaded hair. He'd shown me old pictures of his mother with carefully woven branches of hair and a bladed jaw. I looked nothing like her. Every time I thought of Papa, I became partially eroded, portions of my throat made rare and blue. I didn't know it was possible to cry this much, till there was nothing except a sun burning dry and hot in my mouth.

Our house didn't feel alive now that we were moving out; I had felt the grieving as we packed. I saw how my mother's heart was broken because she couldn't say it with her mouth, so she'd said it in the way she wrapped up the silver they got at the wedding, the way she looked at his portrait for long minutes before burying it in a trunk. She had stroked her thumb over the picture the way she used to stroke it over the lined map of Papa's palm all the time, a gesture that said more than I'd ever heard from her mouth. He would let his hand lie in hers like a captivated wing, like she was telling his future, his knuckles in the cup of hers.

One night after he died, I'd peered around the corner of their bedroom door and seen her kneeling on the carpet with her shoes off and her hair collapsing on her shoulders. I'd wanted to touch her but she was like her fine crystal, forever on a shelf I couldn't reach. We grieved as we took down the lace curtains and sold the dining table, as Grace left and went back to her hometown. When they were clearing out Papa's clothes, I stole one of his favourite shirts from the wardrobe. It was in mild green cotton and still smelled like him, faint threads of cologne that would eventually die like he had. I hid it in my room and, when my mother told me we would spend the night at Aunty Nonye's house once the burial was over, I carefully packed the shirt in my bag under folded underwear, my pyjamas for that night, and a sundress for the next day.

I gasped as Ify parted a section of my hair with more force than usual. She patted my head in distracted apology, rubber thread winding over her fingers as she pulled my scalp taut.

When my mother walked in later, I locked the bones of my mouth, fixing my eyes anywhere but on hers. I had looked up pictures of Uncle Anton and his family in Cologne and they all looked like smooth milk and corn silk. Even my mother didn't look like them any more; her skin was tanned into tiny lines and her hair was less like silk and more like metal.

She went to visit them nearly every year and she must have looked more and more like a foreigner there each time, just like she did here.

I felt the heat of her stare on the branches of thread Ify had created and nervousness coiled in my stomach. There was no time to take the thread out. I could almost taste her calculations, deciding if my small rebellion was worth addressing.

'Let's go,' she finally said. Ify exhaled and, as we trotted obediently past my mother, her fingers brushed against the sculpture of my head.

They held the service at the grave and my mother latched her spine with iron, ignoring the wailing relatives and shielding her eyes with mirrored sunglasses. I saw them curl lips at her, but they couldn't feel the fine tremble in her skin as she ground the bones of my hands together with hers. His sisters were angry because she had refused to let us participate in the wake-keeping, staying in town while the family gathered at Aunty Nonye's house to mourn. She paid for everything but it was a slap, a reminder that she knew how they saw her and she was not going to pretend over his body, that I was hers and she could deny them his only child.

Everyone was kinder to me; I heard broken wisps of conversation about 'that poor half-caste girl' and women were constantly pulling me into their hot lacy chests, patting my face and touching my hair as they unleashed a pattering stream of Igbo over me. I shook my head politely to indicate that I didn't understand, and they were taken aback.

'Ah, ah! You don't speak it?'

'Her mother is white, na. They probably don't speak it in their house.'

'What a shame!'

'Ehn, I'm sure she didn't allow the father to speak it to her.'

'May he rest in peace...'

I broke away from their voices as unobtrusively as I could.

My mother had once taught me how to be deaf. She used to take Grace to the market with her and one day I begged and whined until she agreed to take me instead. We drove down Faulks Road until we were smothered in the noise and life of the market.

'This is Ariaria?' I asked as she parked the car, my eyes greedy.

'Ariaria International Market,' she answered, amused. She knew her way, weaving through the narrow aisles and dodging the grasping hands and calls. A few children started running after us and singing in raucous voices that threaded up into a mocking question as they repeated their lines over and over again.

'Onye ocha/ I biara n'ala Igbo?'

She acted like she had no ears, keeping her fingers locked like a convulsion around my wrist. When we got home that day, she called Grace to unload the car and said she was going to lie down. Papa was balancing a long stick of bamboo, knocking down oranges in the backyard, bright sunlight falling over him. I ran to help him pick them up from the ground, then tried to catch them as he broke them out from the tree, dancing under its branches to arrest them in mid-air. When I asked him what the song meant, he smiled at the way I sang it.

'It means, "White person/ you have come to Igboland?"'

'Poor Mama,' I giggled. 'Do they sing that for her every time she goes out? She must get tired of it.' My father leaned the bamboo against the tree and lifted his hand to shade his face as he looked at me.

'I'm sure she does,' he said. I thought he was sad for her but after he died, I went to the market with Ify and the children sang the song at me. Ify squeezed my hand as tightly as Papa had done that other day as we carried the oranges back into the house, when he spared me the knowledge that I would be as displaced as my mother.

At the graveside, Jachi stood on the other side of her body

with his hand on the plane of her shoulder. Because it was him, she tipped her body weight and rested some of it against him – not a lot, just a little. I stood straight beside her, my weight on myself. The rest of the family stood some distance away from us and the pastor was screaming prayers, his mouth flecked with spit. The rhythm of his words drummed the air around us. I couldn't look over at my uncle. Ever since he had come back, there were nights when I woke up struggling to breathe and clawing the bed sheet off my body because it had touched my chest and it had felt like him. Other nights, he had my father's voice; those were the nights when I did not sleep again. With him the width of my mother's body away from me, my heart was beating so hard that I could feel my pulse stretch from armpit to armpit.

She was speaking softly to him but I couldn't hear her for the wind or the pastor's voice. As she talked, she relaxed and took her hand out of mine, resting it instead on the back of my neck. The touch of her skin flooded me; my mother was not given to caresses. It had been Papa who used to scoop me into his arms when I fell asleep on the sofa, carrying me to my bed while a sock dangled off my foot. He was the one I kissed goodnight, the one who sat me on his knee and bucked it about till I was screaming and giggling in laughter.

They were lowering his coffin and throwing earth over it, white sandy loam. Someone handed me a shovel and I took it numbly. One of my chores used to be weeding the compound, using a small hoe to hack up tangles of roots and patting the soil to even it out afterwards. They took me for a tetanus shot after I cut my foot with the blade and I told Papa that I had not expected it to be so sharp. He told me all useful tools have an edge. I wanted to take the shovel and swing it at my uncle's smile, splatter him over the black pit of her dress. But instead I dug and lifted and threw and a pale mottled rain fell on my father's casket.

Afterwards, almost everyone was in the parlour of the

house and I was walking through the corridor, towards the kitchen, when I overheard Jachi speaking to my mother.

'Think about what I said,' he was saying, earnestly. 'You know I'd love to have you and Gabriele come to London for a bit, spend some time with me.'

My mother was leaning against the heavy curtains. I stood back from the doorway and watched her sigh. 'I'm tired, Jachi,' she answered. 'I just want to go home.'

'I understand.' He twisted his mouth in sympathy and took her hand in his. 'What if Gabriele comes to London with me while you go to Cologne and sort things out there? Take some pressure off you. And then you can come and join us when you collect her.'

Jachi had leaned in to make his suggestion and it dropped across her collarbone, tumbled off her breast and splattered on the floor, where it slithered damply until it found me in the doorway, clawed its way up my body and sank viciously into my head. A briny fear rushed through me and the waves of it battered against my eyes. I watched her tilt her head at him and give him a small grateful smile.

'Thank you, Jachi. That might simplify things a little.'

His eyes were soft. 'It's not easy to grieve and take care of a child at the same time.'

'And Gabriele hasn't been to London in a while.'

'Neither have you,' he pointed out. It had been two or three years since her last trip to Germany, with her usual stopover to see him. Papa had sent Jachi packages through my mother when she flew, books and suya spice and egusi. 'I missed my presents. I miss him.'

'I know,' she said, her voice weighed. 'I miss him, too.' I was listening to them through the storm in me but I was stone on the outside, a hiding gargoyle, with the thought of a few days, a week, two, alone with him in that flat in London making me oscillate tightly on the inside. I wanted to jump out and scream and stop her from sending me away with him, rip that arranged concern off his face, distract the caving sadness on hers. I took deep breaths and steadied myself. I could do it, tell her what happened, right now, and she would never let him near us again. I stepped out, halfway into the doorway, and that was when I saw it, when my gaze dripped down his arm, his arm that ended in his hand, his hand that was cupped halfway and sideways with hers, her thumb that moved in an intimate stroke against the grain of his palm.

I stepped back. I turned with my heart withering and ran upstairs, away from the woman who had touched the thread of my hair and the back of my neck, away from her hand, away from her wine-tipped thumb. I ripped off my dress in Ify's room and put on Papa's shirt, buttoning the gentle green all the way up my throat, then I locked myself out on the balcony and crunched into a tight little ball so that I was buried in the charcoal black of the night, with the smell of my father holding me. I cried and cried forever, a gasping breeze drifting through my chest, bringing in the scent of a slow rot.

Akwaeke Emezi is an Igbo/Tamil writer based in liminal spaces. She was born in Umuahia and raised in Aba, Nigeria. Her work moves through spaces of psychosocial dislocation, traditional spiritual practice, loss and death, and confronts the intricacies of navigating humanity. Akwaeke graduated with an MPA from New York University and is currently enrolled in the Creative Writing MFA program at Syracuse University. Her work can be accessed via her website www.azemezi.com

The Song of a Goat

Pede Hollist

After Stella finished explaining that she had been suspended from school for two weeks for punching another pupil and talking back to a teacher, her mother, Ajuah Danjuma, stood up from the dining table of their two-bedroom flat, glided across the air-bubbled linoleum floor, opened her bedroom door, walked in, and closed it behind her. From the snaps, clicks and thuds sounding behind the termite-riven wood partition separating the bedroom from the parlour, Stella could tell her mother was searching for something. That her mother had not frowned, hissed, or spoken worried Stella. That the sounds from the bedroom included sniffles, coughs, and throat scratches alarmed her, for Stella knew that her mother never left what needed to be said today for tomorrow, especially when it came to school matters. Knowing that, Stella felt her mother must have gone into the room not only to gather herself for a tirade, but also to gather evidence of Stella's prior misdeeds.

Ajuah Danjuma's eyes were cherry-red when she sat back down and slid an off-white envelope onto the table, halfway between herself and Stella. The daughter knew not to touch it. But she sensed it contained a secret – perhaps the name of the father her mother never talked about; perhaps the reason why they steadfastly refused to raise chickens or eat goats like most people in their neighbourhood; or maybe why, some days after a hard day's work at the hospital where she worked as a cleaner, her mother had a distant look in her eyes.

Ajuah scratched her throat and began talking, quietly. As she talked, a woman Stella had never before known filled the room.

***

'When I was your age and quarrelled with my friends,' Ajuah Danjuma stared at her daughter, '*my* mother would say to me, "when a fire erupts, sit on it; it will burn your butt but you will have put out the flames".' Before Stella could ask why anyone would choose to do that, Ajuah Danjuma continued.

I am going to tell you the story of Rika the goat, but it begins with Okuru, the scabies-infested dog nobody cared about that roamed Salibghania, the small fishing village me, my brothers and mother lived in off the West African coast. Okuru probably had rabies too. He definitely had only three good legs. The fourth, right back leg hung by his side like a jacked-up car tyre. Yellow-brown spots, full of pus, and patches of other diseases made up the skin that covered his body. Fat green flies feasted on Okuru and then buzzed over to squat on our food. I hated this. More than that, I hated how every morning, before I left for school and while my brothers ate breakfast, my mother made me clean up the tapeworm-filled shit Okuru had deposited in front of our house. But I hated most seeing Okuru hopping around our village. When I did, I'd throw stones to chase him away. That was what I was doing one Friday afternoon as I walked home from school.

Unfortunately, because of a drizzle, my grip and aim were poor. Some of the stones missed Okuru. A couple landed near Mrs Stevenson and the group named the Daughters of the Catholic Caucus, older women from the Church that funded the school I attended, Holy Angels Girls Secondary School – HAGS, students from rival schools teased us. Mrs Stevenson and her sisters ministered to the women in the village, but after the near misses, they focused their displeasure on me: a disgrace and dishonour to your uniform, your badge as head girl, and yourself as a woman, they huffed and puffed. On my life, I could not understand what these mammies were getting their frilly knickers all twisted about. There I was saving the neighbourhood from dysentery and rabies and they were complaining. Damn! Bet their prayers couldn't do that. But, as I look back, I suppose I could have behaved like the head girl they wanted – you know, say I am sorry, hold their hands and pray, but I just told them the truth: in our village everybody stones stray dogs.

Even though that afternoon I was wearing their precious school uniform and badge, I was truly no longer head girl. After the last paper of our college-entrance exams, Principal had told me I'd be setting an example for the younger girls if I continued attending school and helped out with the shortage of teachers – two had recently started maternity leave, one had taken sick leave, and another had left for a higher-paying job. At the time, agreeing to Principal's suggestion seemed a no-brainer: my classmates whose parents could afford it had or would be going overseas; those whose parents were well-connected had or would be getting jobs in private companies; and the rest of us, whose parents had so little influence they could not even lift their eyelids, would be lounging at home doing sweet nothing, waiting for the September release of our results. Good grades meant college or university to become a doctor, lawyer, or engineer. I wanted to be the first African woman to travel to the moon! Bad grades meant work, marriage and children, and not necessarily in that order. No way!

Truth be told, I was not as anxious about my results as some of my classmates. I had placed first in our monthly report card ever since I began secondary school and was valedictorian. Nice word, isn't it? Has a fullness to it, right? It was one of hundreds I studied for English 1, vocabulary and comprehension. Do you know about 20 showed up on the exam? Bam, Bam, Bam! I know I aced that exam. Everybody expected me to do well; I expected me to do well, to be on my way to university and, one day, to go to the moon. But since September was far away and doing nothing was the alternative, I accepted Principal's suggestion.

I did not teach, though I easily could have. Instead, I made sure pupils completed their class work or that they were not talking loudly or fighting. Sometimes, I covered for teachers who were present but chose not to teach. Instead they yakked away in the staffroom about wearing this and that to school, church, party and cooking this and that for boyfriend, husband, or parent.

✳✳✳

'Here,' Ms Mercy thrusts a thin, three-foot-long cane toward me after my first class.

'No... no... Ma,' I shuffle back.

'Take it!' she grabs my hand. 'These girls don't listen very well. This will be your loudspeaker.' She uncurls my fingers, slaps the cane into my palm, and presses my fingers back over it. 'Nothing like the sting of a cane to open deaf ears.' She snaps three lashes at imaginary rumps and exhales into a satisfied grin.

Ms Mercy was our biology teacher and doubled as our agricultural science instructor, of sorts. She taught both courses the same way – reading from yellow dog-eared notes and cluttering the blackboard with cave drawings and Egyptian hieroglyphics. Classroom teaching was simply not Ms Mercy's strength. Her strength, maybe even mission, was to be our moral compass. Every day, somewhere on school grounds, you would find her, cane in hand, covered from head to toe, hijab style, like a floating guilty conscience, scolding – a single girl here, a group there – about dress, walk, or speech; about being a woman, lady, wife and mother, her favourite topics. Some girls said she covered her body to hide a particularly bad case of scoliosis. They even called her the holy hunchback, but I am not into calling people names.

Of course, in a Christian girls' school faith and fiction have the same mother – imagination. The other Ms Mercy story was that she had been married off to a much older man, to save her, the story goes, from becoming the old cow unfit even for dog chop; that the older man's wife had run away with a Korean fisherman, leaving behind two unruly boys of 11 and 13. Their father's daily rants about women's inherent wickedness fuelled their resentment of the mother who abandoned them, and it spilled over to Ms Mercy. Their behaviour was no story though because I deal in facts. I saw the boys, with these eyes, talk back to her, ignore her instructions, and refuse to do any housework. See, twice weekly I carried Ms Mercy's Ghana-Must-Go bag, heavy with our exercise books, to and from her house.

'Here, take this,' she said, pointing to the bag as I passed by the staffroom one afternoon. 'It's on your way home. I'm too old to be toting a heavy bag full of your stupidity.' Back then, I had complied.

✳✳✳

'You're a disgrace to that uniform,' Ms Mercy points at me.

Maasai tall, Wolof black, and with a neck the girth of an ancient cotton tree, Ms Mercy stands pulpit righteous on the verandah of the beige and brown bungalow-styled school building and wags her finger at me. It is a mid-June Monday morning, the first sunny day after a week of rain and after the Friday encounter with Mrs Stevenson and the Geriatrics. Welcoming the relief, yellow alamanders and purple hibiscuses had reared their heads through the cracks of the ruby-red laterite school grounds, only to be crushed by the stomping feet of girls playing akra before the daily 7.30am prayer. The few flowers that survive the pre-prayer assault are doomed to be crushed by a greater number of feverish feet during the 10.30am recess. The even fewer flowers that had the good sense to grow around the wire-mesh fence marking the school boundary are sure to be nipped to adorn the heads of girls who have rendezvous with boyfriends after school.

'How can *you*, head girl of this school, justify stoning a defenceless dog? Don't you know you should love all God's creatures, show empathy if you can't care for them? And then you have the nerve to tell the women helping *your* people to mind their business!'

The sun must have sided with Ms Mercy that June morning because it suddenly flames over the school building in red glory. Together, they breathe hot fury at me. I squirm like an anguished worm.

'I am the one mama always makes clean up after Okuru,' I blurt out, not really addressing Ms Mercy. 'My brothers never had to.'

'Better get used to cleaning up messes. You'll be a mother soon.'

'I don't want to be a mother.'

Ms Mercy stepped off the verandah and walked right up to me, holding her cane at both ends, flexing it.

'And who should clean the mess you or your children make?'

'Would *you* clean up after Okuru?'

'Talking back to me? I told them you were not fit to be head girl.'

'I never wanted to be.'

'You have no respect for me, your badge, or this school.'

'*You* are the one who has–' I stop.

'Go ahead, vomit it.'

***

It was the story of the disappearing leafy greens and animals. The government had directed schools to develop on-campus activities for its GASP, girls for agricultural science progress, initiative. We showcased our efforts with the garden, growing cassava, potato, bitter leaf or cocoyam greens, and with the pen, raising goats and chickens. And gasp we did, for no sooner did the greens, popular for cooking stews, mature than they disappeared. We were especially disappointed because the Church had promised it would provide rice and palm oil if we harvested enough greens to feed the entire school. But every time we seemed about a week away from our much-anticipated meal, the greens would disappear. Teachers seemed indifferent, even unwilling to investigate the disappearances. Our disappointment mushroomed into hostility when, between Ramadan and Christmas, most of the goats and chickens disappeared. Pupils openly said teachers were stealing our self-help work to feed their families. A blurry black-and-white photograph showing the hunched back of a figure holding a plastic bag near what looked like the school grounds sprung from the manure of our suspicions and spread around the school like wild grass in a vegetable garden. Untended, the blurry figure became, in our minds and in fact, Ms Mercy.

Principal responded to this story with puritanical swiftness at the threat of contradiction: 'Bring the photo to school and let's shame the devil,' she challenged the next morning at prayers. But the photo, too, disappeared, with the same finality as the greens, goats, and chickens. Two days later, Principal called a special midday assembly and paraded two girls, heads bowed, in front of the entire school.

'They've confessed to stealing from the garden,' she said. 'False witnesses and thieves shall not go unpunished.'

The girls were braced on a table by four of their peers, each holding onto an arm or leg. Ms Mercy's rod of correction blasted their rumps six times each: wham! 'For bearing false witness,' she grunted after each stroke. I wondered why she did not show such fury to her sons. I guess that's the way of the world. Beat up on the weak ones when you can't do anything about the powerful ones taking advantage of you. But the display of justice did little to dispel our suspicions, for a new story soon made its way around school that the two girls had confessed to the misdeeds only after a marathon meeting with the principal and the entire teaching staff.

∗∗∗

'You know why our people say okra can never grow taller than its master?'

Of course, Ms Mercy's question is rhetorical, so I say nothing.

'Because a master can cut the okra down to size any time.' She accompanies her answer with a swift, slicing motion of her cane under my throat, hisses, turns, and marches back, Hitler-style, to the verandah.

'It's just another stupid way to say don't change or do things differently,' I shout into her arching back. I must have decided that day I was not going to follow my mother's advice and sit on the fire.

Ms Mercy stops, turns and walks right back up to me. I can smell her hot, rusty breath.

'Be careful, Missy. You may be cleaning up messes sooner than you think. Now, take the goats so they can feed and make up for the way you mistreated that helpless dog.'

∗∗∗

I should have left school that day. To this moment, I don't know why I didn't. Instead, cane in hand, I walk up the 100-yard slope that leads to the pen. From a high of 20 sheep, goats and chickens, it now had only three: Papa Goat, Mama Goat and six-month-old Rika, the star of our pen. Except for those absent, every girl in the school had witnessed Rika's birth. Of course, Principal and Ms Mercy would have preferred a less messy display, but our history teacher, Sister Broderick, old enough to be a museum exhibit, made it a day to remember. She hobbled around the pen muttering: 'You are watching childbirth-o, childbirth-o! Praise the Lord.'

Really? So we named the kid Brodericka, though we later shortened it to Rika.

Every girl in that school loved Rika, black and tan over most of her body with a splash of white on her underbelly. Every girl had played with Rika, caressed her fur, tickled her ears, fed her blades of grass or chased after her. But on that June day, I was in no mood to play nanny.

*** ***

Inside the pen, I smash wildly with the cane, whacking hard – sometimes hitting the goats, sometimes myself, sometimes the air – and enjoying watching them scamper, bleating, maa-maa. 'Nobody,' whack-whack, 'not Ms Mercy nor Mrs Stevenson and the Geriatrics can force me to be nice to Okuru unless they, too, have cleaned up its shit. Simple as that.'

Kuh-chhhh! My cane descends. 'Maa-maa, maa-maa,' Rika and her parents cry.

After venting, I open the pen and prod the goats toward the grassy patch between the north-end fence of the school compound and its pump. Three feet to the side of the pump stands the well, about 10 feet deep, dry and empty, its walls uneven and pockmarked, like its diggers had beat a hasty retreat when the earth and underwater spirits revolted at their intrusion.

But unless you are familiar with the layout of the school grounds, you would not know a well stands next to the pump. Rows of off-white, half-inch plastic pipes and other materials of construction had been stacked all around the well, partly to discourage pupils from sitting on or peering over the rim. The pipes had been donated to install an irrigation system that was supposed to save our necks from carrying heavy buckets on our heads to water the garden. The pipes never got laid and our necks never got saved.

Some 20 yards before we get to the well, Rika turns, looks at me, wrinkles her nose, flaps her ears, and bleats maa maa. The kid wants to play. I oblige her, breaking into a run, forcing her to sprint toward the fence. She zigs. I zag. She cuts, I slash. She hooks, I loop, and all the while I am waving the cane in one hand and whacking the ground with a plastic tube in the other. Hemmed in by the fence and out of real estate, Rika pirouettes, dashes towards the pipes, leaps over them, and disappears, as surely as the greens, goats, chickens and photograph.

I scramble over the shifting pipes to the rim and peer into the well: Rika lies splayed on the ground, spit-ready for a communal feast. 'Maa-maa,' she bares her pink gums. Her disco-ball eyes spool between her ears. Blood trickles from her nostril.

Unexpectedly, she jerks upright on her four legs. They buckle. She collapses onto the ground, 'Maa-maa.' Rika tries her jerky, life-affirming upward leap several more times, only to splay back on the floor, each effort less convincing than the previous, each maa-maa starved of oxygen, faint and pained – the song of a goat, dying.

I slide back from the rim, carefully rolling over onto my back to counter the shifting movement of the pipes under me. I sit up and scan the scene. I see the rusty corrugated-iron sheet roofing of the school buildings, the stained glass showing Him, splayed, on the cross, and the steeple of the church in the adjacent compound. They offer no guidance, no insight, and no passageway to empathy.

I slide down the pipes and hotfoot to the school buildings, a town crier delivering her message: 'Rika has fallen into the well. She is dying.'

Concerned pupils in their white-and-blue uniforms spill out of the classrooms.

'Get a rope, a basket, a bag,' I shout. 'We have to get her out quickly.'

I vaguely remember seeing Ms Mercy shellacking the school bell in a vain attempt to dam the flood my news had unleashed. But I do not care. I have to save Rika. I race back up the slope.

The white-and-blues gather around the well, pushing, shoving, to get a glimpse of Rika. Many are standing on the pipes that slide and shift. C R A C K, one breaks, then another. White-and-blues fall. It seems just a matter of time before someone topples into the well or is trampled.

'Back, back,' I scream, yanking shoulders and uniforms to prevent an accident, but the danger remains. Then I feel the cane in my hand. I whip, poke, swish and slash. The white-and-blues part immediately. Hmm.

I have restored some order by the time Ms Mercy, Sister Broderick and two other teachers, panting, reach the top of the slope.

'Move… down… back, you fools,' they shout in turn.

No-one listens to them.

'Get the fishermen,' Ms Mercy shouts.

'Why?'

'How dare you ask me why? Just do as I say.'

'There are no men in the village.' I stare at Ms Mercy.

'Nonsense. How can there be no men in the village?'

'They have gone fishing with the Korean ferry.'

'Rubbish, there must be some men.'

'Only the old ones.'

'Your stupidity knows no bounds-ehn?'

'Maaaaa-maaaaaa.'

Rika's plea galvanizes me: 'By the time help comes, she will be dead!'

'Rather a dead goat than a dead child. Now,' Ms Mercy pushes out her shoulders, 'you idiots get back to class or there will be hell to pay.'

'No, we have to get Rika out now!'

The white-and-blues stare at us – two rams locking horns – unsure with whom to side. Then they break toward Ms Mercy and the teachers. My heart sinks, but only for a moment, for they are breaking to let a group of their peers, ropes and a big Ghana-Must-Go Bag in hand, through to the well.

Ms Mercy gasps and reaches for the bag as they pass by her.

The just-arrived peers, sweaty and panting from running to and from the village, settle our course of action. We will rescue Rika!

We crowd around the well, overwhelming Ms Mercy, Sister Broderick and their denunciations, forcing them back, out of hearing and sight.

'You, you, you,' I point my cane, singling out the taller, stronger pupils. 'Grab the rope.' They hesitate.

'Do as I say!' I swish the cane side to side. They scamper to the rope.

I swish the cane some more to clear a space around the well. The white-and-blues move back. They grumble, talk. I hold the cane to my lips. A hushed silence follows.

I motion those holding the rope to walk around the well, twice, and to tie a stopper knot around the stand-up pump. With the other end, they make a harness.

'We need someone small, fearless, to go down,' I say, expecting that we will be a while before someone volunteers. Several hands shoot up. I point the cane at Bilkisu, small brave Bilkisu. One set of pupils prepare her for the descent. Another tie the Ghana-Must-Go bag to the end of the second rope.

We ease Bilkisu into the well, the Ghana-Must-Go bag following close behind. The hot air freezes. The scent of sweat deafens. My tongue tastes like 4am static. The world telescopes into this one single event.

The rescue takes only about 15 minutes, but it surely had to have been an eternity because in that time I feel my breasts round out, my thighs soften, and my hips fill out; but most of all, my mind expands and the world stands in front of me, a plaything for me with my cane.

Fortunately, the pupils pull both Bilkisu and Rika out of the well. The brave girl is dusty, a little bruised, but fine. Rika, though, looks in a bad way. Her tongue sticks out in the partial and crooked way of a dead animal at a meat market.

'Let's kill her now-now and cook cassava-leaf soup,' Bilkisu suggests.

'She's already dead,' a voice counters. 'Eating dead meat is wrong, haram.'

'Whoever heard of cassava-leaf soup without creatures?' Bilkisu replies.

Ms Mercy and Sister Broderick jump into the row, trying to shove us back into our white-and-blue uniforms, but they can no longer contain us, define us. The rescue experience has purged us of the toxins of dogma and dirtied us with ruby-red laterite. So we ignore the teachers. Soon after, they slink down the slope, back, I suppose, to fill the walls of their empty classrooms with more cave drawings and hieroglyphics.

Meanwhile, the pupils break into mission groups. Some go to the garden and harvest the cassava leaves; others scour the grounds for firewood; still others go to their homes and to the compound of the diocese to borrow, and, if necessary, 'demand' rice, pepper, onions, palm oil, groundnut paste, beans and fish. Some set out to get the spoons and bowls with which to cook, serve and eat. The final group, led by small, brave Bilkisu, prepare to cut, kill and skin Rika.

'No fauna, no flora,' Bilkisu chants, and repeats a few times before others catch on. Then, a low chant in the background and the Ghana-Must-Go bag as the mat, they kill and skin Rika, wrap up the offal in the mat and throw it away in the garbage pile of desks and chairs.

By late afternoon, just before sunset, the rice is cooked. The soup pot puffs up the last few bubbles of water to leave the pasty green-brown mix of cassava leaves and palm oil. Many of the girls who were part of the afternoon's rescue have left, called home by duty, responsibility, fear and perhaps revulsion. But a hardcore group of 20 remains. We eat and chant again and again: 'No fauna, no flora.'

∗∗∗

Ajuah Danjuma stopped talking, stood up from the table, pushed the envelope all the way across to Stella, but kept her pointer finger on it until the daughter had completed the double take of first looking at the envelope and then at her mother. Ajuah Danjuma rolled her neck and back, stretching out the stiffness, the arthritic pain really, from both. Then, without a word, she walked into her bedroom and closed the door. This time Stella heard no noises coming from behind the termite-riven partition. The daughter opened the envelope and pulled out a legal-size paper with an embossed logo and read:

Holy Angels Secondary School

Tuesday, 17 June 1997

Dear Mrs Danjuma,
We take the academic and moral education of our girls seriously. Your daughter Ajuah has displayed cruelty to animals and a disdain of authority. We will not sit idly by and see our children, girls in particular, devolve into unruly, uninhibited women. Therefore, we the staff members of this school have unanimously decided that, as is within our rights, we must revoke Ajuah Danjuma's enrolment for actions unbecoming of the good name and mission of the school, its church and diocese. This means Ajuah cannot ever claim to have been a student of this school. As a result of this revocation, her college-entrance exam results will be voided, per our admissions and code of conduct regulations.

***

Stella stopped reading, sighed, laid her head onto the table and pressed her right ear into the wood, thinking, then imagining her mother bouncing on the surface of the moon. From somewhere, perhaps from the moon, from within the wood, from behind the termite-riven partition, or even from the pockmarked well she had conjured in her mind, she heard the forlorn maa maa of a goat.

Pede Hollist (Sierra Leone) was shortlisted in 2013 for his story 'Foreign Aid' and is an associate professor of English at the University of Tampa, Florida. His first novel, *So the Path Does not Die*, published in 2012 by Langaa Press, Cameroon, and reprinted in 2014 by Jacaranda Books Arts and Music Ltd of the UK, was named the African Literature Association's 2013 creative writing book of the year. 'Resettlement' (*Matatu* 41-12), 'Back Home Abroad' (anthologized in *The Price and Other Stories from Sierra Leone*), and 'Going to America' (Ìrìnkèrindò: *A Journal of African Migration*) are three other stories that have been well received.

Princess Sailendra of Malindi

Kiprop Kimutai

The sea gives me a hibiscus. The sea places it before my feet, on the sand where I last saw my brother, then hastily retreats. I lift the hibiscus and place it on my chest. The soft petals have lost their scent. Still, I close my eyes and press it in. I hear my brother's deep voice calling me and suddenly I turn into a princess, Princess Sailendra of Malindi. I see myself standing on the edge of a rocky promontory, dressed in a blue chiffon veil that flutters in the wind as servants shield my face from the sun with a parasol. I look far into the ocean, waiting for Chinese junks carrying caskets of my perfume, to appear. As I press in the hibiscus I also feel my breasts: those tough lumps, like kaangumu sold by women in buibui in the narrow Malindi streets; I feel them swell with the magnificence of temples, bursting out of a jungle canopy. I relax my shoulders. My sunken, concave shape reverses.

But this rude boy, in boxer shorts, carrying a ball and running to his friends, knocks me over. I fall hard on the sand, swallowing and breathing it in. I cough and gasp. But on a Saturday, when Malindi beach is full of noisy people, you might as well get on all your fours and bark like a dog as no-one will turn to look. Everyone is unkind. Unlike the sea, they never see. They never give out hibiscus flowers. Never to me at least.

But it doesn't matter. One day they will all know that I am

Princess Sailendra of Malindi. They will know that the palace on that rocky ledge at the corner of the beach is mine and that it is made out of coral and red marble. They will know that my bedroom, inside the palace, is scented with jasmine and lit with rose-scented candles, and that the window faces the east so that I can be woken up by the sun. They will know that in the morning, I only have to snap my fingers and all these male servants, with rippling muscles and washboard abs, will carry me to my bathroom and lay me in sudsy water; they will feed me grapes as they rub honey all over my body. One day I will just close my eyes and march Hitler-style across the beach and they will part the way for me. They will say, 'kwisha leo, Sailendra is among us,' and faint on the shore. Afterwards, they will scoop my footprints, pour the sand into glass jars and display it in their living rooms. One day.

I stand and shake sand out of my two-year-old wig, stolen, for no-one allows me in boutiques any more. I look around. There are too many people scurrying and scrambling all about. Some women have forced themselves into bikinis that are too small and are struggling to find space to lie on the beach. They think they look so cool, like Halle Berry. If I had a giant can of Doom, I would spray all of them dead and shove off their corpses into the sea to be eaten by fish. But as I walk on – passing children eager for camel rides; young men, who talk in deep hushed voices as they check out a girl; women who walk freely through the air, as if it is not the viscous gel that always holds me back – I decide to extend them mercy. But only if one of them turns to look at me. If just one turns and says: 'Ngai Lydia, I haven't seen you in so many days. Usipotee hivyo! We have to catch up. Let us have a soda.'

Then I see him all alone, sitting on a log of wood, staring at the sea. His skin is grey and patches of hair on his mullet-shaped head seem to be falling off. I drag my feet through the sand, afraid to lift them. I turn my head this way and that as

I smile. The children I meet stop playing football and stare at me, their faces frozen. I walk faster to the edge of the log and sit down abruptly. I look at the sea. She too, seems curious. She has slowed down her crashing waves. I lean over to him and begin.

'Do you know I am a princess? That is my palace atop that hill. My father has dhows bearing my name, that sail all the way to India, to bring back turmeric and cinnamon.'

He does not turn. I feel weird. I turn away and lower my head. I try to draw a circle on the sand with my foot but only manage a zigzag line. For a moment, all is quiet as if we are all alone, shielded from the rest of the people by an invisible wall that snuffs out sound. I look at him again, turning my head so slowly for I suddenly feel shy. He becomes stiff as if turning into wood. I stretch my hand and poke his shoulder. The skin sinks in and stays, like a rotten mango. I get angry and shove him hard. That is when he turns, slowly like a settling turnstile. He struggles to open his eyes. A blue syringe dangles from a vein in his upper arm. I drop the hibiscus the sea gave me and reach out with my hands.

He grasps my neck. His fingers are strong and lizard-rough. They sink into my neck flesh and find tender bones not meant to be touched. I turn my head to the side, my tongue out. I feel like a decapitated chicken head that cooks at the palace would throw at the grass to be devoured by ants. Then his eyes turn soft. He parts his lower lip, revealing teeth dissolving into brown mush. He trembles. The shiver runs down his shoulders to his hands and his fingers tap-dance on my neck. He finally lets go of my neck and sits there looking sorry. Only for a moment though, for he raises up his head and purses his lips. It turns him imperial; gives him the look of a pharaoh's son whose statue has been commissioned for a temple.

'Sawa, do you want me to give it to you?' I shout at him.

It's the usual exchange. We only have to hide in the sea. I only have to close my eyes when he enters me and urge him to go faster so as to finish quickly, praying all the time that the tall men in blue shorts and high boots who patrol the beach will not give chase. So I spring up and run to the sea. The sand tries to hold me back by sucking in my legs. I push through into the water. I lift up my skirt and call out to him.

'Si you come for it au!'

I close my eyes and wait for his footfalls. I wait for the air to cloy with the scent of his illicit desires. I wait for his ribs to squash my hard breasts. I wait for the sea to growl like a dog and for that jellyfish sensation of him inside me. All I will think of, as he thrusts into me, is the crown I used to wear. I will wonder if the servants still remember to wipe its sets of emerald and amethyst stones with vinegar. But when I open an eye to look, there he is, still sitting on a log of wood.

'Shoga wewe,' I shout. 'You cannot do it with a woman. Can you even get it up?'

His impassiveness disturbs me and I run back to him.

'Sasa you will give me this dawa for free. Aki I really want it.'

Like pebbles thrown to a pond, his cheeks dimple.

'My name is Lone Voice in the Desert,' he says, in a voice that sends a feeling of cold scales up my back. He sneers. 'Have you found Jesus?'

I wonder who Jesus is and why he is lost in the first place. Then I remember Jesus, the man in a dress, who whipped bankers at Barclays for changing currencies on a Sunday. As I remember, Lone Voice in the Desert lifts a wilted finger and places it on the side of my head. He raises the other hand and flips his fingers through the air, opening pages of a book only he can see. He speaks.

'Come, all of you who are thirsty, come to the waters; and you who have no money, come, buy and eat! Come, buy wine and milk without money and without cost. Why spend money on that which is not bread and your labour on what does not satisfy? Listen, listen to me and eat what is good, and you will delight in the richest of fare.'

My intestines melt then. They drip, hot as candle wax, into my groin. I bend and support myself on my knees. He takes down his hands and holds them before me, palms up and blows.

'Receive,' he shouts.

I fall on the sand and thrash. Later, he tells me, a demon in the shape of a barking seal forced itself out of my mouth and waddled into the sea. Then adds that my sins, which were as red as blood, were now as white as snow.

✳✳✳

Listen:

I had a brother. He fed well on butter and sweetened sesame, swelling till he blubbered like a walrus on the floor. Mum had him take charge of our steed to turn him lean. In time, strong muscles forced out of his shoulders. We would hear his hands ripple in the air as he marched outside, an eager man. His name was Samadra. That is all I have now. Just that name. If you hear me mutter it in the morning, when fishermen are drawing in their nets after a night spent at sea, or shouting it when it rains, just understand.

'Samadra ptooh! That boy is the devil,' said mum, when she was no longer a queen in flowing robes and a high neck, but a woman on a creaking bed, unable to sit up and wipe her nose, a woman whose eyes I had to wipe with a warm, wet cloth each morning.

'Why?' I asked, pressing my bare feet on the earthen floor. I sat on the edge of the bed next to the door, for the cold wind to reach me first and turn warm.

'It is him who threw us into this pit of desperation,' she said. 'A boy with too much greed! Greed all the way up to his neck. Mtoto mtundu sana huyo. Can you imagine a son of mine, meeting with Italians at night? Giving my land away! And have I seen a single coin for that transaction, Lydia? Have I?'

Still I saw Samadra as a benevolent god who performed miracles, who passed through impenetrable walls to offer grace. When mum needed the red pills, found far away in Mombasa, at that pharmacy next to the police station, with grids on the window that sealed the pharmacist like a caged bird, my brother went and got them without paying a single coin. And he got them before six, for mum had to take the pills before six. When mum turned her head on the pillow, eyes open but not seeing, letting out a groan like an echo from a cave, Samadra looked upon the world he created and ordered it to bring forth pineapples and oranges; even the precious sultanas which I would hold to mum's mouth for her to suck on and pacify the demons that tortured her.

I once followed my brother outside one night, when stars sprinkled golden dust on the ocean and the grass. It was hard following Samadra, though. He moved too quickly and disappeared in a coconut grove ahead. For a moment all that was left was his voice, loud and forceful like a crashing wave, then that too quietened. I walked on, though, up a dirt path winding like a thin ribbon. At the top was my palace, surrounded by a concrete fence which was spiked at the top with broken glass. There were noises inside – laughter, clicking glasses, some soft music. I sat on my haunches and stared. A man came outside, an old white man with a greying beard and a belly that settled gourd-like around his waist. He had a cigarette in his hand. I wondered whether he was the Italian.

'Princess,' he said, ever so softly, speaking only to me. 'You are so beautiful.'

I smiled and trailed my eyes to his shorts. They hung awkwardly under his belly, as if he was wearing an immense block of wood. He moved closer and I noticed how tall he was. He was slouching. I imagined him talking to Samadra, hands in his pockets, nodding at intervals. I imagined papers being signed. The exchange of notes. Fresh, clean, unfolded notes. Straight from Barclays.

He tottered closer.

'Why are you barefoot, Princess?' he asked. He puffed in deeply from his cigarette. When he blew out, the smoke filled my lungs with a pang. 'I can give you all the shoes you want.'

He tapped his swollen pocket, then tapped his fly. He leant his head to the side and winked. I slept with him that night. At breakfast, he fed me croissants and hot chocolate, then handed me a thousand shillings and told me to be on my way for his friends were coming. I kept the note folded in my hand for I meant to throw it away. Later at home, though, I slipped it into the folds of my dress. From then I would walk without lifting my legs, afraid that guilt would leak from the soles of my feet and stain the earthen floor, afraid that mum would look at me with cold, stern eyes.

When she died we lost that single room too. I moved to the beach with Samadra and his friends. On the sand, Samadra turned even more handsome, with that sturdy, thickset physique that white women loved. They waved at him as they sunbathed and he would walk and kneel beside them. Later they would walk together back to hotels that security guards forbade me to enter. He would bring me food afterwards. One day, a whole waffle smeared with blueberry syrup. He would lift my chin with a finger and tell me that I was the only princess he had left in the world.

One night he shook too much and I gave him the one-thousand-shilling note. I knew he needed dawa. He unfolded the note and stretched it on his palm and from it, Kenyatta, the first president and a freedom fighter, stared at me sternly. Samadra walked away then, trailing his feet on the wet sand. I kept looking at him till he faded with the darkness. I wanted to call out to him so that he could turn and shout back, 'Take care Princess,' but all the while the pit of my stomach felt heavy as if I had swallowed a stone and I could not talk. I never saw him again. In the morning, I tried following his footsteps on the sand, but the sea had washed them away.

***

I am sitting with Lone Voice in the Desert inside his church made out of twigs. I ask why his church building is so small that only two people can squeeze in at a time and he tells me what Jesus said, that when two or three are gathered in His name, there He will be, among them.

I begin telling him that I am Princess Sailendra of Malindi. I tell him about the rare history books with Parisian binding at the palace library, how I would lie on my back on the Persian carpet, reading about the Straits of Malacca. But I cannot finish this story with him. He is a hard man who turns his gaze far from you to something more fascinating. I stop and wrinkle my forehead instead. I sink my knees deeper into the sand till the sharp grains graze my skin.

Lone Voice in the Desert looks down abruptly, licking his lips.

'You are Mary Magdalene. You washed Jesus's feet with your hair.'

I grasp my stolen wig and hold it firmly on my head, afraid it will fall off and reveal that my hair is short, and I so desperately want to be Mary Magdalene. Lone Voice in the Desert smiles and leans his hands on the sand. He has a nice face, a shapely nose like the statues of Nubian kings in the Sudan desert I would see in books, those who built kingdoms in Kush and Meroe. But then his face turns unclear, as if suddenly hiding behind a veil of fog.

'I know where your brother is,' he says.

That slaps my face. I tremble. He lifts his hand and points out to the sea.

'He is far out there. In an island called Eden. He lives in a garden of apples with a sly snake. He is not afraid of his nakedness and walks on streets of gold. His name is written in the Book of Life.'

'Do you see him now?' I ask.

He leans back on the sand and closes his eyes.

'Verily I say unto you, Lydia. If you had faith even as small as a mustard seed, you could say to this coconut tree, "May you be uprooted and thrown into the sea," and it would obey you!'

I lie beside him. I trail my fingers down his shoulder. I draw the salt road on the landscape of his arm with my fingernail. I turn him into a Berber trader, trudging on a camel across a sand dune, brewing hot coffee at night in a windy oasis.

Later, after we have slept, we melt dawa on a foil and hold our straws ready. I celebrate as I suck in. Narrow is the door to heaven. Peace shall come upon me once the cowardly, the unbelieving, the vile, those who do not see me, have been shut out from the banquet. Peace shall come once they have all been consigned to the fiery lake of burning sulphur. Lone Voice in the Desert and I shall remain, to freely drink from the Water of Life. I hold my breath as the hot fumes burn my throat.

When I finally breathe out, I look at the sea and she is now a tall, regal woman draped in a white robe. She is carrying Samadra on her arm. My brother is sucking on her nipple.

'You are of the world,' says the sea. 'No salvation comes without the shedding of blood.'

'I am going to sacrifice you,' I turn to tell Lone Voice in the Desert. But I see only his eyes. His eyes are huge and far away, as if he has suddenly sunk deep inside a well.

He laughs and his face reveals.

'You are going to sacrifice me, Lydia.'

We both laugh. As I stab him, we laugh out even more. Our laughter turns into sheep that skitter and run. He falls and I lie on top of him. As his blood flows out, it sings my mother's favourite Taarab song, 'Utalijua Jiji' by Afua Sulemani. I try to sing along but I turn to blood and lose my throat. I drip away. I join the sea. We are one now. I want to see mum.

Timothy Kiprop Kimutai is 30 years old. He was the second runner-up for the Kwani? Manuscript Project and his book *The Water*

Spirits will soon be published. Aside from the 2015 Caine Prize Workshop, he has participated in Chimamanda Ngozi Adichie's Farafina Workshop in Lagos, as well as a Granta-sponsored workshop in Nairobi facilitated by Ellah Allfrey and two young British authors, Nadifa Mohamed and Adam Foulds. He is an editor with Jalada Africa and has been able to successfully publish three anthologies so far based around insanity, sex and afro-futures. He believes that if he had been born in Salinas, California, he would have turned out as a reincarnation of John Steinbeck.

Blood Match

Jonathan Mbuna

'Madam Hilda, we have finally got to the bottom of the matter.' Doctor Masamba Asiyana took a deep breath, looked at the results in his hands and proceeded, 'You have kidney failure and...'

He could not continue, as he was interrupted by Osman, Hilda's husband, who stood up, shell shocked, stared at his wife and banged his hands on the chair. Although it was late afternoon in the winter season, sweat trickled down Osman's face.

Hilda herself dropped her hands, as tears rolled down her cheeks. For quite some time she had complained of loss of appetite, body weakness and breathing problems. At first doctors had suspected tuberculosis, then it had gone on to AIDS, leukaemia, and then it was blood tests, urine tests and scans all to no avail. In about nine months, Hilda's body started wearing out. The beautiful, black, slim, dimpled 38-year-old lady, who, when smiling with her milky white teeth, would make some priests forget their celibacy vows, started looking like an old, cragged woman of 79. She was pale and frail.

'Oh no, doctor! Why? She is too young,' Osman whined.

'Let me explain. In medical practice, especially in this part of the world, kidney failure is not something that can be detected at an early stage. In fact we should thank God that we have detected it at this stage. I know you are shocked but we have to act fast. Looking at the level of progression of the kidney failure, there are two options. The first one is dialysis which I would not recommend in her case. The second option is a kidney transplant...'

'What? Kidney transplant?' Osman screamed.

The doctor went over the process, explaining to them in lay language what a kidney transplant mean. He did not dwell on any risks. He explained the necessary conditions and tests required and suggested specialist hospitals outside the country: Apollo hospital in Chennai, AIMS in Delhi, Christian Medical College in Ludhiana and all other private hospitals in South Africa...

When Osman drove home that afternoon, cats, dogs and lizards knew that there was something wrong somewhere. Normally Osman hooted mildly when summoning the guard to open the gate. That day the hooting was not only loud and annoying, but defiant as well. Immediately the gate opened, he drove recklessly towards the carport.

Zakeyu, the house servant, quickly rushed to welcome them. He bowed to the bwana and extended a smile but Osman, who was speaking on the phone in a loud and harsh tone, neither looked at him nor showed any sign of recognizing Zakeyu's presence. He headed to the main entrance of the house. Zakeyu went to the front passenger's seat and helped his madam open the door. Of late, Zakeyu had noted that his madam was becoming frail and looked like a shadow of herself.

'A-zakeyu, take some things from the back seat!'

'Thanks, madam,' he bowed, went to the back seat and quickly took the plastic bag and Osman's briefcase. Hilda, who was in pain, had not yet disembarked from the car.

'Madam, what else can I do?' Zakeyu said, attempting to kneel while balancing the plastic bag and the briefcase in his hands.

'No! No! No! A-zakeyu, I have told you time without number you don't kneel when you are carrying things! Aaaa!' Hilda held Zakeyu's right hand and slowly headed for the house entrance.

'Madam, it seems like the weather eeee... the weather is hostile today,' Zakeyu said while trailing behind Hilda. He was referring to the bwana, who seemed hostile that day.

'A-zakeyu, drop the weather thing. What have you prepared for us this afternoon?' Hilda said as she clapped her hands, seemingly avoiding Zakeyu's remarks. There was a good relationship between Zakeyu and Hilda. Every time Osman was not in a good mood, Hilda would warn all the workers, especially Zakeyu, that the weather was not good.

That evening Hilda slept early because of the tranquillizers the doctor had prescribed but sleep eluded Osman. Immediately after being told that his wife required a kidney transplant, he called his parents in the village some 400 kilometres away. Their response was, to say the least, cold. He also called Hilda's brother, who seemed not to understand the gravity of the matter.

At 44 years old and working as Deputy Director in an energy and mining company, Osman had a knack for solving problems. He had graduated with distinction from university when Hilda was in her first year. He quickly went for his Masters Degree, where he again excelled. In every department that he was assigned, Osman had proved to be a problem solver but that evening he was clueless on what to do about his wife's health. The doctor had made it clear that time was of the essence and he had told him what was required. The doctor fell short of saying something but simply advised him to visit the hospital once again so that they could have a 'man to man' discussion.

As for Hilda, the doctor's revelation that day devastated her. She called several of her relatives and friends. All of them simply offered the sympathetic 'get well soon' message. None of them said anything beyond that. Some came the following day to see how she was, wearing sympathetic looks, but quickly went their way without committing to anything.

'Madam, you said if I want to go back to school I should tell you. Yesterday one of my friends told me that there is a night school some three kilometres...' Zakeyu said.

'Ummm! A-zakeyu, can we discuss that some other time?'

'Oho! But schools open next week, Madam...'

'I know. Let us discuss that later on, or, better still, when I am not around you can talk to your bwana.'

'Umm, Bwana? Maybe you should talk to Bwana on my behalf. Another thing, Madam, I intended to see my friends this afternoon...'

'Oh sorry, I had forgotten. Today we have a function. Our relatives are coming for a family get-together. So although you normally work half days on Saturday, today we will need you for the full day. Can you visit your friend tomorrow?'

'The visit can wait madam. I will go next week.'

'Thank you, A-zakeyu.'

There was more in that thank you than what Zakeyu could read. To Hilda, Zakeyu never complained as the other workers did, especially when asked to work at odd hours. Zakeyu, who was 24, slim, dark, tall and well built, had worked with the couple for three years. Unlike other house servants, Zakeyu was humble, hardworking and honest. He asked where he was not clear and ever since Hilda had employed him, not even a kitchen spoon had gone missing from the house. While Hilda was grateful to her elder sister for finding a house servant of Zakeyu's calibre, Zakeyu too was grateful to Hilda, whom he fondly called 'the madam'. The madam never shouted at him in public and was humane. Unlike the bwana who sometimes, after having one too many, would shout some obscenities at the workers, Hilda was quiet. And, out of the three workers in the house, the two guards and the house servant, Hilda was fondest of Zakeyu.

About 15 people came that day and they included Osman's siblings and uncles. Hilda's relatives were also present and they were mainly her siblings. Osman informed them about the purpose of the meeting. Hilda was in urgent need of a kidney donor. The moment the subject was raised, there was a deafening silence. It was only after some three or so minutes that Osman's uncle cleared his throat and spoke.

'Hilda has relatives. What are our in-laws saying?'

Hilda's brother had been waiting for that opportunity and stood up, pointing challengingly at Osman. 'What has the husband here done?'

Osman's uncle looked at Hilda's brother with disdain and snapped his fingers, 'Osman, tell them.'

'I went to the hospital three days ago to find out if I can donate the kidney myself. The doctor thinks I can't.'

Hilda looked at Osman, surprised. She had asked the past two days where her husband had been after noticing that he came home late, downcast and not giving a satisfactory response. Her suspicions heightened after noting that Osman refused to eat dinner and could not even watch his favourite Spanish football team, which was playing that evening. He just proceeded to the bedroom where he lay, tossing and turning.

'The doctor thinks or knows?' asked Melinda, Hilda's sister. She was a community nurse.

'Well, the doctor said I cannot donate a kidney and he gave two reasons. The main reason is that my blood group and that of my wife are not compatible. She is blood group B negative and I am A positive.'

'What is the other reason? I too work in the hospital and if the doctor told you that there are two reasons, you should tell us the other reason because it is important as well.'

'Well, the other reason is not very important to this meeting.'

'People can't assist you if you can't let them know what the doctor said,' Melinda retorted. It was clear that Osman had had to fine-tune the version he had told his uncle. He feared that Melinda, who had friends at the hospital, knew something. Unbeknown to him, Melinda was just pushing Osman to the wall but she had nothing on him.

'Well, since you insist. The other reason is that the doctor asked me about my drinking and smoking habits. And, as you know, I sometimes drink and he thought I could not be a donor as I would be risking my own health. But believe you me, that was not the major problem...'

'Oho...' Osman's uncle said in disgust, noting that his nephew had somehow been mean with the truth, especially the smoking and drinking issue. The uncle had for quite some time advised Osman against smoking and drinking alcohol. He turned the meeting into a sermon of advising the young ones on 'How not to kill your partner with smoking and drinking'.

Hilda's relatives joined in the fray and threw tantrums at Osman. Osman had been warned by the doctor that he was not an authority on who could be a kidney donor. He recalled the words of the doctor: 'Time is not on our side and if you can't handle this issue properly, bring your people here and I will talk to them. People will blame you if nothing is done.'

Melinda had pushed him against the wall and his explanation had scared people – the very thing the doctor had warned him about.

'Well, let us not just argue for the sake of arguing. This is a matter of life and death and all of us should be concerned. You have heard from Osman that the doctors said preferably the kidney donor should be Hilda's relative because kidney transplant is delicate and we need a cross match,' Osman's brother said diplomatically, trying to minimize people's thoughtlessness.

'We know that but we also have heard of cases in this same country where somebody not necessarily a relative can donate a kidney,' Melinda reasoned. 'The one who donated the kidney to the Speaker of Parliament – was she a relative? Hilda is Osman's wife and we are only her relatives. In the worst-case scenario, hospitals allow kidney swaps. He should provide a kidney or, better still, you the relatives and not us.

Is it not your Imam who, when officiating this marriage that day, said the two are one?'

It was clear the feud, which had sprung up over five years ago when the two were planning to marry, had not died down. If anything it had been in a coma but had now been resurrected. Hilda came from the affluent south and had been raised in a family with a strong Christian background. Osman was from a humble family from the north of strong Islamic faith. Osman's relatives had protested that their son should not consort with a daughter from a different religion and region. Hilda's relatives had hit back that their daughter, beautiful and coming from a wealthy family, would not fit with Osman's poor family. Five years into the marriage, there was nothing to unite these two families and, now that Hilda required surgery and a kidney donation, the feud once again reared its ugly head.

It was clear that, instead of the meeting generating a solution, it was unearthing old scars. Even the house servants, who had been warned to stay outside hearing distance, were getting a feeling that there was tension. When the meeting ended, nothing concrete had been agreed on.

In the subsequent week, two of Hilda's relatives who had volunteered to be donors were turned back because their kidneys were not compatible. Time was running out. As for Osman's relatives, some were hesitant to come forward since the uncle had blown the issue out of proportion. The other reason behind their reluctance was that Osman and Hilda did not have a child. Three weeks had passed since the doctor had advised Osman and Hilda about the kidney transplant. The hospital had already identified a counterpart hospital in India which had a 95-per-cent success rate in kidney transplants. All that was needed now was a donor.

Zakeyu had heard about the kidney-transplant issue in bits and pieces and had noticed a significant change in the house. What surprised him was that nobody seemed to be willing to donate the kidney. The bwana, who previously would come home late at night, had recently changed his lifestyle. He was usually home by sunset. It was the bwana driving the madam to and from work. Hilda was going to work though in pain because she had exhausted her leave days and the non-governmental organization she worked for as Finance Manager had made it clear that if she continued being absent from work in that financial year, her services would be terminated on medical grounds.

The health of his madam was a cause of great concern to Zakeyu and it was clear she was getting worse with each passing day. Should anything happen to her, then Zakeyu would be on his way out. The bwana had made it clear that he had been employed to help his wife.

Zakeyu was a school dropout because his mother was too poor to keep him in school. All his relatives were in school or, if they had dropped out of school, it was not because of lack of fees but by choice. His uncles had refused to bail his mother out. One thing that struck Zakeyu in his village was that all his relatives loved helping each other but, when it came to him, he was usually the odd one out. Was it because his father died in infancy, as he had been told? He had neither sister nor brother, only cousins, nephews and nieces. He could smile at his uncles and aunts but they were never warm. It was only his mother who was loving and caring.

Once out of school, he started selling maize, potatoes and cassava at the trading centre close to his village. However, that line of business did not last long. He ended up broke during the year the country experienced drought. A youth with nothing else to do, he became an active member of the village youth organization which was championing HIV prevention. It was during one of those village campaigns that he met Hilda's sister, Melinda, who was on the HIV prevention campaign. Melinda had been a regular visitor to the village. She asked him if he would be interested in a job as a house boy and, as they say, the rest was history.

From the time he had been employed, he had slowly started working towards alleviating his family's poverty. The madam was kind and during every religious festival, like Christmas, Easter or Eid al Fitr, she would give Zakeyu groceries to send home or even give him extended holiday to visit his mother who was about 280 kilometres away. Zakeyu's mother would advise her son to be honest, noting the many gifts he was bringing home.

The following morning, Zakeyu stopped the couple as they were about to drive out so he could talk to them.

Osman was irritated but Hilda defended Zakeyu. 'Darling, cool down. Can't it wait till this evening, A-zakeyu?'

'No, madam, it's urgent!'

She signalled Zakeyu to say what he wanted but to make it fast. With an open heart, one knee going down, he said, 'Madam, you need a kidney – take mine.'

Hilda's heart sank and tears rolled down her cheeks. Osman, who was rushing to work, explained to Zakeyu that it was not that easy. As Osman drove Hilda to work, the words of Doctor Masamba haunted him: 'Time is not on our side and, if you can't handle this issue properly, people will blame you.' Though Osman had pretended to wear a brave face, inwardly he was shaking and breaking.

During lunch hour that day, Osman and Hilda took Zakeyu to the hospital just in case. Doctors took blood and tissue samples and checked his health status.

Later, it was revealed that Zakeyu's kidney was a perfect match. Since time had already been lost and Hilda was not getting any better, the family quickly organized travel documents. Osman had to process Zakeyu's passport, apply for a visa and get air tickets as Doctor Masamba finalized the link-up with the referral hospital.

Before leaving for India, Osman and Melinda escorted Zakeyu to his mother and his kinspeople to bid them farewell. Hilda was too weak to make the trip. The doctors

had advised her to take a rest. Zakeyu had briefed his
mother before the visit and she had given her blessing to
the kidney donation.

They found Zakeyu's mother, Nyamanda, beside the big
and ancient kachere tree. Nyamanda had had arguments
with her brothers and sisters over the issue, with some
relatives objecting, while others insisted that Osman should
pay Zakeyu handsomely since the procedure was risky.
Nyamanda found it odd that the same people who had
once castigated her, saying that she would bring curses to
the village because of the baby, were now at the forefront
demanding that Osman should compensate the family
handsomely for her son's kidney. It was her wisdom and that
of her younger sister which prevailed.

In India, the surgery was successful. The Indian doctors
were professional and at one time, in jest, asked Hilda the
relationship she had with Zakeyu, the kidney donor.

'I have done several transplants but the cross match
between you and the donor is amazing. Your recuperation
too has been fast. Is he a direct brother?'

Hilda could only afford a smile and simply said Zakeyu
was a relative. Hilda and Zakeyu flew back after two months.
Ideally Zakeyu should have come in earlier but, as somebody
who had not travelled before, it was expedient that he should
only come back after Hilda had fully recovered. Zakeyu was
fascinated with the high-tech hospital, which contrasted
sharply with hospitals in his country. Everything was
computerized and the services were excellent; there was
cleanliness, orderliness and no congestion. The hospital
looked to him like a hotel.

Within those two months, Hilda's health had changed and
she had regained her beauty. Those who had seen her before
going to India and then saw her after her return were amazed.
She had not only regained her soft and smooth body but she
looked younger, lovely and energetic. Hilda's workmates,

some of whom had written her off, were astonished at the wonders and advancements of modern medicine.

Osman, Hilda and this time some of their relatives arranged to visit Zakeyu's mother to thank her and inform them of their return. They went bearing gifts for the old woman, Nyamanda. Osman and Hilda had agreed that the best gift to give to the family was simply to adopt Zakeyu by sending him to school.

When they arrived at the village, they found a small party waiting for them. They had planned to spend at least part of the morning and afternoon at the village. The womenfolk formed their own gathering around the kachere tree. The men formed their own group around a big mango tree.

'I don't know how to thank you, mother. If not for your son's free offer, I don't know what would have happened to me. I was dying, mother...' Hilda started.

'Uumm! My daughter, everybody has a purpose in life. I have seen many rains and gone through lots of challenges in life. This is not something that can make me stand tall before you today. I have not had it easy in life and it has not been easy raising Zakeyu and getting him accepted,' Nyamanda said.

At that moment, Nyamanda, who was very light in complexion and short, unlike Zakeyu, confided in Hilda, Melinda and the other women her sad story, which most elderly villagers knew. She was about 79 now and had been twice married. She had married somebody within the village when she was 25 and after 10 years her husband had divorced her.

'My husband and his relatives divorced me on the grounds that I was barren. He went on to marry another woman and I only learnt after many years that with her too he never had the fruit of the womb.' She paused, shaking her head as Melinda looked intently at her sister Hilda.

'I stayed single for about seven years and then another man from the city came and married me. He was a market vendor. We were married for eight years before he too left me and eloped with a certain young woman. Because I was ashamed to come back home, I decided to stay in the same house he had left me in, close to the trading centre, and work as a market vendor. Five years after my husband left me, one morning I was going to my garden, which was close to the market. I heard the sound of a baby crying.'

Silence engulfed the women as Nyamanda stopped speaking and wiped away some tears.

'When I followed the cry, I discovered that it was a baby crying under a mango tree. I took the baby. In our days, girls, especially bar girls or schoolgirls, would at times dump babies in latrines or even in gardens. I took the baby home, nursed him, and then decided to bring him here. That baby is this Zakeyu, who you are hailing me today for being an excellent mother to. For 24 years, I have been with my child. I could not give him money but just gave him love. Of course, some people in this village did not accept him but today, look, they have come to celebrate with us and were even telling me to charge you for my son's kidney.'

While everybody was following with keen interest Nyamanda's story, something had pricked at Hilda's heart and she also remembered the doctor's question: 'I have done several transplants but the cross match between you and the donor is amazing...Is he a direct brother?'

'By the way, mother, precisely where was this? I mean, where did you find Zakeyu?' Hilda asked, shaking and sweating profusely.

'Oh yeah! It was some place in Makedzana trading centre.'

'What? Oh no!' Hilda screamed, much to the amazement of everybody, including the men who were seated some distance away. It was a hysterical cry. Melinda's heart thumped when her sister screamed and then she connected the word 'Makedzana'.

Hilda was a former student at Makedzana Girls Boarding School.

Jonathan Mbuna lives in Blantyre, Malawi, and is a management development consultant. He has written radio plays, short stories and one novel, *Meeting Point*. The manuscript of a second novel, *Pilgrims Together*, won the third prize in the 2013 Malawi Peer Gynt Award and will be published soon.

Coloured Rendition

Aisha Nelson

George told Aku Shika about all the things she had missed at school that day. The coming of the whites. And especially about the white lady, Marcia. When smiled, the whiteness of her teeth outshone Father's cassock. The brightness smudged into her flying golden strands of hair, and the colour of the arduous sun. This reminded George of the halos that always hung around the heads of the saints – especially the Virgin Mary.

The only images of saints which George and everyone else in Namɔale had ever seen were the hastily painted ones on the mud walls of the village's only chapel.

Then George told Aku about the special, plain, white sheets of paper. And the colour pencils.

The pupils had just returned from break and everything about the schoolwork dragged through a quagmire of lethargy. With no solid classroom walls, the breeze cooled down sweating little bodies. The teachers sat. They were busy doing nothing – or rather, something, which was counting the time to closing, their lot of ill-luck and woes for having been posted to Namɔale, of all places, to teach, of all things.

Then normalcy died. The bell rang again. Soon, there was Father, walking separately from the trio of two whites and the all-peacock headmistress. With their classrooms doubling as the school compound, the pupils quickly arranged themselves in tidy rows. Planted on the fringes of the assembly were suddenly alert teachers wielding ready canes.

Marcia and the headmistress addressed the pupils in turn, the headmistress rashly translating everything Marcia said. The need for the translation surprised Marcia and affected the cadence of her speech. Father decided not to be amused by what he deemed theatrics, not even when he could tell that the headmistress's translation was longer, compared to Marcia's actual words. As for disinterested Craig, he frantically tapped his feet and let his eyes stray and drink in the dusty bleakness of Namɔale. Maybe Craig would have looked with different eyes if he had known that the name of the village, Namɔale, meant – or rather, asked – the existential question, 'Who knows?'

Craig's irritation scratched a part of Father's bitter impatience and his pet pride, the pride in treating one's own self with dignity. Not bothering to clear traces of these from his voice, but taking care to adjust his clerical collar, Father intervened: 'Mr Craig and Madam Marcia, welcome. Ours is a country with different peoples, with different languages. The medium of instruction for the lower primary school years is the mother tongue. At this level, the English language is just one of the subjects in the curriculum. It is impossible to exaggerate the myriad benefits of this policy. I say this so that you understand the necessity for translating your address, especially because of your kind of accent.'

After Father's explanation, the teachers clapped in a neat chorus. It was obvious to all that the pupils really needed the translation. Some of the teachers, who might not be so honest as to have admitted that they too needed the translation, exchanged winks and grins.

Marcia said many things about the purpose of their visit, but the pupils were happiest to know that the whites deemed them friends, and that they brought them gifts. Marcia was not sure the pupils heard her – or clearly enough. So she drew closer to the first friendly-looking pupil in the front row, George. 'How are you?' Before the boy could even answer, Marcia was tugging three of the white A4 sheets and three colour pencils from the arms of a bewildered Craig. She gave them to George.

'Thank you, Madam Marcia and Mr Craig,' was what George had meant to say but, in wonder at the paper and the colour pencils in particular, he accidentally dragged out Craig's name. He took the /-g/ away added a /-yon/. So '*Craig*' became '*Cra-a-a-a-y-yon*'. Quickly realizing his near-blasphemy, George covered his mouth with his hands. Much quicker, sharp whacks of the canes of two teachers rained on his skull. Not deterred by the cane wielders, those pupils around, and soon, almost all the pupils, were scrambling to have a look at the papers and colour pencils. The whacks rained again. They surprised Marcia as much as what became of the papers.

The headmistress feared that Marcia would give everything away too quickly, so she urged Craig to give her what was left of the packet of paper and colour pencils. She urged Father, too, to take part in the grand occasion that she considered the handing over of the gifts to be. Father hesitated. The headmistress turned her head in time to see a curious, fleeting look on Father's face. The look was ripe with a queer mixture of resentment and sympathy for the headmistress's lack of pride. If she had known what the look meant, she would not have eagerly urged Father to receive the stationery on behalf of the school.

Marcia was not so sure she understood what Father's look meant. More out of courtesy than spite, she offered Father the only gift she had left, a pencil which was black – barrel, pigment and all. Father played along. With a crisp 'Thank you, Madam', he took the pencil. Marcia sealed the drama with a broader contrived smirk.

Later, the plan was that class teachers who thought any of their pupils artistic would report to the headmistress, who would, in turn, write a note for the said pupil to send to the Father's rectory for an A4 sheet and a colour pencil. The chosen pupils were to submit their drawings at the headmistress's office, a rickety shed that would have long ago collapsed in despair of more things than age, had it not been propped against a gnarled guava tree.

***

Months before, when Craig and Marcia had been doing their online orientation, the pupils from a school at Jade Luxurious Estates had sounded smart. Now, Marcia and Craig wondered if Namɔale and that *Something International* School were in the same country.

However, the two did not feel duped. Marcia and Craig felt pity – not exactly simple but certainly raw – for Namɔale. They were two teenage white lovers on a sham student exchange programme somewhere in the middle of Africa – a white boy and girl who were out to save the world, by just scouting for younger African boys and girls who had talent enough to paint their worldview.

***

Shouting her surprise at seeing Father, Awo Fio emerged from her room. Aku Shika was pointing at and explaining something in the textbook to George. On seeing the children, Father's mouth opened. Awo Fio explained to Father how, most times when he sent Aku Shika over, she helped her son with his homework. This surprised Father even more.

'But they are in the same class.' Father added, 'and she was not even at school today.'

'Oh, Father. And how is that strange?' Awo Fio gently rebuked. 'Everyone who visits you so often at the rectory must be intelligent.'

Father shrugged.

'And, what's more, you two are related. You are her uncle,' Awo Fio added.

Father smiled.

'Ever wondered why I seek out excuses to send my son to

the rectory?' Awo Fio asked.

'Now I know, I think. And why do you often give me extra bottles of the corn drink and sometimes even refuse to let me pay at all?'

'You would not like to know the reason for that. Not if I were to tell you. Especially because you are a Father,' she whispered, with a sly smile dancing at the ends of her lips.

✳✳✳

George was praying that he had one of those sheets of paper. Aku got up and ran. Father's eyes followed her, but she disappeared beyond the rounded edge of one of Awo Fio's huts. Shortly after, Aku returned from behind the hut with a crumpled and slightly dirty version of the paper. George was still praying. Aku roughly tapped him. George smiled his surprise.

He asked, 'Where did you get this?'

'It's a secret,' she mumbled.

Then she whispered something into his ears. His smile grew broad and curious. Aku tore the paper into two. She gave George one half. George wished he had the whole, real paper, and a gold colour pencil. With a rugged stub of some colour pencil, Aku started to copy a picture from his textbook.

It was the picture of a bright-eyed, dirty-nosed boy with a halo bob of shiny jet-black kinky hair. Grains of moist earth graced the peak of his nose. Beneath his nostrils was something that glowed with eagerness, something far from a film of mucus. His ears, like an afterthought, jutted out of his head. The boy was basking in sun, dew and fresh green.

Aku did not get to finish the drawing. Yet, in her mind, it was already done.

✳✳✳

Father made ready to leave Awo Fio's house. His eyes could

not miss the basket – containing the bottles of fresh corn drink – beside Awo Fio's soot-coated kitchen shed.

The bottles were the most divine things in the whole of Awo Fio's compound. Originally, they used to contain communion wine. The sight of the bottles nagged Father with that part of the scriptures about putting new wine into old wineskins. The thought of what he made out of the contents of those bottles was far from divine. This made him uncomfortable, but only secretly.

Father could surely use some alcohol, as a Christian and even as a priest, but he carefully waited for days in order for the sweet corn drink to ferment, until it acquired the character of alcohol, to sting and to scour all at once. Again, he convinced himself that whoever admonished us in the scriptures to not be drunk with wine but to be filled with the Holy Spirit, did not mean that to be taken literally.

Awo Fio would not listen whenever he asked her not to fill the bottles to the brim, since the now-fermented drink naturally spilled immediately the bottle was uncorked. Neither would she refrain from giving him more than his money's worth of corn drink – and sometimes refusing to take any money at all.

Despite all this, Father always pitied Awo Fio because her husband had died a drunk.

❋❋❋

George has always been the pride of Little Mother, Awo Fio. She calls him mibləfonyo, 'my white one'. The first time George had seen Marcia and Craig, proper white people, he could not tell if what his mother has been calling him was an insult, a hollow appellation or a mere wish. Yet he was sure that whether it was for good or otherwise, it was one long lonely course he would have to chart in order to become, to remain white…

❋❋❋

Father was on his way out when George too came to the rectory. The boy had a note from the headmistress, and two bottles of corn drink and some foodstuff from his mother. Before he finally left, Father gave the boy a few sheets of the A4 paper and a yellow colour pencil.

Hidden under the foodstuff in the basket was that textbook. Both George and Aku knew that this was the only way she could have had the textbook, in order to finish the drawing she had started on the day she had missed school and the visit. Both children were not sure if Awo Fio would have allowed George to bring the textbook along with him to the rectory. For Awo Fio jealously guarded everything – especially things that went into the making of her son, blɔfonyo. This textbook was one of those things.

George told Aku about how he too had been chosen to draw for the visitors. He told her how he would rather draw the white lady, than a picture of some 'bush' boy in some African primary school textbook. At the thought of this, Aku simply smiled. The thought and the smile melted and mixed. The mixture dripped into the beginning of a reverie.

Before long, Aku had stepped back into reality from her reverie and was telling George about how Father recently discovered one of the secrets that she had always been hiding in her panty.

'Really?' squealed George.

'Really!' said Aku, with glee.

Then Aku told George about her change of mind. She would not need the textbook any more. Maybe the girl was so naïve that she believed she could finish her rendition of the picture just by using her own imagination.

***

Father knew that Aku was timid whenever he was anywhere close to her. He never knew what it was about him that made the girl so fearful.

One late afternoon, Father noticed something unusual. Instead of playing and daydreaming, Aku was eager to finish her little chores in the rectory. She flitted about the house like a happy ghost. She hummed a song about how God takes pleasure in painting birds, flowers, and galaxies, and how He finds greater joy in the dainty curve of a child's smile. Maybe it was because she could not forget about her uncompleted rendition of the picture in George's textbook. When Aku finished the chores and Father asked if she would like for them to leave the rectory together, Aku was still not eager to return home. Perhaps this was because she had been finding it hard to sleep these past few nights, since George had told her about the visit; and night always seemed to fall quicker whenever she returned home from the rectory.

Soon, Father left for his usual house-to-house visits.

Aku ran into her favourite corner of the rectory, a large makeshift box which used to be the church's pulpit. She always had her now-threadbare straw mat laid at the base, inside of the pulpit. In the half-darkness, on the cold wood and straw floor, and with her back taut up, Aku let her hand slide down her abdomen, then under her panty. She felt for and fondled it, inside her panty. She closed her eyes and let her imagination run wild with lofty dreams of worlds trapped between many a slip, masterly strokes and shades, of pencil lead on scrap paper.

Suddenly, it was too late to even pull back her hand from her panty. For there was Father, towering above her. He must have arrived much earlier from the home visits than Aku had expected. Father's eyes sternly questioned where her hand was. Aku's hand was bulged into a fist, inside her panty. And even after she had withdrawn her hand from her panty, there still remained a fist, only this time, the new fist was smaller and rounder. Father stared on, at the fist.

Then he beckoned Aku to let him have a look at it. Reluctantly but fearfully, she gave him the dirty piece of crumpled scrap paper. He carefully straightened it. Father had a hard, long look at the paper. He smiled. He beckoned her to follow him. This time, for the first time, into his study.

Aku timidly mumbled, 'I-I-I took the paper from your waste bin.'

Father ignored her. Aku continued to explain.

Father groped for his lantern. He lit it when he found it. Then Father fumbled for something on top of the high bookshelf. He used the keys he had found on the shelf to open a special drawer. He pulled out a rectangular tin box from under the bottom of the pile of files in the drawer. Aku heard some objects make a guttural sound, as Father lifted the tin box.

Gently, Father began to bend his frame sideways. He beckoned Aku, with the index finger of his free hand, to draw nearer. Aku took no more than three short steps forward. He beckoned her again, this time with a pleading smile playing at the tips of his lips. Aku only came as far as the long end of the table. She shyly let one foot scratch up and down the other leg.

It was enough that Father's refreshingly human breath and the deliciously edgy smell of his freshly shaved moustache wafted around Aku's head. The minty scent of the talcum powder he was wearing, and the sensual smell of the fine beads of warm sweat on his temple made Aku dizzy. The boldness of his facial features and his strong steady gaze burrowed into her very soul. Aku's legs turned wobbly, but she did not fall yet. Then there was also this manly, yet divine aura about Father's very person, and the subtlest of his mannerisms and movements. These and many other indescribable things sent Aku's legs crumbling. To steady herself, Aku held on to the edge of her end of Father's desk.

Not wanting to spoil the solemnity of the moment with Aku's pettiness, he quickly reached across the table, picked her up, and set her on the table, right in front of him. He then sat on his chair, behind the table. He used the little key he had found under his cassock to open the box.

She watched. She waited.

Father lifted the lid. He dipped his hand into the tin box. Aku saw him gently shove some of the objects inside the box to one side of it. Father pulled out some yellowed sheets of paper from the tin box. He showed them to her. One after the other. On each piece of paper was a silhouette of one sama, an ideogram of the Ga people. He never stopped smiling. Aku was infected with Father's smile, and its warm radiance seeped deep into her being. As Father taught Aku the name of each sama, their smiles bloomed. And as he explained the moral wisdom behind each sama, their smiles unfurled and generously shed their fragrances.

Then he asked her to choose the one sama she liked best. Aku did, only she selected three: 'Alagba tɛ', 'Abii wo ni ahe nu' and 'Akpokpolonto'. Father gave her three fresh A4 sheets and his black colour pencil gift. He had already given Aku the yellowed sheets of the three samai she had chosen.

Then he said to her: 'I have always trusted you, and believed in you. So you need not show them to me when you finish drawing. Go ahead and give them to your headmistress.'

He did have reasons to trust Aku. For one thing, only God knows how many of his secrets that the girl had burdened herself with, without his so much as even asking her to. A secret like his being a notorious drunk, in private. And even with her fear of him, Father discerned that Aku simmered with a promise waiting to spill any time soon, given any outlet. And he was willing to wager that her quiet penchant for drawing would be one such outlet or, possibly, one of many.

* * *

Aku drew a long ladle with a tricky curve in the middle of its handle. Inside the bowl end of the ladle sat a bird's nest. The heads of two little birds shot out the nest. A smile shone in the eyes of one bird. The beak of the other bird was wide open, frozen in an inconsolable cry.

The headmistress had no difficulty choosing between Aku and George's drawings. She thought Aku's was original, masterly and silly. It was even sillier because she did not remember having given Aku a note to take to the rectory, unlike all the other pupils whose class teachers had recommended that they be given a chance to draw. Or did Aku think that just because her uncle was the one who kept the drawing materials, it made her an exception to the procedure?

'Nepotism. Breaking protocol. Corruption. All part of the things killing our country. Politicians. Priests. Everyone plays a part,' the headmistress chuckled.

The headmistress liked George's drawing far better. And she found its theme more relevant and universal, as compared to Aku's. Besides, the person in George's drawing looked very much like...

Marcia
wearing a golden halo
clothed in the blinding brightness of sun –
an instant beauty, a new deity.

Much later, when they came for the drawings, Marcia and Craig received only one. Marcia thought of the drawing as an honest compliment. Craig, on the other hand, did not mince words about how the drawing was the worst insult Marcia, or any other person from her part of the world, could have been given by a person from George's part. To Craig, even the 'inspiration' of George's drawing was blasphemous.

So, before he and Marcia left, Craig reiterated to the headmistress that what they had expected was a drawing, if not drawings, of anything that was 'actually not above the truth, the reality, of Namɔale, and of Africa'. So whoever did that 'best' drawing would have to do another drawing, a different one altogether. And more such drawings. For more times to come.

Marcia and Craig made arrangements to supply all the needed stationery. And more.

***

When George asked Aku for help with his new task, Aku told him he could draw her rendition of the picture that she had copied from his textbook.

'Was that not what you submitted?' asked George. 'And... and... it was not even selected by the...'

'No. I kept that drawing for myself. Together with another copy of the drawing I actually submitted.'

'There was another drawing? Which you submitted?' George frowned.

'The drawing of a ladle with...'

Angry, George would not let Aku finish. He tried not to raise his voice. 'Aku, you disobeyed Father. It is a sin to do so. And you know it.'

'You once hid a textbook under foodstuff you were asked to bring him. Was that not a sin too?' returned Aku.

'I had a good reason. It was because of you. Remember?' defended George.

'He will never know that I disobeyed him,' shrugged Aku. 'And George, Father must not know any of this,' warned Aku. Then, almost to herself, Aku added, 'Headie will never tell him. I know. And he will never ask her what I submitted. They don't seem to like each other. They talk to each other only because they have to, because of the relationship between the church and the school.'

George did not try to understand Aku. It was convenient for him to mentally write her off as a girl gone crazy with the excesses of wilfulness and too much thinking. Besides, George still had to think of how to go about something far more important...

While at his drawings, George always kept in mind that there were people to please: from Awo Fio through the headie to Marcia and Craig...

***

That George had talent was as stark as fat dirt in clean water. His first drawing was almost a picture. It was a coloured rendition of Aku's completed version of that 'bush' picture in his textbook. And it just happened that George's rendition, even though it was coloured, lacked all the details and lustre of Aku's.

The hair of the boy in George's painting looked unkempt. The boy's nose was moist and dirty. His ears drooped. The brightness in his eyes was no brightness at all; it was jaundiced. And the boy sprawled on the ground, chasing after crawling insects and earthworms.

Later, George graduated from drawings to paintings, all of which took after the bleak character of his earlier pieces. His paintings roamed the world over. Maybe George's paintings told the truth, in that they were not pretentious, not romantic about the African reality. And, as Craig would rightly say, there was no need to mince words about that truth. But George's paintings were nowhere near the truth, the reality of Namɔale. Who knows?

For a long time to come, Marcia continued to believe that a white A4 sheet was a very precious thing on George's side of the world. For another long time, the headmistress kept Aku's drawing for her amusement, and for a memorial of the visit. Sadder still, and maybe forever, Father and Aku hid their evergreen portfolios from each other, and from the world.

On Aku's part, her portfolio grew slowly, steadily, as the tortoise that the 'Akpokpolonto' sama signified. In keeping with the spirit of 'Alagba tɛ', the bellows of the master goldsmith's refining furnace, every next drawing was bolder in scope and brighter in depth than the one before. Aku's pieces spoke of 'Abii wo ni ahe nu'. Aku refused to accept water when it was honey that was asked for. She refused to let her art be reduced to mere objects robbed of their voice and dignity in mid-sentence, objects to tickle other people's fancies and feed their prejudices.

As for Father, it was enough that he found himself to be a fine gentleman who, in his closet, was a finer drunk. No-one else needed to think of, or judge him an idolater, just because a priest like himself had turned so pagan as to draw samai and collect cowries and other queer, native artifacts. Also, enough suspicion already hinged on his christening every newborn child in Namɔale yet insisting on calling his niece by her real, original name: Aku, whose appellation is, Shika.

Shika. As in Precious. As Gold.

Aku. Shika.

Meanwhile, everywhere else on the globe, George's paintings continued to represent the reality of Namɔale.

And of Africa.

Aisha Nelson dreams, writes, thinks and lives in Accra, Ghana, where she is also a tutor of English Language and Literature. Her works have featured in weeklies, literary and academic events, radio and other outlets, including Accra Theatre Workshop, *OneGhanaOneVoice*, *Kalahari Review*, *Saraba Magazine*, *Munyori Literary Journal*, *Phillis Wheatley Chapter* and *Prairie Schooner*. Her poem 'Revolt' was shortlisted in Poetry Foundation Ghana's 2012 POLITICAL poetry competition; 'Steg-nation' was the winning entry in Akwanto Writing's inaugural Harmattan Poetry Contest. Her blog Nu kɛ Hulu (Water and Sun) is at aishawrites.wordpress.com

The Caine Prize rules of entry

The Caine Prize is awarded annually to a short story by an African writer published in English, whether in Africa or elsewhere. (The indicative length is between 3,000 and 10,000 words.)

'An African writer' is taken to mean someone who was born in Africa, or who is a national of an African country, or who has a parent who is African by birth or nationality.

There is a cash prize of £10,000 for the winning author and a travel award for each of the shortlisted candidates (up to five in all).

For practical reasons, unpublished work and work in other languages is not eligible. Works translated into English from other languages are not excluded, provided they have been published in translation and, should such a work win, a proportion of the prize would be awarded to the translator.

The award is made in July each year, the deadline for submissions being 31 January. The shortlist is selected from work published in the five years preceding the submissions deadline and not previously considered for a Caine Prize. Submissions, including those from online journals, should be made by publishers and will need to be accompanied by six original published copies of the work for consideration, sent to the address below. There is no application form.

Every effort is made to publicize the work of the shortlisted authors through the broadcast as well as the printed media.

Winning and shortlisted authors will be invited to participate in writers' workshops in Africa and elsewhere as resources permit.

The above rules were designed essentially to launch the Caine Prize and may be modified in the light of experience. Their objective is to establish the Caine Prize as a benchmark for excellence in African writing.

The Caine Prize
The Menier Gallery
Menier Chocolate Factory
51 Southwark Street
London, SE1 1RU, UK
Telephone: +44 (0)20 7378 6234
Email: info@caineprize.com
Website: www.caineprize.com